THE
FUNDRAISER

THE FUNDRAISER

PAUL STRAND

AMBER LEAF
Publishing
Seattle

The Fundraiser
Copyright © 2020 Paul Strand

ISBN: 9798560049997

Printed in the United States of America

Independently published by Amber Leaf publishing.

For Karen
My encourager

"One who deceives will always find those who allow themselves to be deceived."

—Niccolo Machiavelli, The Prince

CHAPTER 1

Sol Solomon sat at a small table in the bar of a luxury hotel waiting for his host. His thick black hair and mustache were short and freshly groomed. He wore a lightweight, grey Italian linen suit over a pearl white shirt open at the collar. The bar's air conditioning offset the hot desert air with the sense of a cool breeze, but it did nothing to cool Sol's anxiety. To add to his discomfort, the bar protruded from the hotel some six-hundred feet above the Arabian Gulf. The high perch made him giddy. He looked across the city of Dubai. What was he doing here? He only met his host once and now he had traveled halfway around the world at his invitation. But it was the promise of wealth that drew him. He knew that such a promise must include risk, but he had no way of knowing the enormity or its consequences.

Tall and slim, Ibrahim Bin Jabar strolled easily to Sol's table, wearing a white suit, and sporting a bushy black beard parted by a wide toothy smile. Had it not been for his dark complexion and black hair he may have looked like a tourist. He bowed slightly and extended his hand. Sol rose to greet his host.

"Did you have a nice trip, Mister Solomon?" Ibrahim asked.

"Very nice thank you."

What made it nice was last night's private jet from Grand Bahama Island, and the helicopter ride from the airport to the helipad above the hotel. However, the anticipation of today's meeting, and a serious case of jet lag, kept him awake into the night wondering if he had made the right decision. Now he would find out.

Only a few weeks earlier, Sol was working the crowd at a Republican fundraiser in Miami. He noticed a tall dark complected man bidding unusually large sums of money on minor items, just what a fundraiser wants to see. After the auction, the man came to the front of the banquet room where Sol sat with members of the Republican National Committee and other dignitaries.

He addressed Sol, "may I speak with you alone?"

Sol eagerly rose to his feet. "Of course, you may."

The two exchanged introductions on the way to a side door. He said his name was Ibrahin bin Jabar. As they stepped into a hallway, a local celebrity gave the closing speech.

"Mister Solomon, I live in Dubai, but my home is in Damascus, to which I cannot return because of political and military conflicts. I am part of an independent movement that would bring stability in the Middle East. We believe this can be done with the cooperation of the dominant American political party, and that with your help, we can provide large political contributions to congressmen sympathetic to our cause."

Sol did not know that Ibrahim had done his homework. That he knew about Sol's sketchy real estate investments, his overextended credit, and his love for luxurious living. Ibrahim also knew that Sol arranged illegal campaign funding, then skimmed what money he could for himself. Sol was vulnerable.

"I can be of great help in your fundraising efforts," Ibrahim continued. "And your own business interests as well. I can make you a rich man. Would you be interested in meeting with me where you will not be recognized?"

"Yes, of course."

"It would require four days of your time next month, for a most enjoyable holiday out of country where we can safely discuss my proposition. You would enjoy a short but splendid stay at one of the finest hotels on earth. All at my expense. Can you do that?"

Sol hesitated for a moment. Nothing seemed more interesting. "I'd be happy to meet with you. Where might that be?"

"I have chartered a boat for four days of fishing next month. It starts at six a.m. the first Monday in January and will be waiting for you at the Salt Breeze Charters in Miami. Tell people you are going on a fishing trip. Once aboard the boat, you will be given more information. Expect to enjoy an unforgettable holiday." He smiled and extended his hand to Sol. In it lay a gold coin. "Please accept this as a token of my sincerity. Now return to your companions and say nothing of our meeting." Ibrahim excused himself and left the building.

Early on the appointed January morning, Sol arrived at the Salt Breeze Charter Service in Miami. By mid-morning he was well out to sea heading toward Grand Bahama Island. There, he boarded a private jet for a flight to Dubai and a meeting that would change the course of American history.

Now, after weeks of anticipation and a fake fishing trip, Sol stood in the luxurious hotel face-to-face with the man who had promised him wealth. Smiling eyes of black steel carefully assessed Sol as the two engaged in light conversation. The waiter served tea and cakes.

Ibrahim picked up a berry tart and got to the point, "How would you like to offer Republican congressmen ample campaign money, and also provide them with a compelling reason to be re-elected?"

"How can I do that?"

"It is something you, as a fundraiser for your party, are in a unique position to do. Let me explain. It is inevitable that the Middle East will become a caliphate. It is our destiny. We do not expect western nations to help us, but we would like to be left alone to achieve it. If American forces stay out of our territory, we will do no harm in America or to Americans."

Sol's brow furrowed with curiosity. "But, how would I fit in?"

"I can help you provide money to congressmen who are willing to keep America out of our territory. You would receive ample amounts of cash for their campaigns as well as plenty of under the table cash as an incentive to keep everyone interested. All we want in return is that congress not authorize any actions that would interfere with our goals. Your congressmen can take credit for keeping the peace and protecting Americans. They can run for re-election on the reputation that they kept America out of the Middle East, and terrorism out of America. We will even leave Israel alone."

Ibrahim sat a tall stack of gold coins on the table. "We have studied your past and found good reason for you to give us your loyalty. If you are willing to commit to this cause, take the gold."

Sol watched Ibrahim's stoic face. "You're making it hard for me to say no."

"We hope to incentivize you to help us establish our goals."

"You're willing to buy off Americans?"

"It is cheaper than military solutions. Congress as well as the American people have sickened of wars in the Middle East. They want peace. We can give them that peace."

Sol picked up an American Gold Eagle coin. It felt heavy and smooth — solid gold. He held it lovingly, then moved the whole stack next to his martini glass. "Okay. Tell me more."

"Here is how it will work. You confront Congressmen who have something to hide. Offer them wealth and an enhanced opportunity to be re-elected. Maybe someone has a paramour or some dark secret. Maybe it is lust for money or gambling debts gone unpaid. Whatever it is, use their transgressions as a threat to their well-being, while offering them the opportunity for wealth. They are already cheating and hiding secrets. It should be easy for them to hold one more secret when wealth is at hand. The money alone may be sufficient for some to follow our cause. These kinds of people are especially vulnerable.

"But be careful. There is a risk to exposing the dark side of one's life. Let them know that their trans-gressions are safe with you no matter what. But be sure to keep their secrets close at hand should you ever need to remind them of their agreement. Above all, they must promise to keep America out of the Middle East.

"Right now, you have an account in a Cayman Island bank in the amount of five million dollars. It is yours." Ibrahim removed a small account book from his folder that lay on the table. He put it next to Sol's drink and stack of coins. "Additionally, we will deposit one million dollars more for each congressman you recruit. The same bank will set up a one-million-dollar Cayman Island account for each recruited congressman.

"Just as I have given you gold as incentive money for your trust, you will offer gold for the same purpose. The offer of gold is an open door to a greedy heart. It is hard to turn down. If, however, a congressman threatens to report your offer, you must threaten public exposure which could ruin the congressman's career, or personal life. Such serious consequences may be unavoidable. You should be prepared to act on any threats you make. We will back you up with personnel trained to deal with such circumstances."

Ibrahim leaned back and smiled. "We have solicited the services of a Washington based governmental relations firm—lobbyists—to seek out vulnerable congressmen for you to approach. The agency is well paid and have their own secrets to worry about. They do not know who employs them or our motivation. They believe an organization interested in uncovering corruption in government has commissioned them. You will present yourself to them as Arthur Bishop, the executive director of The American Anti-Corruption League. This is a real corporation that we registered in Virginia, and with the IRS as tax exempt. This is so we will look legitimate in case there is an investigation. We have an old store front office in a strip mall for an address. A young Syrian woman sits at the only desk. We even have a website and a phone tree.

"The lobbyists will provide you with the names and transgressions of the congressmen you will attempt to recruit. So far, you are known only through correspondence. You must go to them in Washington and sign an already agreed upon contract. Your contact is Marion West, of Leonard Governmental Relations. We also have a separate organization that employs them to lobby in favor of bills that our select congressmen will propose. In short, they will lobby for any bill that keeps America out of the Middle East and you will recruit the congressman who will sponsor those bills."

Sol could hardly take in all that he was hearing. Was this really happening?

Ibrahim went into further detail about how he expected Sol to achieve their goals. He explained how, through large donations to the President's charitable foundation, and huge speaking fees to members of his family, the President would sign bills favoring the caliphate. Congress must now provide those bills.

"We have enriched the President's business interests through our relationship with important financial institutions and governments. As long as he favors us, he will continue to enjoy opportunities for greater wealth. Should he not, we can do him great harm. Dare I say it? He is a selfish man with much to hide. You see, when you know one's inner most secrets and cater to their greed you can control people, nations and events.

Ibrahim's expression conveyed the seriousness of the plan he broached. "Remember this, we do not communicate in writing, by phone or any electronic media. All communication is by voice, in person and free of surveillance. And finally, we have operatives on American soil who will assist you when needed. They will also inform me of your activities. They are there to protect our interests even unto death."

Sol hesitated before addressing what was on his mind. "Pardon my asking, but what is your position with your caliphate?"

I am like an ambassador. I am also the registered owner of a small British oil company that contracts with the caliphate. That is as much as you need to know."

By the time Ibrahim completed his presentation, the bar was filled with guests and the sun hung low on the horizon. Ibrahim handed Sol one last thing: a set of false identification. "This will establish your identity as Arthur Bishop, Executive Director of the American Anti-Corruption League. You can use this identity in case of an emergency, but for no other reason. Your stay here in Dubai has you registered as Arthur Bishop. We must be careful that the name Sol Solomon is never in any way connected with me.

"You will be contacted very soon by a man with a gold coin. Examine it carefully. It will be an American twenty-dollar coin dated 1932. Anyone who approaches you about our business who does not have such a coin is an impostor. Also, your contact will never divulge his name. This man is my emissary. Of the utmost importance, never tell anyone how you were transported in and out of the United States. That must be our secret. After all, you were just on a fishing trip."

A man sitting at the bar turned toward Sol's table. He surreptitiously snapped several photos of Sol with the Dubai skyline behind him. A corner of a recognizable paper containing confidential Syrian Information protruded from Ibrahim's folder where it lay next to Sol's coins. It, too, was in the photos.

CHAPTER 2

Sol was in Ibrahim's private jet as it rolled to a stop in the dark of night. It was the same runway on Grand Bahama from which he had left, two nights earlier. He was the only passenger. He deplaned and walked to the edge of the tarmac where an old jeep waited. He tossed his bag in the back and climbed in next to the driver. They drove slowly by moonlight on a narrow gravel road, until they reached a paved road that led to the coast where a charter fishing boat was anchored.

On the way, Sol chatted with the driver who worked for Ibrahim's organization. This was the man who took care of the abandoned runway, and drove people from there to the fishing boat

As a salesman, Sol knew how to engage others in conversation. "How do you like your night job?"

"We always work at night. We can fly in and out of here most any night we want."

Offering the driver a cigar, Sol asked, "How's that?"

"It has to do with surveillance systems. The planes fly low. The pilots know how to avoid detection. It's kind of risky but our planes are all registered to a small British oil company. so, if we do get caught, we'll be locals. No one pays any attention to the old runway. We own it, and a large chunk of land around it. Nobody ever comes around. My tax returns show my family's income as caretakers. Pretty clever aye?"

"Ingenious."

"That's not the half of it. While the Americans are busy checking airports and border crossings, we send in as many people as we want. All anybody knows, is we run a fishing charter. We like to call our operation The Midnight Express."

In his casual conversation, Sol had no idea how much information the driver would disclose. "Do people just come in and out of The United States whenever they want?"

"Whenever the caliphate wants. We can also fly people and material by helicopter from one of our ships to one of our fishing boats. Not everything that comes ashore, is fish!"

"What about passports?"

"We do well at that. After all, millions of identities have been hacked from prominent American companies. We buy what we want on the dark web. When we sneak someone into the United States, they have all the ID they need; passport, drivers license, credit cards the works."

"Isn't it easy to get caught using fake ID?"

"Not really. Our identity engineers are experts. Have you been given fake ID?"

"Yes, I have."

"Me too, in this business you need a set of fake ID. You never know when you might need it. Let me give you tip. Never carry your fake ID on you. If you must use it, be sure your regular ID isn't on you at the same time."

It was still dark when the Jeep pulled into the gravel lot of the High Tides Charter Service on the shore of Coral Beach. As soon as Sol boarded the fishing boat it left port and sailed toward the coastal waters of Florida. He changed into shorts and a polo shirt, then leaned against the stern rail to watch the sunrise turn broken clouds to gold against a pale blue sky.

A crew member bent over the stern and replaced the boat's name. When finished he went to the bow. There, he replaced the registration numbers. The captain leaned against the rail next to Sol. "Come on down to the galley and grab a bite to eat. It's going to be a long day."

"But what's that guy doing with name changing?" Sol asked.

"It's part of how we operate. The name and number of the boat is registered in Bahama, but when we dock in Miami the boat will have Florida registration numbers. We do this to avoid the appearance of a foreign boat coming into port. This way it looks to both countries like we've only been fishing in nearby water."

A full breakfast of fried fish, eggs, hash browns and toast waited in the galley. One of the crew plopped down next to Sol. "We'll be off the coast of Miami soon. We'll have to kill some time so we can dock at five. We'll spend the day fishing. After all, that's what we're supposed to be doing."

Sol lingered over a second cup of coffee, then stretched out on the galley seat and napped. In the early afternoon he joined the others on deck. One of the crew was on hand to show Sol how to use the large rod and real needed for ocean fishing. He had no sooner thrown a line in the water, when his pole bent strongly forward.

A deck hand yelled out instructions. "Lower your pole and reel in. Don't let the line go slack!"

Sol did as told. The deck hand shouted more instructions. Sol's arms began to tire as he pulled the fish closer to the boat. When it broke water, the deck hand gaffed it and pulled it aboard. The sheer joy of reeling it in made Sol a convert to deep sea fishing. He eagerly tried for another.

They docked in Miami at five p.m. Sol stepped onto the dock with his luggage in one hand, and a plastic bag of cleaned and butchered kingfish in the other. Sol's friend from the Dade County Republicans drove Sol to the train for an overnight trip back to Washington. He left the fish in the car.

The next morning started in the offices of Leonard Governmental Relations. He introduced himself as Arthur Bishop. The middle age lady at the desk showed Sol to a small conference room. Sol waited. A tall, slim woman entered the room. She introduced herself as Marion West then, laid out a contract for their signatures. "Mister Bishop, I'm curious. Why is your organization interested in uncovering corruption in congress?"

Sol had practiced his response all morning. He had a role to play. "We believe that many of the bad decisions made by congress are sponsored by deal making and by profit incentives. In other words, greed and avarice drive bills through congress. There are all kinds corruption. All you have to do, is follow the news. For example, just recently, a congressman was forced to resign from office after he was caught trying to arrange a meeting with an under-age girl. Another was found taking large sums of money from a lobbyist. We also think it's odd, that so many congressmen become rich after taking office. We believe there are many in congress that the American people suspect of wrongdoing. With your help, we hope to force congress to be a more honest body of law makers. That's what the American public expects." Sol knew that Leonard Governmental Relations was a company that profited from inside connections made while its founder, Elliot Leonard, was a congressman.

After signing the contract, Marion gave Sol a Manila envelope. "We've started our investigation and have already found four congressmen for you, with photos and incriminating evidence. We are considering several others.

There were four packets. Each contained information about a congressman with something to hide. One of them, he knew well; Senator Lyle Bates of Florida. He would be attending a retreat in Miami with him the coming weekend. Another was Congressmen Roger Carlson, the President's pal, a lesser known congressman named Hugh Bireley, and finally, Senator Melvin Case, the Senate Majority Leader. A man whose popularity helped the Republican party raise substantial money. "I'm impressed. These are important men."

"There will be more. Our investigation has just begun."

Sol thanked Marion, gathered his documents and stepped out to the sidewalk and a waiting car. The driver dropped him off at his real estate office.

He had to arrange meetings with each of his new candidates. His first meeting was already scheduled for a Republican retreat in Miami the next weekend with Senator Bates and a few other senators. Next, he scheduled a meeting with congressman Bireley, then with Senator Melvin Case at the Senator's office, followed by a meeting the morning after with Congressmen Carlson at the Capital Grind Coffee Shop. That gave him the rest of the week to get used to being rich.

First, he contacted his Cayman Island bank to make sure he had access to his money. Thrilled to see the extent of his new account, he transferred several thousand dollars to his personal checking account. He left his bank with a fresh wad of bills in his wallet. Next, he went condo hunting. He had spent years showing other people lovely homes, while he lived in a simple apartment. He knew where all the good condos were, and he was going to get one.

As a single man, he wanted to live in town where the action was and be close to his brokerage. He wanted to live where the rich people live. But first, he stopped at the Arundel Men's Ware store where he picked out a new black wool overcoat, a black Italian wool suit, shiny black wingtip shoes and a matching black fedora. Sol believed that expensive black clothing made the wearer look important, maybe even a little dangerous. He also picked up a cheap blue suit for when he met with people at Leonard Governmental Relations. He believed that a man in a sky-blue suit didn't look like much of a threat — maybe even religious. This was by design. Sol didn't want people to find out about his two personas. Next stop was a rare coin dealer. Sol needed a supply of gold coins to offer his prospects. American Gold Eagle coins came in tubes of twenty coins each. He bought four. The dealer placed them in a small box. It weighed over five pounds. Sol hefted it up and went to his car. He was being chauffeured in a black Lincoln belonging to Republican National Committee.

By Sunday afternoon, he was the owner of a brand-new condominium with balconies and a view. It even had a pool and a secured parking garage. At the street level was a large well-appointed lobby next to a small café and coffee bar. Sol had arrived.

On the first morning of his residency, he stepped out of the elevator into the lobby of his new home. A young, dark complected man rose from his chair and approached Sol. A gold, twenty-dollar coin dated 1932 lay in his hand, face-up. He spoke with a middle eastern accent, "Mister Solomon! May we talk for a moment?"

"Of course, Mister?"

"Never mind that."

The two moved to a couch near the gas fireplace. No-one else was in the lobby.

The coin bearer spoke first. "Welcome to your new home. And your new responsibilities. Ibrahim sends his best wishes. I am his emissary. I will convey his messages to you and, in turn, apprise him of your activities. I trust you have contacted our lobbying firm?"

"I have. They had four names for me."

"Who are they?"

From his briefcase, Sol handed the coin bearer the packet of information provided by Marion West. The coin bearer studied all of it. "I am especially interested in Congressman Carlson. It says here that he is a long-time friend of the President. I want you to take this opportunity to use Carlson as a conduit to the President.

"You should know that the President is not living up to deals he made with Ibrahim. He is being paid to sign bills that favor our cause and to withdraw from our territories, but he slanders us. This could be a dangerous conflict of interest. We may have to take actions to correct his behavior.

"The President needs to be more respectful." The unnamed man continued, "He doesn't say good things about us even though he benefits from us. I want you to take every opportunity, through whatever contacts you make, to get the President to speak favorably of our cause.

"You may approach congressmen who behave in the same manner as the President. You will be expected to take action, when this happens. We are here to help you with this. We may also call on you to help us with the President."

"How would I do that?"

"We will let you know. For now, tell me your plans."

"My first contact will be in Miami next weekend." Sol explained how he would approach the four men referred to him. He explained the role of each one and how they could influence congress.

The coin bearer smiled with satisfaction. "You must be very careful that you keep a low profile. Don't let your new wealth cause you to become well known. Now that you are living a double life you must be careful not to let anyone know you are one in the same."

"Of course."

Then, without another word the emissary rose to his feet and walked out to the street. Sol wondered how he could have anything to do with the President of the United States.

Sol booked a flight to Grand Cayman Island. He flew to Atlanta where he boarded a small jet to the island. It was late afternoon when the plane landed. Sol enjoyed a leisurely walk to the car rental. He rolled the windows down to let the warm sea air blow through the car. He did a little sight seeing on his way to a hotel on the beach where he had reservations. Sol found a small table on the deck. He relaxed looking to the horizon across the Gulf of Mexico. When the waiter came, he ordered parmesan crusted scarlet snapper with a tart passionfruit vinaigrette. After dinner, he sipped martinis and nibbled on deep fried calamari while listening to waves advancing on the shore. Once again, Sol dreamed of how he could live the life he'd always wanted. He was rich! But He knew that someday his newly found cash flow would end. In preparation for that day, he would establish his home here on Grand Cayman. where he could live in comfort and anonymity as Arthur Bishop.

After a restful night, Sol got ready for a busy day. He dressed in tan shorts, a mostly black Hawaiian shirt, sandals, and a very expensive pair of Cartier sunglasses. He returned to the deck, where he enjoyed a light breakfast, then left for the bank where he checked his balance. True to his word, Ibrahim had all the deposits up to date. With a sizable bank account and an address on the island, he could apply for residency as Arthur Bishop, his new alternate identity. To apply for residency, he needed an address. He called a real estate broker who drove him around to look at some homes. The one he settled on was a small two bedroom that overlooked a large marina. It had its own dock. Buying it took all day. By the time the papers were singed, it was time for another peaceful evening on the deck.

Next morning, Sol returned to the marina where he had seen a yacht dealership the day before. When Sol announced he was there to buy a yacht a very dark completed man in khaki shorts and a maroon polo was quick to oblige. The salesman opened a portfolio of yachts. they looked more like ships.

"No no," Sol said. "I want a small personal Yacht."

"What do you plan to use it for?"

"I've never owned a boat. I just want something seaworthy that I can take out by myself, or maybe with a couple of friends and do a little fishing."

"Maybe you should look at something a little smaller." The sales rep turned to the back of his portfolio. He showed Sol some cabin cruisers.

"Yeah, that's what I'm looking for."

"How much money do you want to spend on one of these?"

"Depends on the boat. Can I look at that one?" Sol pressed his finger against a full-page photo.

The two men went to the docks. There were lots of boats of every kind. They climbed aboard the boat Sol Chose.

"Want to take it out for a spin?" the salesman asked. Sol spent the rest of the morning trying out boats. He settled on a pre-owned thirty-three-foot Starfisher inboard cabin cruiser complete with galley, two berths, and a flying bridge. They signed papers over a late lunch at a dockside cafe. Sol paid cash for the boat just as he had for his house. The sales rep would take care of the registration and paperwork. After lunch they moored the boat at Sol's dock.

Sol's next purchase was a shiny, black Miata roadster for getting around the island. His last purchase furnished his new house. He was now established on Grand Cayman, but he couldn't stay any longer. He was due at a Republican retreat in Miami where he would approach his first prospect.

CHAPTER 3

The Conquistador Hotel on Ocean Drive in Miami Beach was restored Deco, painted in pastel green and pale yellow. The high-ceilinged lobby was decorated with 1930's art and furnished with brown leather sofas tucked under potted palms. The morning sun angled in through wide front windows that framed a white beach bordering the pale aqua of the Atlantic Ocean. The fragrance of Cuban food filled the room, and gently drifted through the open front doors, to be lost in a cloud of Cuban cigar smoke. The perfect place for a handful of Republican big shots to take a weekend break from the chill of Washington's politics and its winter weather.

Senator Lyle Bates, chairman of the Senate Homeland Security and Governmental Affairs Committee, chatted with Sol at a small table in the hotel's sidewalk café. He smiled as he tapped his cigar with his forefinger and watched the long fat ash fall into a small ashtray. Across the table, Sol smiled back. Overdressed for the occasion, he wore a short-sleeve black shirt with a white silk tie. He smiled before continuing.

"I'm about to make a proposition to you that could ensure your reelection and make you a wealthier man at the same time. It's not exactly honest. Shall I continue?"

"What kind of proposition?"

"You may find my introduction embarrassing or unkind, but it is an important part of the proposal."

"Go ahead."

Still smiling, Sol handed him a photo; a lewd photo.
"What's the big idea?" Lyle demanded.
"Don't worry no one needs to see it."
"But, where did you get that?"
"Now that I have your attention, I'd like to explain my proposition."
"People who take candid pictures of US Senators can get into some serious trouble." Bates warned, as he snuffed out his cigar.
"Senators who bring girl friends to their room can get into a lot of trouble too."
Bates paused and stared at the horizon before answering. "So, what do you want?"
"Your loyalty."
"You have a poor way of asking." Bates now glared into Sol's narrow dark eyes, about to go into a rage. "Listen Solomon, you'd better get rid of that picture."
Sol laid his cell phone on the table. "Before you do something impulsive I want you to know that with one tap of my finger that picture you're holding will be in your wife's possession."
Bates couldn't believe he was being blackmailed by a party faithful, someone whom he regarded as a friend.
Solomon's Washington real estate brokerage contributed to the Republican National Committee, and Sol worked hard to raise money. He even helped manage one of Senator Bates campaigns. It was not unusual to see him at retreats like this one. In fact, it was Bates who invited him. Bates had wondered how Sol's small real-estate brokerage could afford some of the large contributions Sol provided, but he knew better than to ask. Sometimes small fish like to swim with the big fish, in hopes of looking more important. Bates figured that was what Sol was doing, but because Sol was faithful to

the party, he had stroked Sol's ego and the contributions kept flowing.

Bates felt a chill in the otherwise warm beach air. He continued staring into Sol's eyes. "So, what do you want?"

"Your loyalty."

"You have a poor way of asking." Bates now glared into Sol's narrow dark eyes, about to go into a rage. "Listen Solomon, you'd better get rid of that picture."

Sol laid his cell phone on the table. "Before you do something impulsive I want you to know that with one tap of my finger that picture you're holding will be in your wife's possession."

Bates couldn't believe he was being blackmailed by a party faithful, someone whom he regarded as a friend.

Solomon's Washington real estate brokerage contributed to the Republican National Committee, and Sol worked hard to raise money. He even helped manage one of Senator Bates campaigns. It was not unusual to see him at retreats like this one. In fact, it was Bates who invited him. Bates had wondered how Sol's small real-estate brokerage could afford some of the large contributions Sol provided, but he knew better than to ask. Sometimes small fish like to swim with the big fish, in hopes of looking more important. Bates figured that was what Sol was doing, but because Sol was faithful to the party, he had stroked Sol's ego and the contributions kept flowing.

Bates felt a chill in the otherwise warm beach air. He continued staring into Sol's eyes. "So, what do you want?"

"I need your help. Congress is in a position to make important changes that could ensure relief from terrorist intrusion into our country and even in Israel." "That's nothing I know about. Just how is that supposed to work?" Sol carefully placed ten gold coins in front of Senator Bates. "Just listen to what I have to say." Sol spent the next several minutes explaining his proposition that would keep the United States out of the Middle East and provide a bunch of cash in the Senator's pockets.

Hooking game fish in the torrents of the political current has all the excitement of watching a trout jump as your fly glides above the water of a mountain stream. When Sol finished, the Senator relit his cigar and again smiled at his companion. The coins were in his pocket, and he was in Sol's.

Sol's next contact was scheduled for Monday morning in Washington. He had plenty of time for a relaxing train ride from Miami back to Washington.

Republican Representative Hugh Bireley of Nebraska narrowly won election by cheating. Sol had copies of absentee ballots that Bireley submitted for residents of state institutions who, themselves, were not able to vote. He also had a statement from an institution employee who saw him do it.

Monday morning, Sol was right on time for his appointment to discuss fundraising for Bireley's next election. The congressman kept him waiting in his outer office for more than fifteen minutes, before an aide showed him in. The congressman was a slim forty something. He wore an ill-fitting navy-blue suit, with a loose brown tie. His comb over left streaks of white pate showing through. His expression was deadpan. Sol glanced around the room. Papers and books were scattered about and stacked on his desk. No family pictures or awards — nothing personal. A granola bar wrapper lay next to the waste basket.

"I'm a little short of time, Bireley said. "You'll have to be brief."

Sol removed a piece of paper from a chair and sat down. "I want to talk to you about ways to increase your campaign funding."

"So, let's hear it."

"You almost lost your last election. With more cash you could have had a more decisive win."

"So?"

"During the course of my fundraising activities, I found someone willing to fund Republican congress-man, such as you, who can help reduce the threat of terrorism in our country."

Bireley's expression showed a hint of suspicion. "And whom might that be?"

"He likes to remain anonymous."

"Everybody has to declare their contributions."

"Yes, there are limits to how much a person can donate, but those limits don't apply to candidates giving to their own campaigns. This contributor wants to make you personally wealthy enough so you can help fund your own campaign."

Bireley squinted at Sol, "Would you explain that?"

"I'm sure you know that Congressmen and their families can pick up a lot of extra cash from Speaking engagements, book deals, trust funds, consulting, real estate, insider deals, and so on. Our anonymous benefactor can help with this as well as arrange donations from several political action groups at five-thousand dollars each which is the legal limit. Want to hear more?"

"Keep going."

"I have a proposition for you that could result in personal wealth, as well as a compelling reason for you to get re-elected next term." Sol reached into his coat pocket and produced a gold coin. He handed it to the congressman. Do you know what one of these is worth?"

"I have no idea."

"Well over a thousand dollars." Sol reached into his coat for a few more coins that he placed in the congressman's hand. How would you like to have all these?

Bireley closed his hand around the coins. "Okay let's hear it."

Sol explained about the need for legislation that would pull troops out of the Middle East and the freedom from terrorism that would follow.

"Still interested?" Asked Sol.

"But how would that get me re-elected?"

"You understand that the Middle East is a volatile place. People in that region of the world long to have a caliphate—one nation that would bind them together. Some of those countries also sponsor international terrorism."

"Yeah, I know. Get to the point."

"Alright, I'll get to the point. If you sponsor or support bills in Congress that keep Americans out of the Middle East, our benefactor will make you a rich man."

"That doesn't sound right." Bireley grumbled.

Sol looked at the congressman's hand gripping the coins. "Look, your constituents want us out of the Middle East. Any legislation you can take credit for that pulls us out of there will get you re-elected, no sweat. Then there's the campaign money you'll get."

"I'm not convinced."

Sol unzipped his black leather folder and pulled out two pieces of paper. He shoved some books out of way and laid them on the desk. One was a copy of a voter registration form that the congressman had forged. the other was a signed and notarized document stating that Hugh Bireley was seen committing voter fraud.

"Where did you get these?" Bireley demanded.

"Right now, I'm the only one who has evidence of what you did to get elected, and who helped you. That can remain our secret. I just want you to agree to help keep us out of the Middle East."

Bireley looked shocked. He lay the coins on the desk. "I said, where did you get these?"

"A private investigator got them for me, but you know where they came from."

"What are you going to do with them?"

"Nothing. I'm not here to accuse you of anything, I'm here to offer you a proposition. If you agree, keep the coins."

Bireley picked up a coin and studied it. "Okay. Suppose I agree to go along with this, what would I have to do?"

"Like I said, sponsor or support bills that would keep us out of the Middle East. That's it. There are other congressmen doing this, so you'll have others to work with."

"What about these papers."

"They will go into a safe deposit box. No one will ever see them." Sol told him about the Cayman Island bank account and the million dollars. Bireley picked up the coins.

"Later on I'll introduce you to other congressmen who have agreed to the same commitment," Sol said. Bireley dumped the coins into his briefcase and snapped it shut. "I really do have to get going. Thanks Mister Solomon. Thanks a lot."

"I'll be in touch," Sol said. Then he exited the office. He had to get ready for his afternoon meeting with a more important prospect.

Senate majority leader Melvin Case watched his TV monitor as it kept up with action on the Senate floor. His phone rang. It was his administrative assistant. "Mister Solomon is here."

"Show him in."

Sol looked around Senator Case's spacious office. The Senator stayed seated. "Sit down. Care for some chocolate?" Case waved a huge hand at a bowl of truffles on the corner of his desk. "I have a constituent who is a chocolatier. She keeps me well supplied."

Sol delicately chose a dark truffle with a raspberry stripe across the top. He glanced out the window at a cold, sunny sky. "It's supposed to snow tonight. Strange how the sun can shine so bright just before a storm."

"A little snow never hurt anyone," Case said. "I remember once when we were playing the Packers at Green Bay when snow was so thick, we couldn't see the goal posts. Passes would just disappear into the stuff."

The glass case behind the Senator was filled with football memorabilia. Trophies and plaques surrounded the jersey the Senator had worn at a Super Bowl win several years earlier. At six-foot-six he was one of the tallest offensive linemen in football. Since then, overeating made him even bigger.

Sol got to the point. "We need to talk about campaign money. I'm setting up a fundraiser luncheon for Senator Maxine Byte at the Sonoma. I'd like you to host it."

"Why me?"

"People admire you. You're well known. You help attract donors. These luncheons generate a lot of money. You've benefitted from them yourself."

"You're right. Let me think about it."

"While you're thinking, let me explain a proposition that could get you a ton of campaign money. Even more than you've been getting from those under-the-table contribution deals you've been making."

Case leaned his massive shoulders forward as if back on the line of scrimmage. "What do you know about any deals?"

"What about that Florida offshore drilling bill you pushed through congress? The only people who wanted it were oil companies and their investors. You weren't even truthful about it. You not only took their money, but you invested it in their stock, which skyrocketed as soon as drilling permits were awarded."

"You don't know what you're talking about."

"Oil company accountants haven't hidden their transactions. Neither have the investment companies." Sol took some folded documents out of his coat pocket and handed them to the Senator.

Case slammed his huge fist on his desk. "Where did you get these?"

"I'm just showing you this to let you know that I can get you even more money and assure that you win your next election. I already know you can keep quiet about financial matters. Want to hear more?"

"Maybe. Sounds like you're the crook and you're trying to call me one."

"How would you like to run your next election on the reputation that you passed bills that got the US out of the Middle East and protected Americans at home and abroad from terrorism?

"Sounds like a pretty tall order."

"You wouldn't be the only congressman doing this. Other Republicans in congress are getting on board with this and will be capitalizing on the same reputation. I will see to it that each one has plenty of campaign money and then some. You can be part of this. This can also enrich you personally".

Senator Case narrowed his eyes. "What do you mean, personally?"

Sol laid a gold coin on the Senator's desk. "Do you know what gold is going for these days?"

Case picked up the coin. He rubbed it between his fingers, then spun it on his desk. Sunlight filtered through the office window and across his dark walnut desk causing the coin to glisten. "I don't know. Well over a thousand an ounce, I think."

Sol placed several more gold coins in front of Case. "If you want in, help yourself."

"What do you plan to do with that oil company information?"

"Nothing, if you accept my proposition. Remember, that's my proof that you can keep a secret. So can I." Sol explained about the campaign money and the tax free million just waiting for him to take.

Case opened his pencil drawer and scooped the coins into his desk.

As the first storm clouds rose on the horizon, Sol explained the details of his proposition.

CHAPTER 4

Since Sol's return from the Cayman Islands, he picked up three million dollars from his recruitments. Tomorrow looked like another million-dollar day. He stayed up late watching the snow fall on his balcony. He turned on the TV to the Night Show with Archie MacArthur. Archie loved to pick on politicians. Tonight, it was President Townsend.

While his band played a jaunty tune, Archie bounded on stage. He went into his monologue featuring President Townsend's latest gaff at a fundraiser. Archie motioned to a wall sized screen. On it, was the President seated at a large table with some dignitaries. Cocktail glasses were everywhere.

"Now watch as the video plays," Archie said, "Listen carefully, the President is liquored up and bad mouthing everybody he can think of." The low-quality video ran. Townsend could be heard talking to others at his table about pulling troops out Afghanistan. He said, "I don't give a damn what happens to a bunch of Middle Eastern whack jobs We're pulling out of there."

"Another example of Townsend's vitriolic attitude," Archie said. He closed his monologue with one more video of the President climbing into his limousine after the fundraiser. Another poor-quality cell phone video catching the President losing his footing and falling headfirst into his limo.

Certain individuals in the Middle East were also watching Archie. They seethed at how unappreciative the President was of their support.

Sol knew that President Thad Townsend's election was close. If the popular vote mattered, he would have lost, but the electoral vote put him in office. False promises helped. Although it's no measure of character, Townsend's good looks and charisma went a long way to winning the election.

Just as important as personality is money, and running a successful campaign required more than he had. To fill the shortfall, he made deals with anyone who would donate. He promised to award people positions as ambassadors, department secretaries, bureau chiefs, any position could be bought. One of Townsend's best friends, Congressman Roger Carlson, had the support of an underground organization willing to pony up large sums of money. That is, if Townsend would promise to keep out of their hair and promise to grant certain pardons and sentence commutations. Townsend was all for it, but that money could not be reported as campaign donations, so he claimed he was spending his own money. He could get away with this because the IRS was auditing him, which would prevent him from having to disclose his tax returns. But he still needed more money. Then, good fortune struck.

It happened after he gave a rousing campaign speech full of promises nobody could keep. When he stepped down from the stage to greet supporters, one of them introduced himself as Ibrahim Bin Jabar the CEO of a small oil company. He wanted to meet Townsend at his hotel. "I have a very large donation for you," he said.

Surprised and curious, Townsend agreed. At Townsend's hotel, the candidate and the donor spoke privately.

"I can fill the short fall in your campaign chest, and help you win the election." The donor said. "All you have to do is stay out of the Middle East, and sign bills that would pull America out of the Middle East."

Townsend listened intently. "How much money?"

"You can have as much as twenty million dollars given to you, as you need it. Some of it will come through legitimate sources, and some must be hidden." The man explained that he represented the formation of a caliphate in the Middle East. "It's important to us that Republicans stay in office long enough for our caliphate to form."

"But, what do you want from me?"

"I want you to campaign to get America out of the Middle East. Inform Americans that some two trillion dollars have been spent over there, money that could be better spent to fight terrorism at home. Base your campaign on ending terrorism and you will win votes."

Townsend eyed his visitor with suspicion.

"How do I know you're on the level?"

"I've anticipated your question. Thursday at three p.m. your time, two bombs will explode, one near the UN building in New York, and one near the Wailing Wall in Jerusalem. Shortly thereafter your phone will ring. At that time, you will know my sincerity. Then we can negotiate a deal."

"Okay! If what you say, actually happens."

"It will." The donor handed Townsend an antique United States twenty-dollar gold coin dated eighteen-fifty-seven, minted in San Francisco. "Please accept this coin as a token of my sincerity." Jabar and Townsend parted, leaving Townsend to study the valuable coin.

Thursday came and so did the explosions. Townsends new campaign mantra was, "we can end terrorism."

Once in office President Townsend reneged on several of his promises. He did bring some troops home, but many of his donors missed out on government appointments causing dissension in the Republican Party.

During his first months in office, Townsend spent much of his time on what he called diplomatic trips to places like London, Paris, Moscow, Seoul, and Dubai. All had golf courses. By now, the American public had become disgusted with his conspicuous waste of public funds for his pleasure. His approval rating nosedived.

Sol understood why Ibrahim's coin bearing emissary was unhappy with the President.

The next morning, snow crunched under the wheels of a black sedan as it stopped at the curb. The back door opened. Sol, dressed in a black wool overcoat and a black hat, stepped into the cold January morning. A swirl of heavy snow ushered him across the freshly shoveled sidewalk to the door of the Capital Grind Espresso Shop. He hurried into its warmth.

At the counter, Sol ordered a cappuccino and an apple Danish before taking a seat across from an older man in a grey suit. The two men had arranged the meeting to discuss fundraising, but Sol knew he knew he had to talk about President Townsend.

Sol shook snowflakes from his hat before laying it on a chair. After an exchange of pleasantries, Sol said, "I want to talk to you about campaign funding, but first I want to address the president's unique way of discouraging donors. Roger, we can't have the President talking the way he does about The Middle East. There are a lot of friends of those countries who give generously to our campaigns. He is supposed to raise money, not drive it away. Did you watch the Night Show last night?"

"Sure." Roger Carlson had been in the House of Representatives for decades. He served as Chairman of the House Committee on Homeland Security. He was also an old friend of President Townsend. Both were Republicans from New York and alumni of Columbia University.

"I don't think he meant it the way it sounded," Carlson said. "These kinds of slip-ups happen." To warm his chubby fingers, he wrapped them around his cup of double shot vanilla latte.

"I think he meant it. It's not the first time he's made a stupid remark. The man has got to watch his mouth. What about that dumb remark he made about Afghanistan last month, and how he'd like to turn the whole place into glass?"

Roger was edgy. "I can't do anything about what the President says."

"You know him. You can talk to him. It's vital that he lays off his remarks and stops making disparaging comments about the Middle East. Maybe he can make an apology."

"I'm not going to ask the President to make apologies. He has his own agenda in the Middle East. An occasional slip of the tongue can be expected. Give him some space."

"The President isn't supposed to get liquored up and loose tongued."

"I didn't say that."

"No, you didn't. Archie MacArthur on the Night Show did. They're making fun of the President on TV and it's seriously ill willed. Do you know what that does to campaign contributions? Don't you see the need to talk some sense into him?

"The President oversees this situation. I can't help what people say."

"You need to help. That man is running off contributors and risking serious reprisals from organizations in the Middle East. We're supposed to be soliciting contributions. The way he's going, we'll lose the House and Senate and there will be no Republican in the White House. His remarks could even be putting his life in danger."

"Go easy on that kind of talk. No one wants to assassinate the President."

"Don't be so sure. I know that he is involved with Middle East interests. Those people expect favors from him. Who do you think is paying for his family's speaking gigs and donating to their foundation? Surly you know that presidents don't get rich on their salaries, alone."

Roger said nothing as he nervously worked two fingers a little too tightly into the handle of his cup. Sol glanced out the window at the accumulating snow. "If Townsend doesn't cooperate ..." Sol paused and looked over his shoulder to see who might be listening, then said, "they'll kill him."

CHAPTER 5

Standing at a darkened second story window across the street, Fred Ferguson made a phone call. "Something interesting just came up," he said. "You want to hear about it?"

"Sure." the woman said, "Can you meet me at lunch?"

"Where?"

"Napoleon's."

Because the work Fred did for her wasn't legal, his meetings with her were always clandestine. "Alright. See you at twelve."

Fred was a private investigator whom the woman had hired. His job was to check the background of members of congress, looking for illegal or immoral activities. Representative Carlson was easy to observe, because he frequented the Capital Grind two or three mornings a week. He sometimes met with other congressmen and constituents, some of whom were also suspected of corruption. Fred had already provided the woman with photographs of Carlson meeting with known underworld figures.

Fred rented a small office across the street from the Capital Grind. It sat vacant for a long time until Fred came along. It worked well for surveillance of Carlson and his guests. He moved in some equipment and went to work, his only light a small TV tuned to a twenty-four-hour news channel in Washington. The lease sign still hung in the window. It continued to look vacant.

A high fee had been offered for illegal surveillance of members of congress, and Fred had succumbed. The woman on the phone had been introduced to him by an old army acquaintance from his Military Police unit Fred retired from. She hired him to find dirt on as many congressmen as he could.

Now, Fred stared intently at the window across the street, his long lens video camera focused on two men. He knew what they were eating, what they were drinking, what they were wearing and with luck, what they were saying. Laser listening equipment was focused on the same spot; sophisticated enough to pick up voices from window vibrations, but thick snowfall was getting in the way.

The snow fell silently. Large, fluffy snowflakes settled onto a thickening layer of pure white. A cheerful young woman stepped out of the coffee shop door and swept away a patch of snow. She tossed a cup full of salt on the sidewalk, then ducked back into the warmth of her shop. She picked up Sol's order and brought his cappuccino and Danish to his table.

"Care for anything else?"

Sol didn't appreciate the interruption, "No!" He snapped.

She quickly retreated behind her counter of pastries. Business was slow.

The man-in-black stared at Roger's complacent pink face, waiting for him to say something. Roger just sat there warming his hands on his cup. Finally, he said, "I hate this weather. My hands hurt when they get cold."

"Roger, I know I'm here to talk to you about fundraising, but do you think you could give some thought to helping the President understand what he's doing? People are tired of conflict in the Middle East.

Congress is thinking up ways to keep us out of there. The president is supposed to help."

Roger sighed. "It's not a congressmen's job to direct the office of the President."

"But he knows you. He'll listen to you. Don't you see that his remarks are not only bad politics, but may even endanger his life? Those Middle East guys are more than ticked off."

"I'm sorry about what he said, but I'm out of it. Besides, how do you know leaders in the Middle East are angry with the President?"

"Roger, there's more to this Middle East problem than presidential politics. How would you like to be able to help eliminate the threat of terrorism through legislation, and pick up some serious campaign funds at the same time?"

"I don't know what you're talking about."

"Campaign money. Lots of it. I know that you are involved with certain people who may function outside the law. That's fine with me, but if that information got out it could ruin you. I'd like to explain something that would make you less dependent on their support and make you richer at the same time." Sol then placed a stack of gold coins on the table. "If you're interested help Yourself. There are lots more where these came from."

Carlson studied the raised figure of an eagle bringing an olive branch to its nest. The coin was a work of art. He knew its value. The little stack was worth thousands of dollars. "What do you know about anyone operating outside of the law?" he said.

"I know who's been contributing some unreported money, but that's not important. Just let me explain my proposition."

"Don't tell me that's not important. You just threatened me."

"It's not a threat. I'm offering you an opportunity."

"I'm not biting. If you breathe one word of what you're talking about, you'll be finished. Do you understand me?"

"Let's be reasonable. There's no need to ..."

"Are you deaf? I can't control the President and I don't like being bribed. I don't need anything from you." He shoved the coins across the table.

"Please let me explain."

"No! As for anything you might know about, what you call 'people outside of the law', you better be careful".

Sol felt a million dollars slipping away. With a raised voice and a twitching eyelid Sol blurted out, "I don't like being threatened either. The President is destroying his presidency and the Republican party. He' s endangering his life and the security of our nation. He's toxic. Frankly, I wish you'd both drop dead."

"I'm sorry you feel that way, but making threats is a foolish thing to do." Carlson looked directly into the dark eyes of a man he no longer wanted anything to do with. He, in fact, wanted Sol to drop dead.

With thick black eyebrows pinched into a knot, Sol drained his cappuccino to the bottom, leaving a large dab of foam on his thick, black mustache. Then, raising his voice even more, he leaned across the table and jabbed a finger into Roger's chest, "I could stick my finger in a phonebook and find a better president."

With that, Sol, stormed out the door, tapped the snow off a shiny black wingtip and slid into the back seat of his car, disappearing into the worsening snowstorm.

Roger stayed at his table long enough to control his temper and get his stuck fingers out of his cup handle, then he grabbed Sol's untouched Danish and sauntered out the door. Sol's black fedora lay on the chair where he left it.

Fred noted that the man-in-black's fedora lay forgotten on a chair. Then, he turned his attention to his equipment. He ran the audio data through software that used refinement techniques to coax out otherwise unintelligible words. Software designed to interpret lip movements, helped clarify the audio recording. Unfortunately, the falling snow interfered with both methods. Under more favorable circumstances the value of lip-reading software was enormous. In fact, it was used to give voice to a silent film of a Teddy Roosevelt speech. Some used lip reading at football games, causing coaches to hide their mouths when communicating with their quarterbacks.

Fred spent the rest of the morning squeezing out every word possible. Most of what could be translated into words came from the man-in-black, because he kept raising his voice. The few other voices were weeded out. He copied his new information onto a flash drive.

Fred turned his video recorder on and left it aimed at the espresso shop, in case the man-in-black returned for his hat. Then left his darkened office and stepped out into the falling snow.

Napoleon's restaurant occupied the second floor of a building only a few blocks away. Fred entered the dining room and walked toward his client, Marion West, a slim young woman with wavy blond hair picking at a Cob salad.

Fred lay the flash drive on the white linen tablecloth next to her plate. "Some guy dressed all in black met briefly with Representative Carlson at the Espresso shop this morning. Unfortunately, I didn't get a good look at him. The only time he faced me was when he came out of the shop. The snowstorm blocked nearly everything."

"So, what was the meeting about?"

"What I got from the man-in-black is that he is angry about the President's remarks about the Middle East, angry enough to threaten the President's life. I had trouble with the conversation because the snow messed with the surveillance equipment. Carlson mumbles, so I got nothing from him, but he seemed defensive and angry. What the man-in-black said to Carlson was, 'I wish you'd drop dead.' He also said, 'they'll kill him.' I didn't get who 'they' might be or whom might be killed, but surmised he was talking about the President. Then, when he got up to leave, he jabbed his finger into Carlson's chest, and said, 'I could stick my finger in a phonebook and find a better president.'"

"I think a lot people might agree with that statement. You ever see this man-in-black before?"

"No. He could be another congressman or maybe an underworld figure. I just can't tell. He's a short, stocky guy with a dark complexion, lots of black hair, and a thick black mustache – white on one side. The car is a black Lincoln. I couldn't read the license plate – too much snow. Everything intelligible is on that flash drive along with some photos. Carlson may be into more corruption than I reported earlier."

"Who can get away with talking to a congressman that way? Did you get anything else?" Marion asked.

"No, but it should be apparent that Carlson knows this man-in-black quite well."

"See if you can find out who this man-in-black is."

"I thought I was to report on the activities of certain congressmen not their contacts."

"It could all be part of the same thing. This man-in-black could be, as you say, a congressman or maybe an underworld figure. Who knows? I can give you a cash bonus for the extra work. I have a bad feeling this guy is trouble."

"I'll see what I can find out." Fred got up without ordering and went back to his office.

He wished he had a bug at Carlson's table. With it, he could have heard everything the man-in-black and Carlson said. Gathering information about other people was Fred's business, but bugs are risky. He didn't want anyone finding any of his bugs, but after weighing the odds, he stuck a small bug in his pocket.

Fred had to keep a low profile. He didn't want to be seen in the Capital Grind, but he had to see if the black fedora was still there. It could provide information. He crossed the street to the espresso shop, where he was enveloped in rich moist air, and the strong aroma of coffee. On an overhead TV monitor, a large array of coffee choices was shown in full color video. It was confusing.

"Hi. What'll it be?" The young woman smiled broadly awaiting his order.

He paused glancing at the black hat on a shelf under the side counter. "I'm not sure. I ah ... Just want a cup of coffee."

"May I suggest something?"

"Sure."

"What kind of coffee do you usually drink?"

"I usually just order a black coffee." He thought about his two-cup coffee maker that sat in his tiny office. "At home, we have a Mister Coffee."

"You might want to try a Café Americano. It's half strength espresso. It tastes a lot better than anything your Mister Coffee can make."

"Okay."

Fred sat down at the table where Carson usually sat. As he waited, he surreptitiously stuck a small bug under the table. It was smaller than a wad of gum but could transmit as far as the receiver in his office across the street, where it could also be turned on and off. When the coffee arrived, Fred asked, "Do you remember a man coming in here this morning dressed all in black?"

"Nope. I don't work mornings."

"He said he left his hat on a chair. He asked if I would get it for him."

"Sure. I'll be right back."

The barista lay the black fedora on the table. "Is this what you're looking for?"

Fred reacted appropriately for someone who was glad to retrieve a friend's hat, but he wondered what the man-in-black would think about this.

"Thanks," he smiled.

"No problem." The barista walked away leaving Fred to enjoy a good cup of coffee. He stuffed a five in the tip jar on his way out.

In his parking stall in the basement garage below his office, Fred wondered what to do with the hat. It was an expensive fedora lined with white satin, stamped "Biltmore President" A little tag read, "size 7¼." An additional tag read, "Arundel Men's Ware, Washington." It looked brand new. Fred had a clue.

CHAPTER 6

That afternoon, Marion met with the principal at Leonard Government Relations. Her boss, Elliot Leonard, had started this business after leaving the House of Representatives a few years earlier. Her job was to learn about the activities of certain politicians; ones who might be involved with immoral or illegal activities. This information, she would pass on to their client, The American Ant-corruption League.

"Elliot, today I heard that the President's offhand remarks about the Middle East may have brought a death threat against him."

"Who told you?"

"The guy I hired to help us identify corrupt congressman."

"But who said it to Carlson?"

Marion handed Elliot the flash drive. "So far, all we know is that the man is short and stocky. He dresses in black and is chauffeured in a black Lincoln – looks like a hood. A few details are on the flash drive, but the snowstorm makes the pictures hard to see."

"Any idea who this man-in-black is?"

"No. But I think he's dangerous. My detective said the man-in-black jabbed a finger in Carson's chest and said, 'I could find a better president by sticking my finger in a phone book.'"

Back in his office, Fred turned his attention to looking at pictures of the man-in-black's car. There were likely hundreds of Lincolns like it in the Washington area. He had to find something unique, like a dent or maybe a bumper sticker. As Marion had said, the falling snow almost obliterated the pictures.

Fred opened several successive photos of the Lincoln, using Photoshop. He layered the photos one on top of the other, then erased the snowflakes from the top picture. This exposed parts of the car on the photo beneath it. He continued this process, then merged the photos together, producing one photo with much of the snow removed.

The result showed a Lincoln MKX, two or three years old. It had an oversized shark antenna on the roof, tinted windows, and a white oval in the upper left corner of the rear window, possibly a parking permit. The license plate had a red line on it like a District of Columbia plate, but the numbers remained covered with snow. Not much to go on, but at least a start.

With that done, Fred studied pictures of congressman. After an hour, he found no one that could be him.

It was getting dark. Fred had to check out a man who had made a suspicious insurance claim. These kinds of jobs were the bread and butter of his private investigation business, but his contract with Marion West provided the gravy.

He carefully inched his car out of the parking garage and onto the snowy street. From now on, he would study every black Lincoln he saw, for the few features that could lead him to the man-in-black.

By the next morning, the storm had passed. Washington blushed in an apricot sunrise as the temperature slowly rose above freezing. From his office window, Fred watched Carlson sitting alone in the

Capital Grind. When he turned on the bug, he could hear a television and the chatter of customers. Even Carlson's eating noises. The bug worked perfectly.

Carlson's phone rang, but there wasn't much of a conversation. All Fred heard, was "yes" and "no". The call ended with "We need to talk in private. We have an unpleasant job to do." Because Fred's bug only got half of a conversation, it left him thinking about what could be unpleasant. Shortly thereafter, Carlson got up and left.

Fred turned his attention to finding the black Lincoln. Driving around town, he eventually saw two cars with white oval stickers mounted in the rear windows. Both had the name of the same DC parking garage. Fred located the large multilevel garage in an area dominated by office buildings. Parking could be paid by the hour or leased by the month. Fred took a ticket from the automatic parking gate and drove in. Several cars had the oval parking permits, but there were no black Lincolns.

Now, Fred hatched a plan to find the man-in-black. Just after midnight, he put a small box of portable surveillance cameras on the passenger seat of his car and headed back to the parking garage. He placed his cameras at a few intersections where traffic would most likely travel going to or from the garage. He stuck them on the sides of posts and buildings, being careful to avoid security cameras. Each of his cameras were positioned to photograph the rear of the car so the license plate would be included. They were motion sensitive, set to record only a couple of seconds at a time. Each camera recorded to a chip. He made timing adjustments until they photographed each car correctly.

By the time Fred finished, morning traffic covered the streets. He drove through McDonald's for coffee and a sausage biscuit, then parked where he could watch the entrance to the parking garage. Between sips of weak coffee, Fred Googled up five Lincoln dealers in the Washington area, hoping the Lincoln being sought was purchased or serviced at one of them.

A steady stream of cars entered the garage, but not the one he was looking for. Fred watched until ten o'clock then left for the closest Lincoln dealership. On his way, he pondered what Marion and her organization knew about his activities. Surely, her boss told others about the death threats. Maybe lots of people. Fred wondered how much Marion knew that she didn't share with him. Recording the activities of those in Congress is, after all, illegal.

The mechanic at the Lincoln dealer service counter listened patiently.

"Do you service many Lincoln MKXs?" Fred asked, knowing it was a dumb question.

"Sure, quit a few. Why do you ask?

"Well, I'm trying to locate a guy who drives a black two or three-year-old MKX with tinted windows and a white oval parking sticker from the Stonehill Parking Garage. Does that sound familiar?"

"Maybe, most of the MKXs that come in here are black."

"This one also has an oversized shark antenna and is chauffeur driven. I want to return a hat that his passenger left in my office. It's a rather expensive black fedora." Fred showed it to the mechanic.

"I think I know whose car that is."

"Who?"

"We don't give out that kind of information."

"So how do I get his hat back to him?"

"I can call and leave a message that you have the hat. What's your phone number?"

Fred grabbed a pen and pad from the service desk and wrote down a fake name and his untraceable cell phone number. The mechanic found the service record then punched the numbers into a phone. Fred memorized some of them.

"Okay, I left a message that you have the hat. They'll tell the driver."

"Thanks. I'm sure he'll appreciate it."

Fred couldn't be happier. Now all he had to do was wait for a phone call.

On his way back to his office he stopped by the Arundel men's shop, hat in hand, and asked if anyone remembered who purchased it.

"It's possible, but we don't usually know the names of our customers, and we never talk about them."

Fred showed the clerk his credentials and said he was investigating a man's whereabouts. A short, stalky man with a black and white mustache.

"I'm sorry we just wouldn't know who that customer would be."

Fred handed the clerk a fake business card. "If He should come in again, would you give me a call? It's really important."

"Of course, Mister Wilson."

Fred spent the afternoon in his office anticipating a call from the owner of the Lincoln. While waiting, he brought up a reverse telephone directory on his computer. He tried variations of the numbers the service manager dialed, hoping to find the number of the Lincoln owner. But it was getting dark and he was having no luck.

A distant explosion suddenly jarred the office. Fred jerked toward the widow where he saw a tower of glowing orange smoke bulge above the buildings a few blocks away. He looked toward his TV. A news announcer quickly reported, "Whoa! What was that?" Then she said, "There has been a large explosion. We could hear it right here in the newsroom. As soon as we have any information, you'll be the first to know." She then looked to her teleprompter and continued. "There's been a huge blast somewhere on 14th street. A crew is on the way. We'll bring you more news as we get it."

Before long a picture appeared on the oversized monitor behind her. It expanded to a full screen view. A reporter and cameraman were approaching the blast scene on foot, doing their best to run and narrate at the same time. The street looked like a picture straight out of the Middle East. Store windows were blown in, parked cars were wrecked, and people were injured.

"It looks like a car bomb, and a big one", gasped the reporter as the camera scanned the wreckage. The picture zoomed in on the ripped apart car. Fred's heart thumped hard. He saw the flaming remains of a black SUV only a few blocks away. He could be there in minutes. Grabbing his coat and camera, he shot out the door.

Out of breath, Fred reached the blast scene. There was no getting close. A half-block away, he zoomed in on the blast with his telephoto lens and began shooting. He moved closer for a better look.

"Hold it. This is as far as you go." A cop had his hand on Fred's shoulder.

Fred pulled out his private investigator's ID card.

"You can go as far as those officers who are unrolling yellow tape. No farther. And, stay off the street."

Fred ran as far forward as the TV cameras, only a short distance from the calamity. He scanned the area with his camera. Emergency vehicles were everywhere, and more were coming. Medics and cops were triaging the wounded on the sidewalk. Bits and pieces of the car were all over; a wheel in front of a mail drop, chunks of metal scattered about the street, a car door on the sidewalk, and glass shards reflecting the flames. Firefighters had just begun putting out the blazing wreckage of the split open Lincoln.

Fred had all he needed. He hustled back to his office and studied the pictures on his computer. It was a black Lincoln MKX. The plastic window tinting of the black Lincoln held enough of the glass together to see an oval sticker being consumed in the flames. The roof gaped open, but an oversized plastic shark antenna remained right where it should be. This was the man-in-black's car.

Fred got home late. His wife, Lilly greeted him at the door. "Fred where have you been? Why do I even bother to fix dinner anymore?"

"I know, I'm Sorry, but you won't believe what I saw. Turn on the TV, it should be on the news." All the news channels were covering the bombing. Fred told Lilly about his experience at the scene of the explosion. He wished he could tell her more, but he kept his business to himself. Jason, his twenty-six-year-old son, was glued to a laptop video game, oblivious of anything else.

Fred flipped channels into the night, eventually he saw a casualty report. Two dead and seven injured. Only one casualty in the Lincoln. What happened to the man-in-black? Fred fell asleep on the couch with the TV still on. The last news he heard, said law enforcement concluded it had to be an assassination attempt.

With three hours of sleep to sustain him, Fred went out before dawn and pulled the cameras he had set up. He made it back to his rented office in time to see if Carlson would show up. He didn't. After a few minutes of skimming through the new pictures from his cameras, he found what he hoped for; a picture of the Lincoln on its way to destruction.

Later that morning, Fred pulled into the Denny's parking lot. Marion sat sipping a Diet Coke nervously waiting for Fred's arrival. He slid into the booth across from her.

"Hi Marion, I found the man-in-black's Lincoln."

"Where?"

"Blown to pieces on fourteenth yesterday."

"What?"

"That's right, it was the man-in-black's car that got bombed. Photographs of the wreckage match photos from outside the Capital Grind. See for yourself." Fred slid an envelope across the table.

Marion opened the envelope and studied the pictures. "Was the man-in-black in it?"

"No. Only the driver."

Marion shoved her Coke aside and spread the pictures out in front of her.

"It had to be a timed explosion. Maybe started with a remote control. After a preset amount of time, Boom! The car blows up."

"With no passenger?"

"There was a passenger, but I think he got out along the way. I also believe the passenger had to be the man-in-black," Fred said.

Marion thoughtfully sipped her Coke. "What makes you think so?"

"This morning I checked some cameras I had set up near the garage where the Lincoln parks. I found a clear shot of the black Lincoln just minutes before it blew up." He pointed to one of the photos in front of Marion. "Notice the silhouette in the back seat." The outline of a hat brim. "He must have more than one hat, because when he stormed out of the Capital Grind, he forgot his hat. I have it in my car."

"So, what are you going to do with his hat?"

"It's one more piece of evidence to help locate him. For instance, it's new. He purchased it at a local men's store. They may know who he is."

Marion tapped her finger on the picture of the Lincoln. "Who do you think wants him dead?"

"Maybe Roger Carlson knows. He and the President were both threatened by him. Maybe someone inside the Republican Party did it, which could be a way to mitigate the man-in-black's death threat, or maybe Carlson's criminal friends were involved."

Fred knew he was in over his head. He and Marion knew more about the car bombing than the police. What if the law found out about them? Illegal surveillance was bad enough but withholding information in a capital crime could put him in prison for a long time. All he knew about Marion, was that she worked for a lobbyist and was interested in information about congressmen who may be corrupted, including Roger Carlson. In fact, she knew enough to get them both locked up.

"Marion, when we hear of a threat to the President, or anyone else, it's our responsibility to tell someone."

"I know that, but how can we explain how we found out? Don't you think the President already knows about the man-in-black and the threat? After all, Carlson is his friend, and knows who the man-in-black is."

"We're in too deep, Marion. Why don't we just drop the whole thing and forget the man-in-black?"

She frowned. "My organization thinks he's too important to forget about. He may be involved in illegal activities at high levels in government, maybe activities that could influence the outcomes of elections, or careers of politicians, or even the laws of our land. Influencing politicians can be a high stakes business and it looks like this guy might be right in the middle of it. He may also be one of Carlson's underworld contacts. We want to know what he's up to. And who he does business with. He may be involved with other congressmen."

Fred paused and gazed out the window. "I didn't sign on for this. It's one thing to investigate a dishonest congressman, but quite another to get involved with an ongoing criminal investigation. This is a job for the proper authorities, not us."

"Just find out who he is. Nothing else."

Fred pressed on. "So far we know he is the intended victim of a car bombing. He also committed a felony with his death threat. The guys a criminal. The authorities must believe the bombing targeted someone who wasn't in the Lincoln. Let them find him."

"I want to know who he is. that's what we're getting paid for."

"It's one thing to eaves drop on members of congress but to witness criminal behavior and not report it is felonious. What if you have to answer questions about what we know, that could get us arrested."

"Don't worry about me Fred, they have prison cells for women, just as they do for men."

"Okay Marion, you win. But before I do anything else, I need to know more about your organization, and I don't want to have to investigate you to find out. My association with you is making a criminal out of me. I want to know to whom I'm giving information and why?"

"Okay, I guess it's time you learned more about my organization. As you already know, I work for a large lobbying firm. We get paid to influence policymakers. We represent special interests in the decision-making process in the legislative and executive branches of government. The information you give us about congressmen is important to our client, The American Anti-Corruption League, who employs us. We receive substantial bonuses for each congressman identified. They in turn use that information to rid congress of corruption."

Fred frowned. "You want to know what I think? I think you guys want information so badly that you're willing to risk anything to get it. This client of yours must be paying very well."

"Do you want, more money?"

"No. I just want this to end before we all wind up in prison."

"Just keep quiet about this and we'll be fine. I am authorized to pay you an additional thousand dollars for each congressman you identify, if that helps."

"And for the man-in-black, what's he worth, five to ten in a federal penitentiary?"

Fred went back to his car. He knew that even if he found the man-in-black he would still be linked to a criminal organization. He was being sucked into an evil black hole in the center of Washington.

CHAPTER 7

Fred went home and threw himself on the couch. Lilly smiled seeing him home early. Jason looked up from his laptop. "Hi Dad, you hear about the bombing?"

"I did."

Fred flipped on the TV In time to see President Townsend send condolences to the nation for those harmed by the car bombing. At the end of his address, he said that the next week he would entertain a delegation of European Union businessmen, adding that the weather looked good enough for golf with his guests. The rest of the news covered the bombing. No witness information had yet been found. Speculation surrounded a variety of terrorists, but no organization had claimed responsibility. An assassination gone wrong topped the theories. The big questions were why was this car bombed, was there a particular target, and who would assassinate someone at the cost of so many innocent people? In one segment, the Chief of Police said, "If anyone has any information about this bombing you are urged to come forward." Fred's heart sank. He wished he could help the police. Instead he feared them. The guilty hide even when not being sought.

In the kitchen, Lilly whistled a happy tune as she put together a family dinner for the first time in a few days. Fred stretched out on the couch and propped a pillow under his head.

The news anchor came back on, "The investigation into the bombing found that the black Lincoln left the

Stonehill parking garage shortly before the bombing. Surveillance cameras showed only the driver, Harvey Westgate, exiting the garage alone. Police believe the bomb was intended for someone expected to be in the car, but for some reason was not."

To Fred, that meant the man-in-black got in the car after it left the garage. The assassin must have followed it until the man-in-black got in the car, then arm the bomb remotely. Fred would check his street photos to see which cars were following the Lincoln.

As Fred drifted into sleep his thoughts followed many rabbit trails. How could the killers know when or where their target wanted to be picked up? Did the assassin's car continue to follow the Lincoln, even after the passenger got in? Probably not or they would have seen him get out, then they would deactivate the bomb. Could the bomb be deactivated? Was the assassination threat against Carlson and the President the reason the Lincoln was blown up? How did the bombers know about the threat? Did Marion's people tell them? Did Carlson arrange it?

Then Fred dreamed he saw the man-in-black climb into the backseat of a black Lincoln, tap the driver on the shoulder and say, "let me off at the Arundel men's store. I need a new hat." He visualized the man-in-black getting out and disappearing through a double door. Then, out of the fog of his sleep he heard two men in a car. One saying, "Turn off the timer," and the other saying, "I can't. Once it's triggered it goes until it blows up."

"Dinner", Lilly yelled, waking Fred from his nap. Fred and Jason arrived at the table at the same time.

"That chicken looks delicious," Fred said.

"Thanks. But I'm worried about you Fred; you spend too much time at work."

"It's temporary. Things will get back to normal soon."

"I hope it's real soon. Your retirement job was supposed to give us more time to do things together."

Sol knew Representative Carlson had given him a stern warning. Now the Lincoln he used was blown to bits. What would he try next? He had to get Carlson off his back. But how?

Sol walked out of the Arundel Men's Wear store, gently bending the brim of his new fedora. A man stepped in front of him with a gold coin. He showed it like a cop flashes his badge.

"Mister Solomon, May I have a few minutes with you?" The man held out the coin long enough for Sol to see the date, "1932."

"Of course. What's your name?"

"You don't need to know that." The man pointed at Sol's rental car. "Can we talk in your car."

Sol learned that a small contingent of Ibrahim's men were in Washington. The man with the coin gave Sol the name of the group leader, a Syrian immigrant named, Jameel Hasan. Sol could call on these men if he needed help with his recruitments, whether to enhance a deal or to mitigate a threat. They would be Sol's personal goon squad, but they would also assure that Sol didn't stray from his obligations. Most of these men were illegal aliens brought in via Ibrahim's Midnight Express.

Sol updated the coin bearer with the news of who he had recruited and how many more were on his list. They agreed that any congressman who refused Sol's proposition had to be exposed, but the danger of Roger Carlson's assassination attempt on Sol's life superseded that and had to be dealt with immediately and permanently.

"Something else," the coin bearer said. "The President has been dragging his feet on deals he made with us. He knows the gravity of failing to carry out his promised allegiance to our cause. He receives great compensation for this. He also makes public statements against our people and our region. He needs to be significantly warned. I want you to meet with Jameel and his men to work out the means of effecting this. It should be done very soon."

"When will I see you again? Sol asked.

"When I choose. If you must contact me, Ask Jameel. He can alert me. Since we usually know where you are, I will come to you."

Sol was dumbfounded. What did the coin bearer mean by, "He needs to be significantly warned?" Does he expect me to do something to the President? Sol felt a twinge of fear. He would do anything to preserve his wealth.

The meeting ended. The coin bearer got out and walked away. Sol called Jameel and arranged a meeting. It took place informally at a small bar on 14th Street. Jameel arrived with two other men, one young, one old. All three looked and sounded Middle Eastern. Over a few cocktails they planned a series of events that would satisfy the requirements of the coin bearer.

The next morning, Sol called a fellow real estate broker who had a trusted employee who would do any job. All anyone had to do is act like they liked him.

He asked his broker friend, "do you still have that funny looking guy working for you?"

"Sure do. Why?"

"I need someone who can buy me a car that can't be traced to anyone."

"He might do it."

"Good. I'd like to meet with him in your office."

"Sure. I'll set it up."

Long before he went to work for Sol's friend, Delmar Fawcett won a Silver Star in Iraq. He didn't do it out of bravery. He just wanted people to like him, so he took foolish risks at any opportunity trying to achieve that end. To his credit, he knew how to shoot straight. One night on a rescue mission to save a captured journalist, he and his buddies were stopped by a group of Al-Qeada that blew a track off their personnel carrier. Delmar jumped out and started shooting – one shot at a time. He killed five enemy combatants and captured an anti-tank gun. He was credited with saving his platoon as well as his commanding officer, Major Tory Thorson, who rode in the personnel carrier with him. He received the Purple Heart for a wound that took off half an ear and a chunk of scalp to go with it. A knee wound gave him a medical discharge and a small pension.

His bravery didn't have the effect he wanted. To add to his perpetual goofy half grin and pockmarked face, his injury resulted in a hairless white streak across the side of his head where the top of his ear used to be. In fact, few ever liked him. As a kid, his classmates called him leaky Fawcett because he was a bed wetter and had no friends at all. Even his siblings shunned him. As a teenager, they called him dummy Delmar. He had acne so bad that it permanently scarred his face. To add to his problems, he grew to six feet two inches but weighed only one-hundred-sixty pounds.

For treatment of his scalp and knee wounds he evacuated to Landstuhl hospital in Germany, then on to

Walter Reed in Bethesda Maryland for scalp grafting and a knee replacement. After his discharge, he found work for a real estate brokerage in Washington, doing property clean up and odd jobs. He worked hard, and people seemed to like him. For the first time in his life he felt like he had friends. He would do anything they asked. No job was too hard, too dirty, or too dangerous.

Eventually, he worked directly for the principal broker. This meant a step up financially for Delmar, but also meant he had to do jobs likes evictions, repossessions, and some illegal activities in addition to his usual property maintenance work. His boss profited from criminal enterprises, but that was okay with Delmar because his boss liked him.

On a cold January morning, Delmar walked into the real estate office. His boss introduced him to a man in a black overcoat who sat behind a brand-new fedora that lay on the table. The man needed someone to buy him a used car.

"What kind of car?" Delmar wanted to know.

"A reliable, older, full sized sedan," Sol said. He then put five-thousand dollars in cash on the table. "This should get you a pretty good one."

Delmar's boss laid out the deal. "I have a fake driver's license for you. Buy the car using the name on the License. Don't do anything else. Don't register it. The car will be used illegally so I expect you to keep your mouth shut. As soon as you buy the car, drive it to the address on the license and park it."

Sol handed Delmar's boss five-hundred dollars. "Give that to Delmar when I tell you I like the car." He then grabbed his hat and walked out.

Delmar went online to search for a car. One lot in Northeast Baltimore had plenty to choose from. He took public transportation to the lot where he bought an older grey Chrysler sedan.

While Delmar searched for a car, Sol met with his Syrian goon squad. They discussed ways to threaten or intimidate the President. They spent most of the day planning until they had it right. They knew how to convince the President of his mortality.

The next day, Delmar picked up his five-hundred dollars. Sol arrived at the same time. He had a new request. "How would you like to pick up a quick ten-thousand bucks?" Delmar couldn't believe what he just heard. *What do I have to do this time, buy a cruise ship?* "What do you want me to do?"

"It would require you to wound a man."

"Who?"

"Your boss tells me you're trustworthy."

"You bet."

"It's important that everything said here is never repeated. Can you do that?"

"Yes."

"The man I want you to wound is the President of the United States."

Delmar could not believe what he just heard, but the words that came out were, "That sounds impossible! Why me?"

"You're known as an expert shot. I need someone who can shoot well enough to inflict only a light flesh wound."

"Why?"

"The President is about to cause great harm to many people. He has been warned to stop or face assassination, but he continues with his agenda. We think that if he gets shot and wounded, he will believe the threats and change his behavior, thereby saving the lives of many innocent people. This requires a good shot like you."

"If I do this I'll either be killed or imprisoned for the rest of my life."

"We've got it planned better than that. The President goes golfing almost every week and almost always at the Grovewood, here in the district. We've already practiced dry runs at the golf course. Here's how it will work. We've prepared an in-ground hiding place sixty yards from the fifth fairway. It's a hole in the ground with a camouflaged lid. You could stand right next to it and never see it. As soon as we hear that the President is ready to go golfing, we'll sneak you in. You will hide in the hole overnight until the President is on the course. Then you will step into a simple blind where you can't be seen. All you must do is wing him while he's on the fifth fairway. As soon as you fire, jump back into the hole and cover it. There's enough food and water to last as long as needed. There is also a comfortable place to sit and plenty of blankets. To throw investigators off the trail we have a trampled spot in the brush that will look like someone waited there to target the President. We'll even leave an empty cartridge from the same rifle you will use, and some cigarette butts."

"I don't smoke."

"That's all the better. When the Secret Service rushes to the direction of the shot they will see evidence that a shooter waited in the bushes. They will also see broken brush leading to a cut in a chain link fence next to the highway. They'll see that, as the shooter's escape route. As soon as we can, we'll come take you out. You can go back to work ten-thousand bucks richer. No one will ever know what happened to the shooter."

"I don't know."

"Delmar's boss cinched the deal by telling Him, "you'll be praised by people who, while they don't know you, will be thankful for what you did for them. Ten-thousand bucks, Delmar."

"Okay boss. I'll do it."

Just after seven the next morning, Fred went over pictures of cars he had photographed with his surveillance cameras, the day before. Close behind the Lincoln followed a blue Ford Escape. Could that be the bomber's car? Fred glanced out the window and saw Roger Carlson walk into the Capital Grind. He flipped on his surveillance equipment and put on his earphones. As usual, Carlson ordered a double latte and went to his preferred table. Fred switched on the bug under Carlson's table. A few minutes later an old gray Chrysler pulled up to the curb. Two men got out, both dressed in jeans, sweatshirts, and baseball caps. They walked briskly into the espresso shop. One pointed an automatic pistol at the customers.

"On the floor, I'll shoot the first one who looks up."

Fred's eavesdropping equipment caught it all.

The other man went behind the counter and ordered the baristas to the floor. He reached into the cash register, stuffed his pockets with cash, and then yelled, "Let's go."

Carson quivered with fear, then dared to look up at the gunman. A quick burst of three deafening shots killed Carlson instantly. The men ran to their car, pulled the nylon stockings from their heads and took off. A third man drove.

Fred had the whole thing recorded; sound, video, and photos. He grabbed his evidence and started packing. He had only a few minutes to clear out his stuff, leaving only an unused office behind. He could hear the sirens coming as he ran downstairs to the garage. He unloaded armloads of gear into the trunk of his car and ran back for more. It wouldn't be long before cops started looking for witnesses, and he wasn't going to be one of them.

Totally out of breath he threw the last of his incriminating evidence into the trunk of his car. He slowly drove out of the garage. Fortunately, the cops had just arrived and hadn't turned their attention to witnesses. Because of his work, Fred drove one of the most common cars in Washington – a five-year-old silver Toyota Camry. It's good for private investigators not to be noticed. He drove straight home.

When he arrived, he unloaded his trunk full of equipment into his garage office, installed a spare hard drive in his computer, and destroyed the old one. The camera chips were replaced with last summer's vacation photos. Thankfully, he didn't have a cloud backup to worry about. All the surveillance evidence was gone except the bug under the table. That made him nervous. He sat down, switched on a TV and watched the news reports. All the reporting channels said that Representative Roger Carlson died from gunshot wounds during a holdup. Two masked gunmen got away with a small amount of cash. The gunmen and the getaway car were both described. The Police had the details, but they didn't have pictures. Fred did.

His cell phone rang. "How about lunch at Napoleon's?" Marion asked.

"Sure, see you there."

Before leaving, he listened to the recording from the bug under Carlson's table. He heard the whole thing right down to the gun shots and the screams. The two men had a Middle Eastern accent. He then dropped the recording chips and photo chips into a plastic sandwich bag along with the recordings of the holdup. He slid the bag under a shingle on his garden shed roof. He'd find a better hiding place later.

At twelve sharp, Fred sat at Marion's preferred table at Napoleon's. Two minutes later Marion walked in.

"Good afternoon Fred. How are you?"

"I'm glad you called."

"Did you see what happened this morning?"

"I did."

"Well?"

"The news reports have it just like it happened."

"Do you think Carlson was targeted?"

"I do. Carlson wasn't the only one to look up, but he was the only one shot. Furthermore, the gunman never took his eyes off Carlson from the moment he entered the shop. This was an assassination. I think it was a retribution killing for the botched bombing. The way I see it, Carlson took the man-in-black's death threats seriously. Someone in Carlson's orbit must have arranged to have the man-in-black killed. The man-in-black may have perceived that his life was in danger and acted unpredictably to avoid trouble. When he missed getting bombed, he decided to kill Carlson. This is how the mob does things."

"It's also the way the drug cartels and terrorist organizations work," Marion added.

"It could be. Years ago, after the Kennedy assassination, people all over the country including the FBI, CIA, the Secret Service and even Congress suspected the mafia because Robert Kennedy was trying to put them out of business. Even President Johnson and Fidel Castro were suspected. These suspicions persist."

The waiter arrived and Marion ordered a salad. Fred ordered a Rubin sandwich. He hadn't eaten since his wife's fried chicken the night before. After the waiter retreated Marion said, "Do you have any more information on the man-in-black?"

"No. But I know his hat size!"

When lunch arrived, Fred wolfed down his sandwich as he contemplated terminating his contract with Marion. But he didn't know how.

"If I were the man-in-black, I'd disappear," Fred said, as he wrapped the remains of his sandwich in a napkin and stuck it in his coat pocket. He was anxious to leave.

"Unless his next job is to carry out his threat to kill the President."

Chapter 8

On Friday morning, President Townsend addressed the nation from his oval office. It was clear that he was grieving over his friend of forty years being murdered in a common holdup. To reporters, he expressed deep sadness for Carlson's family, and would make every effort to bring his killers to justice. "We need to do something to get guns out of the hands of criminals!"

As he stepped away from the podium he was overheard saying, "I'd like to personally blow their heads off." That remark became the lead story of the day. It was only one in a long line of thoughtless remarks, ensuring the unlikelihood he would be re-elected.

That afternoon held chilly, but sunny weather. An afternoon on the golf course with his European guests, would help President Townsend burn off his anger. They arrived at the golf course at one o'clock.

Well down the fifth fairway, the President and his company stepped out of their golf carts. He chose a club and approached his ball near the edge of the fairway. "When he commented on the chill in the air, a German business mogul who led the game by one point, replied, "Not too chilly for golf!"

Townsend lofted the ball toward its target just as two gun shots rang out. Secret Service agents pushed the President to the ground and covered him with their bodies. Other Secret Service ran toward the direction of the gun fire. The President's doctor jumped from his cart and ran to him. No one noticed the President's ball roll to the rim of the hole and drop in, one under par. Nor did anyone notice a blue Ford Escape pull onto the highway north of the golf course.

Fred Ferguson killed time listening to his car radio, while watching the home of a certain congressman suspected of keeping company with young women. This, while his wife was out of town. Fred had his hand in his lunch bag, when news of the shooting broke in, "just minutes ago, an assassination attempt was made on the President of the United States. He was shot and injured at the Grovewood golf course in the District." Fred dropped his sandwich as the news went on. "The extent of his injuries are not yet known, but he is sitting up on a bench receiving aid. He looks alert and is talking." The anchor continued, "We just learned that the would-be assassin was himself shot. He was found dead some sixty yards away in a wooded section at the edge of the golf course. The bullet that killed him came from a second gunman firing from the highway just east of the golf course. The question being asked is, 'how did the shooter escape detection by the Secret Service?' The answer? A camouflaged hole in the ground, from which he emerged."

Fred let out a long sigh. First Carlson gets it and now someone's trying to kill the President, just like the man-in-black threatened.

The news went on to say, "The President is being carried to a waiting helicopter for evacuation. Several other helicopters are in the area. The fairway is being overrun by vehicles as officials arrive on the scene."

Fred got out of his car. In the distance, he saw helicopters over the golf course.

The President sustained only a shallow wound to his arm and left the hospital the same afternoon. Back in the White House he went into a rage about who might have shot him.

"It could have been anyone," he told his wife. "Probably the Israelis, I know they'd like to see me dead, or maybe the Vice-president wants my office, seems like everyone hates me. What about those demanding generals. I bet they'd like to see me dead too. Maybe the Russians had something to do with it. Maybe some Middle East wackos." No one escaped his tirade. "I want to know who did it. Had that assassin been a better shot, I'd be dead. Or maybe he was a good shot and my injury is a warning."

"Warning about what?" The First Lady asked.

"Roger told me Someone had threatened his life and said mine was in danger too. He said if I didn't lay off criticizing Middle Easterners, they might kill me. Now Roger is dead, and I have a bullet hole in my arm. What am I supposed to think? This wasn't any nut job shooting either. Whoever shot at me was organized. Someone needs to call the FBI. They should be looking for that guy who made the threats."

"All that's been take care of. I'm sure they'll update us on their findings."

The press secretary came in. "Mister President, I'll need to say something to the public."

"I don't care what you say. Can't you see I'm wounded? Leave me alone."

"Yes sir."

The White House press secretary made a statement just in time for the six o'clock news saying, "The President has only a flesh wound and will be back in the Oval Office tomorrow. He is resting and is in good spirits." But in the White House, the President plotted revenge.

The next morning, President Townsend awoke with a very sore arm and a very bad attitude. Arriving late to his private office. He immediately drafted a letter to the director of the Secret Service. It began with, "You're fired." He gave the letter to an aide for immediate hand delivery. He then logged into Twitter and made the firing public.

While directing his investigation at the Grovewood golf course, the director of Secret Service received the news from a reporter who asked, "Do you know that the President is tweeting that he fired you?"

At the morning press briefing the Press Secretary could only say that the President had his reasons for the firing. Reporters pounded him with questions. "No, it had nothing to do with retribution. The President is reviewing the circumstances of the shooting with security agents whom he trusts completely."

"No, no one has claimed responsibility." The press secretary continued.

"No connection has been made to the murder of Representative Carlson."

"We know nothing more about the shooting than what has already been reported."

"The President's wound is superficial, but uncomfortable. He has canceled all appointments for the next few days."

"You will be kept informed as we learn more."

The briefing ended.

President Townsend stared at a gift he had received shortly before taking office. An antique twenty-dollar gold coin. He knew now that he must keep his mouth shut and follow every promise he made.

After several weeks, law enforcement still had no arrests in the President's assassination attempt,

Carlson's assassination, or the car bombing. If authorities made a connection between them, they hadn't let on. So far, they knew what kind of car the Carlson assassins drove, their weapons, approximate age, and size. About the bombing, they knew the Lincoln was leased to the Republican National Committee, but that shed no light on who could have bombed it or who they targeted. The dealership that leased it was heavily questioned, but all they could offer was a pile of service records and the descriptions of the man who leased it and the unlucky driver, both employees of the RNC. The employee who leased the car didn't drive it. He said the dead driver used it the most. Everyone who used the car had to sign it out with a log entry of how it would be used. The log entry for the day of the car bombing said, "transport passenger." Nothing else. None of the many entries made by the killed driver gave a name.

About the President's close call, law enforcement knew the type of weapons used and how the crime was carried out. The dead assassin was a thirty-seven-year-old handyman from Fredericksburg Virginia, employed by a local real estate brokerage. He was a single army veteran with a Purple Heart and a Silver Star. He was being treated by the VA for Post-Traumatic Stress Disorder. His weapon was a 1903 Springfield 30-06. The same kind of weapon used by Sergeant York, the famous World War One Medal of Honor winner. The shooter had no criminal history. Not the kind of person anyone would think of as an assassin. They had no leads on who shot the shooter. The bullet that killed him was a full metal jacket 7.62 NATO round that could have been fired from a number of different weapons. barrel groove marks narrowed the field, but nothing conclusive. There was no DNA found on any of the cigarette butts left near the hole in the ground.

The Secret Service took heat for not providing better security for the President. In their defense, they argued that the President should have kept his mouth shut about going golfing. The President spent several weeks hiding out at Camp David letting everyone know his anger for the Secret Service, the FBI, the CIA, and all the local law enforcement agencies for their perceived ineptitude in the shooting incident. The President appointed a new Director of the Secret Service.

Through it all, Sol continued to gather recruits. It seemed the congressmen he approached didn't worry much about any threats but loved the idea of a quick million bucks. Fred continued to provide a stream of crooked congressmen that would keep him busy. However, Fred was amazed at how many congressmen were cheating on their wives. He found one law maker's indiscretions just by looking at his Facebook. Another on a dating website. He suspected some were receiving large sums of money from criminal organizations; others were receiving illegal contributions, still others were interested in salacious activities with minors. Fred suspected one of having two wives. There seemed to be no end to the crimes some congressmen were hiding, or not bothering to hide.

Fred checked out one last lead in his search for the man-in-black, then the trail went cold. It was about the driver killed in the car bombing. The driver worked for the RNC and drove a variety of cars as an on-call chauffeur. Fred learned that he frequently drove the ill-fated Lincoln. The RNC told Fred that the car transported people to places where it was impractical to park, or when the passenger needed only a one-way ride. Fred asked the RNC office manager, "Are you familiar with a stocky man in his forties or fifties who is, say, five-feet-six, dark complected, with black hair and who may dress in black suits and a black hat?"

"You just described a fair percentage of everyone we know. Men in Washington like to wear black suits. It's like a uniform, and in the winter many of them wear hats. In fact, several men matching your description are associated with this office."

Fred wondered if anyone knew about the man-in-black's threat, or that he was the target of the car bombing. Certainly, the President must know, but why would he keep it quiet? Fred would like to make an anonymous tip to law enforcement but feared what might happen if anyone figured out who made the tip. He worried about Marion's handling of the surveillance information he had given her. Until these crimes were solved, Fred would have to live with the nagging worry that he may be found out. The guilty always have to look over their shoulder.

CHAPTER 9

With Fred's surveillance subject assassinated, he decided to move his garage office into the small one across from the Capital Grind. He had already spent much of the past few weeks purchasing equipment and setting up his new business location, on the second floor. Lilly suddenly took an interest in her husband's new office. She dug right in painting walls in green and maroon and replacing the worn linoleum with dark walnut laminate. An old-style carpet graced the center, and bargain local art hung on the walls. She even found a well-seasoned set of leather chairs. She lined the inner office with bookshelves and an old armoire to store Fred's equipment. An antique oak desk of some long-forgotten Washington bureaucrat sat in the outer room. Lilly carefully picked out the best that Washington's thrift shops had to offer. When finished, the office appeared well established. Bright chrome lettering on the outside window read, "Ferguson Investigations LLC."

Fred kicked off his first full day in his new office with a visit to the Capital Grind.

He greeted the auburn-haired barista and ordered a Caffe Americano. He walked over to the table where the late Representative Carlson had been assassinated. He sat in the same chair. While he waited for his coffee, he slipped his hand under the table. There it was. His bug. He popped it loose into his hand, then into his pocket. While he admired his new office, he realized that anyone looking across the street, could see his place of business. He decided to add his phone number to the chrome lettering.

Marion West entered the office of Ferguson Investigations for the first time. She smiled politely at Fred's wife Lilly, at the reception desk. She announced her name and said she had a ten o'clock appointment. Lilly got up and knocked on Fred's door. "Hey Fred, there's someone here to see you." Fred hadn't yet established office protocol.

Marion glanced out the window at the Capital Grind Coffee Shop across the street. She watched customers chatting. No wonder Fred knew so much about Representative Carlson. Fred motioned Marion in. Lilly had a tinge of jealousy, as the attractive Miss West disappeared into Fred's inner Office.

"I have a lead on a congressman who has a suspicious bill before congress," Marion said.

"What kind of bill?"

"It's a land exchange bill. My boss thinks it's an opportunity for corruption."

"If your boss thinks it's corrupt, why wouldn't those in congressmen think so too?"

"It looks good, but it's a real estate bill and the sponsor is a real estate broker."

"So, who's the congressman?"

"Representative Stuart Burke, a Republican from New Mexico."

The folder Marion handed over held a copy of the bill, plus a minimum of other information.

Lilly was glad to see Marion leave. "Fred, why didn't you introduce me to your client?"

"It's just business. She's the one I research congressmen for."

"That's your largest account. Don't you think I should know more about her?"

"There's not much to know. I research the background of a congressman. If I find corruption, I let her know. Sometimes she has a lead for me. That's why she came here today."

Lilly paused, a slight frown crossing her forehead. "Don't you think there's something wrong with photographing and eavesdropping on members of congress?"

"No big deal, the paparazzi do it all the time."

Fred went back into his office and read the bill. It looked straight forward. It would trade private land to be preserved as recreational land, in exchange for public land. But, the sponsor of the bill owns a real estate agency. How could he benefit from this?

To find out, Fred had Lilly book a flight to New Mexico for the next morning.

He visited the land described in the bill. Neither the private nor the public land looked valuable. After that, he entered Representative Burke's real estate office, saying he owned land in the area described in the bill, and wanted to know how he could get in on the trade. The agent explained an acre for acre trade.

"But can I choose the acreage I want to trade for?"

"Sure, but there are other landowners asking for parcels they want to trade for. You can register your request at the county clerk's office. But the best acreage is already spoken for."

"Could I sell the land after the exchange?"

"Yes."

"How about mineral rights"

"You would have mineral rights."

At the county clerk's office, Fred looked up the owners of the private land. It didn't take him long to learn that part of that land belonged to members of Representative Burke's family, and some local businessmen. Most of the land was recently purchased. When he checked the public land to be traded for, he found It sat on a natural gas field. He photocopied all he found and took it home with him.

Back in Washington, Fred joined Marion for lunch at Napoleon's, where she had already ordered. He was anxious to share this new information. "You wouldn't believe what Burke is doing with his land exchange! If that bill passes, his family and his buddies will trade some worthless rock outcroppings, for some other worthless looking land that just happens to sit on top of natural gas." He handed some of his documents to Marion.

"Not if the bill passes. It passed while you were away. The land exchange will become law."

Fred shook his head. "It looks like some people in New Mexico will be getting rich."

Fred gave Marion his travel expense invoice and photocopies and went back to work.

Sol's cell phone buzzed. Marion had a new prospect for him. They would meet in her office the next morning. He arrived early and was sitting in the Leonard Government Relations Office reading the Washington Post, when the receptionist called his name. "Mister Bishop. Miss West will see you now."

"Thank you," he said, as he stood and buttoned his tight-fitting sky-blue suit coat.

Marion had one folder for him. If Sol knew anything, he knew real estate. He studied the information, then looked up at her. "How did he get away with it?" he asked. "This is the most blatant scam I've ever seen. We should have no trouble exposing this guy."

"Good," Marion said. "Nothing would make me feel better."

With another million-dollar prospect in his briefcase, Sol set out to meet Representative Burke. Elected officials are always interest in campaign money. Representative Burke would see him right away. Sol couldn't get his mind off the real estate scam. Burke was scamming the government for millions, and nobody suspected anything except Marion West. Sol admired Burke's hubris.

Representative Burke's office showed off the natural beauty of New Mexico in photographs and paintings. Burke dressed to match; blue jeans with a big silver buckle, a white shirt with a silver tipped black bolo tie, and a black blazer. A black Stetson hat lay on the corner of his desk. He stood tall in his ostrich skin boots, as he greeted Sol. He presented a powerful handshake and offered him a chair.

Sol began as he had with others. "I have a confidential offer to make. How would you like to get some serious campaign contributions?"

Burke was stoic.

"The Republican Party has a very wealthy benefactor," Sol said. "He wants to be sure certain Republicans like you stay in office."

"Who is he?"

"He wishes to remain anonymous."

"That doesn't sound right."

"That doesn't matter. The money can be distributed by legal means."

Burke hesitated. "How so?"

"Through political action committees, speaking, land deals, and so on. All the usual ways."

"So, what do I have to do?"

"Our benefactor, as well as some members of congress, want us to get out of the Middle East. In exchange for the campaign funds, you would vote for, or enact, legislation that would keep the United States out of the Middle East."

Burke leaned back in his chair and threw one booted leg on his desk. After a long silence, he said, "How much?"

"Enough to get you re-elected." Sol explained a few specifics, then placed a small stack of gold coins on the congressman's desk. "If you're interested, we can seal the deal with these coins. Then I can tell you more. Go ahead. Help yourself."

Burke stared at the coins for a while before speaking. "I better not. This just doesn't sound right."

"Let me rephrase the offer." He opened his briefcase and pulled the maps Marion West had given him. "Here's something else that 'just doesn't sound right'."

Burke sat up straight. He recognized the maps.

"Recently enacted legislation is about to make you a rich man. If you can profit from your own legislation, what's wrong with supporting legislation that keeps us out of the Middle East?"

"I gave up a prosperous real estate business so I could represent my district in Congress.

Burke answered. "Now you want to bribe me into something that goes against my morals."

"Your real estate deals are safe with me. Please take some time to reconsider all that my offer entails."

"No thanks. I don't think I need your help." Burke grabbed the maps and told Sol to leave. Sol scooped up his coins and left. He waited to see if Burke would reconsider. He didn't have long to wait. The next day, Sol got a call from the Republican National Committee. Representative Burke had been asking about the unknown donor Sol mentioned. The manager at the RNC asked Sol for details. Sol feigned innocence. He convinced his manager there was a misunderstanding, and that his visit to Representative Burke was routine fundraising business.

Sol hadn't told Burke about the million-dollar Cayman Island account or who was involved with his proposition, but he did offer a few gold coins that could be seen as bribe money. There was no confirming evidence that Sol did anything wrong, but Burke could still cause trouble. Now he had to be convinced to keep his mouth shut.

Sol was surprised when Burke took his call, inviting him back to his office. "Representative Burke, I thought the conversation we had the other day would remain confidential."

"You accused me of making fraudulent land deals. It's just coincidental that some of my land is included. I am, after all, a real estate broker with several holdings. The government could have claimed eminent domain. That would harm rural landowners. The exchange offers them a fair trade, their land for unused federal land." Burke crossed his arms over his pearl buttoned shirt.

Sol looked him straight in the eye. "Acreage used for rock climbing has far less value than acreage sitting over natural gas. Who do you think you're kidding?"

"I don't know what you're up to with your mysterious rich benefactor, but I'm going to find out, and when I do, you'll be finished. However, we can both stay out of trouble if you stick to your fundraising and let me do the legislating."

Others in congress knew much more about Sol's propositions than Burke knew. They had reason to keep their mouths shut, but if Burke questioned enough of them, he might find out too much. Sol felt the agony of intimidation Just like he had imposed it on others. He had to get Burke off his back. He would distract him using his alter ego.

So, Sol drafted a news release concerning the land exchange scam. He put it under the letterhead of his phony American Anti-Corruption League. with the signature, "Arthur Bishop, Executive Director." on the bottom. He mailed copies to newspapers in New Mexico, and to Marion West at Leonard Governmental Relations.

Eventually, an investigative article appeared in a small New Mexico paper. It outlined what the bill in congress did, who sponsored it, and who would benefit from it. A few days later, major news organizations had the story, with even more incriminating revelations of Burke's criminal behavior. Representative Burke became the subject of a House investigation. He was asked to resign from congress.

Sol's successful exposure of Burke was credited to Arthur Bishop of the American Anti-Corruption League without anyone knowing that Sol had anything to do with it. Marion West followed the Burke news until he resigned. She then emailed congratulations for a job well done to Arthur Bishop.

CHAPTER 10

Sol was reading_the Wall Street Journal over breakfast at Lincoln's Waffle House on 10th Street, when a man sat down across from him. When Sol looked up, he could see a familiar man holding a gold coin. A closer look reveled the date, 1932. "Good morning, Mister Solomon," he said.

"Good morning. I've been expecting you, but how did you know where to find me?"

"You are a valuable investment. We keep track of you."

"That's flattering, Mister...?"

"Never mind that. Ibrahim sends you his best regards. He is happy about the President's new complacency. A job well done. He is most pleased with your recruitment efforts. They seem like easy pickings."

"Yes, they are. I receive regular referrals from our lobbyist."

The man leaned over Sol's plate of eggs and home fries. "It's time we see legislation that keeps America out of our business."

"Those things take time and opportunity, but we're working on it," Sol said.

"We want to see bills that will get America out of the Middle East. But we have a more immediate problem. How can the American public be convinced that terrorism is being controlled, when a car bomb goes off in the middle of Washington?"

"The perpetrator of that fiasco has been eliminated," Sol explained.

The coin bearer's voice was firm. "Blame the fourteenth street bombing on terrorists. Congress should use that unfortunate event to pass anti-terror legislation. This will make Republicans look good in the eyes of voters. Your party must stay in the majority to affect the legislation that will allow our caliphate to form. You should also focus your attention on security measures closer to home. If you put effort into building walls on your borders, you can distract attention from the Middle East. Also play up the danger from North Korea and other maverick nations. Find a way to move aircraft carriers from the Mediterranean to the Sea of Japan. While you're doing this, begin legislation that would remove the United States from the Middle East. Now that you have enough Congressman in your stable, it's time to fulfill your promise."

The time had come when Sol must organize a corrupt congress to fulfill his agreement. "Of course, we are ready to do just that."

"You have the Senate Majority Leader in your confidence. He can affect all that Ibrahim wants."

"You're right. Senator Case has enough popularity in the Senate to influence not only our cooperating senators, but many others, plus he has a good relationship with the Speaker of the House."

"How soon can I expect to see some results?"

"I'll go see Senator Case right away. He has taken charge of your legislative requirements. I'll keep you posted."

"You can't contact me. You must relay any important information to Jameel. Ibrahim has more than one emissary dispatch to the US. Your next emissary contact may not be me. Remember the gold coin."

"One more thing. We need a remote location for our Washington based agents. Some place secure and private were we can come and go without anyone being concerned. Since you are in the real estate business, you should be able to find us a place nearby, yet private."

"I may already have what you want," Sol replied. There's an old lodge on the Potomac river that hasn't been used in decades. I only recently acquired it. It sits on a few wooded acres, and it's close to town. It can accommodate several guests. If you're interested, I can have a realtor show it to you."

"No agents. You will show it to me, just you and me, and I want to see it now."

The man with the gold coin waited quietly while Sol wolfed down the remainder of his breakfast. The two men then left to see the property. They drove south of town to a remote location on the west bank of the Potomac river. At the end of a long dirt driveway stood a large forgotten building. A moss-covered grey slate roof protected the antique lodge where it slumbered away the years waiting for new life. Though the building was old, it was livable. The two men walked through the lodge. The coin bearer liked what he saw. He especially liked the dock that jutted out over the river. It was large enough to accommodate a sea going fishing boat. The coin bearer said it would do.

"Let's go to my office and draw up a lease agreement," Sol said.

"I'm not going to your office nor am I signing anything. You are already compensated. I want complete use of this property without any encumberances. I want you to make this place livable as soon as possible, so I can move our people into it. No one is to know who occupies it. As far as anyone is concerned this is your private holding, not for sale or lease. We must insist on complete privacy."

"Okay. I'll get right on it."

Both men returned to Washington. The coin bearer got out of the car back at Lincoln's Waffle House. Sol went to his office where he arranged for a contractor to inspect the house and make it ready for occupancy. After that, Sol went to see Senator Case.

When the Senator walked in, Sol spoke right up. "Today I met with our benefactors. They expect us to get started on legislation that will keep us out the Middle East. Now that we have several congressman agreeing to help, and the President is in line, they expect to see some action."

"Well, it looks like it's time to pay the piper. How about we start with getting support for a law that would require anyone entering the country to be photo-graphed, fingerprinted and give a DNA sample, all of which would be cross matched against existing data bases?"

"Not so fast. Those kinds of things are already being done. We risk being duplicitous if we don't have a good and real reason for legislation. These guys want to see us do something meaningful for them — and soon. They've got a nation to build."

"Okay. While we're finding ways to get us out of the Middle East, how about we get to the bottom of why we've lost drones in combat? We can call in some generals for questioning and ground all the drones while the issue is being resolved. That's quick and will give us some time for more powerful legislation. We have a senator on the Armed Services Committee who can start on that right away."

Sol paused for a moment. "I like it, but the first order of business should be to limit entry into the United State from certain Middle Eastern countries. This will give us credibility in our efforts to protect the American people from foreign terrorism. The caliphate people don't care anyway. They have the means to bring people across our border any time they want. We should also support a spending bill to complete the Mexican border wall. That would be highly controversial, which would detract from activities in the Middle East, focusing the terrorism threat on a porous Mexican border."

Case would call a meeting with other senators in his confidence, to discuss how to move forward with these ideas. Sol grabbed a truffle on his way out. He had an appointment with Senator Craig Kirk (R) of Connecticut regarding campaign funds and his communication with minors on the Internet.

There were several new millionaires in Congress, all of whom made Sol even richer. Now Sol had to find ways to match his income to his purchases. How would it look if his tax deductions exceeded his income? He spent most of his money in the Cayman Islands using his false identity, but in the United States he still had property taxes on a rather expensive condo to worry about, among other expenses. Sol decided it would help to expand his real estate business. He hired a manager and some new agents, registered his Mercedes as a company car, and his driver became an employee of the brokerage. He opened two satellite offices in the wealthiest suburbs. He could never have done this without using some of his Cayman Island money.

Income from his business expansion made Sol look legitimate. The lodge provided another opportunity. He decided to lease it at a high price to his alter ego, Arthur Bishop. This provided two benefits; the appearance of a few thousand dollars a month in lease income, and someone else to be responsible for its current occupants. His expanded finances required accountants. He hired one to keep track of his real estate brokerage, and another to handle the financial affairs of the extraordinarily rich Arthur Bishop of the Grand Cayman Islands. Yet another one would take care of his personal finances and advise him on how to hide his ill-gotten wealth. With his real estate business and financial worries managed for him, he became free to be the kind of fundraiser Ibrahim Bin Jabar expected him to be.

When renovations at the lodge were finished, a Salt Breeze fishing boat arrived at its dock. Several Middle Easterners disembarked and walked up a freshly graveled pathway to the front porch. They were welcomed by Jameel and two others who arrived earlier, to oversee the installation of a security system. Jameel's Chrysler minivan sat in the carport by the kitchen. Next to it stood the blue Ford Escape used in the golf course shooting incident.

Ibrahim Bin Jabar's new Washington contingent included the man who shot Delmar Fawcett and the two assassins of Representative Carlson. The house would be managed by an aging Palestinian from New York.

Also, Ibrahim saw to it that one man always knew Sol's whereabouts. This was typically easy duty, but back in January when Sol first went to the Cayman Islands, he lost his followers completely when he disappeared into the Airport. To prevent this from happening again, Jameel's crew used Sol's absence to bug his condo and real estate office.

The coin bearer told Jameel that Sol had an appointment in Miami the Saturday after he disappeared with Senator Bates. Jameel had one of their Florida agents from the Salt Breeze Charter check it out. He found Sol's reservation at the Conquistador hotel and bugged his room. Through recorded eavesdropping, Ibrahim's crew learned that Sol had been to the Cayman Islands.

The coin bearer went to Grand Cayman to investigate. Through public records he learned that Sol purchased a house using the false identity provided by the caliphate. When he went to see the house, he also saw a cabin cruiser moored in front of it. Sol may have thought he had a secret hideaway, but there was no keeping secrets from the caliphate.

CHAPTER 11

While Sol gathered a cadre of corrupt congressmen, Democrats in the Senate were taking notice of recent events.

Two senators, Morris Weinberg and his friend Tory Thorson, were finishing lunch in the Senate dining room. They, as were many others, discussed the recent violence in DC. Thorson washed down the last bite of his sandwich with lukewarm coffee. "You know what bothers me the most, is the man who shot the President. I'm the one who nominated him for a Silver Star. He was a soldier in my unit. A good man. But for him, I might be dead. I feel like I should do something, but I don't know what. Maybe he has family somewhere."

"You had better leave this one alone, Tory. He was, after all, the would-be assassin of the President."

"This whole affair has the earmarks of organized crime," Thorson said.

"Maybe it's a good time not to be president," Weinberg said, half joking.

Senator Weinberg, a democrat from California, cringed at the reminder. Last September his hopes of ever being president ended in a Bakersfield California auditorium. What he thought was a plan for better irrigation water distribution, was seen as discrimination against farm workers and even anti-immigration. People were yelling him down and swearing at him in two languages, until he gave up and left the podium. The news people wouldn't leave it alone. They called him anti-farmer, anti-Mexican, and pro big business, just another fat-cat who didn't care about regular people.

In fact, Weinberg grew up on a farm in California's Salinas Valley where he gained intimate knowledge of the work and hardship in the agricultural community. He learned the language and ways of the field hands, as he worked long summer days with them on his family's farm. His father used to tell him, "No one should hold himself above the ones who put the food on his table."

"Yes, maybe it is a good thing," Weinberg continued. "I probably won't get re-elected to the Senate again, either." He continued with his thoughts about organized crime. "In the past, presidential assassins were loners with physiological problems. Not this time. I believe someone is getting paid to kill certain high-ranking officials. The question is, why? And will there be more?"

"Maybe the President was wounded purposely, as some kind of warning. I know that Fawcett was an expert rifleman. It was his accurate shooting that saved my unit in Afghanistan. I think if Fawcett wanted the President dead, it would have happened. And, what about Representative Carlson? And who was that car bomb intended for? I think we are seeing only the tip of the iceberg."

Senator Weinberg picked up his plate and headed back to work. "You might be right," he said as he walked away.

Back in his office, Senator Weinberg sat at his assistant's desk. Ann Mercer had been with him since he was an assemblyman in California. She looked and acted like someone's mother, with her sweet smile and comfortable attire. But behind her soft brown eyes and high arched nose was the strength and determination of a businesswoman with a UCLA Master's degree.

"Ann, do you think that car bombing, the Carlson killing, and the attempt on the President's life are related?

"I most certainly do. Who wouldn't?"

"Everyone I talk to thinks so too, but no one can make the connection. Reporters are writing plenty of stories, but they don't really have much beyond the obvious. Most of it has to do with the security screw up at the golf course and the President's offhand remarks about the Middle East. They report the other incidents separately. But what bothers me even more, is how much is being reported about the Super Bowl. People are more concerned about football than they are about their elected officials. Apathy has become a lifestyle in America. If the people don't care what their elected officials do, then government will do whatever it wants without accountability to the people."

"You have a committee meeting," Ann urged.

Senator Weinberg's day dragged into the early evening. He went home to a microwave dinner. It didn't matter. His wife was back home in the Salinas Valley visiting her aged parents, and probably wouldn't be back until the weather warmed up; the kids were off to college, leaving Weinberg by himself. As he ate, he looked at the family photo on the china cabinet. One son and a daughter in their twenties, standing next to their still young-looking mother who could have passed for a celebrity - and Morris, dark haired and tan, standing next to them. The picture of happiness last summer, with Monterey Bay spread out behind them.

He sat alone with his thoughts. Why is there so little interest in the recent horrific events? What, if anything, would be done about it? It had to be apathy. Maybe disgust and disappointment mixed in. Why should people care when all that comes out of Washington are broken promises, more debt and inaction? Recent polls showed that people felt politicians didn't represent them. When it came time to vote they had little choice but to vote for the lesser of two evils, or not vote at all. Their democratic system wasn't working. He knew something had to be done, but what? He thought about the axiom of bringing about positive change through a controlled crisis, but how could a crisis be engineered that would rekindle the American spirit?

Senator Weinberg arrived at his office in the predawn darkness. When he walked in, Ann had a plate of Fig Newtons and a cup of tea on the Senator's coffee table, just like any other morning.

"Ann, I've been thinking. How does one do something about elected officials that aren't liked or respected? People who legislate by greed, corruption, and maybe even murder?" Weinberg settled into his couch. "These aren't crimes of passion or the mayhem brought on by mental problems. These are organized crimes. I believe that national politics has become so corrupt that ambition for high office has become a deadly contest, one that threatens those who seek it and excludes the American public."

Ann pulled up a side chair. "We can't legislate morality."

Senator Weinberg stared into his teacup as if something important lay deep inside. "Whatever happened to the spirit of public service? Like, Kennedy saying, 'Ask not what your country can do for you', and Reagan's vision of a shining city on a hill, or Truman's 'The buck stops here'. There are so many more. It seems like we have nothing to be proud of these days. People are tired of bailouts and unemployment, unpayable indebtedness, inflation, and an encroaching world of terrorists. Now we have assassins in the middle of Washington DC and shootings across the country. People are tired of it.

"Do you remember," he went on, "that little girl from Monterey who came to town for the national spelling bee last spring?"

"Sure, I do. She sat right there on the end of the couch."

"Well, I've been thinking about her. She said she was president of her class and wanted us to help her student body do something about money for a music program. I didn't know what I should say, so I asked how she became class president. Do you remember?"

"I do."

"Her answer kept coming back to me last night. 'How did you come to be class president?' I asked, and she said, 'My name was drawn from a baseball cap.'"

"Yes, I remember."

"Student politics can be nasty, so her principal asked those wanting to be class president to write their names on pieces of paper. He would draw the winner from his cap."

Ann's fingers stopped just short of a fig bar. "Where are you going with this?"

"The Monterey school principal had one thing right. He stopped election politics."

"Are you serious?"

"Imagine a presidential campaign without the multimillion-dollar price tags, the favoritism, the bad mouthing, the corruption, the hype and all those empty promises, followed by paybacks and cronyism."

"Are you trying to tell me we should pick our next president out of a hat?"

"Couldn't be worse than we have now, and who knows what we're in for next term. I think the public would agree."

Later that day, Senator Weinberg sat down in Senator Tory Thorson's office eager to share his new idea, as he and Thorson often did.

Thorson was a farm boy from Texas who went on to become a West Point graduate with a promising career ahead of him. Soon after his promotion to major his career ended on a battlefield in Afghanistan. The trouble started when he learned that a journalist from a Huston Texas newspaper was held by enemy forces. It was thought that the journalist faced execution. Major Thorson disobeyed orders and led a troop of cavalry into an enemy stronghold. He rescued the journalist, but in process, he lost a vehicle and sustained one casualty- Delmar Fawcett, the man who shot the President. His unauthorized action caused him to lose his commission.

Back in Texas He enrolled in law school. After graduation, he took a job as a public defender. He gained a good reputation defending Harris County's poorest defendants, both guilty and innocent. Folks in Texas loved him -- especially the press. When he decided to run for congress, every major newspaper in the state endorsed him. When he ran for the senate, voters happily voted him in.

His underdog orientation attracted Senator Weinberg as a friend. Weinberg too had a heart for the oppressed and forgotten. Having both grown up on working farms gave them a passion for a class of people who had little voice of their own.

"You know what I think?" Morris began, "We should hold a lottery to elect the next president."

"Do what?"

"A lottery. You know, put names in a hat and draw a winner. I'm serious. Think of the benefits. With a president selected at random you might get someone more responsive to the people, and less distorted by powerful special interests. A lottery would limit the influence of money in politics, and the divisive rhetoric that candidates use to hook voters. It would solve the problem of ducking big issues like entitlement reform and immigration. Think of the months of campaigning and the billions of dollars spent. That would be eliminated. We're not a democracy anymore, anyway. We're an oligarchy where only a privileged class and their interests rule the nation, and everyone knows it."

"Novel idea, I trust you're not serious."

"I am serious. I think anything that would put this election madness on hold would be worth trying."

"You'll never pull this off, Morris. You'll look foolish trying."

"I already look foolish. The closest thing we have to a democracy is letting citizens vote for whomever big money manages to get on the ballet. Even then, the popular candidate may not get elected. What about Vice-president Gore getting the popular vote and then losing to Bush because of a Supreme Court decision? Or how about Clinton's popular vote and electoral vote loss? Our current president didn't get the popular vote either. Now we even have hackers interfering. On top of that, less than sixty percent of registered voters even bothered to vote for a president in the last election, and a whole lot more didn't vote because they didn't register at all. There are even some who wished they hadn't voted. What kind of democracy do we have?

I think more people would vote if they could vote people out of office."

As he looked into Weinberg's pleading eyes, Senator Thorson shook his head. "Your points sound fine but even if you think the American people would go along with such an idea, it would require a constitutional amendment. Do you know how much goes into a constitutional amendment? It's overwhelming. You must get two-thirds of the House and Senate to go for it. We haven't had that kind of a majority in decades. Then, three-fourths of the states must ratify it. Even if everything goes your way, it could take years. The last time this succeeded was in 1971. That's the one that lowered the voting age from twenty-one to eighteen. The reason none have been ratified since then is that Democrats and Republicans fight each other on such things, and majorities can't be had. In the vacuum of indecision, the Supreme Court has had to impose constitutional change. You can bet that the Supreme Court would have nothing to do with a lottery. Then there's the problem with setting up a lottery. How's that going to work? No, Morris. This is not a good idea."

"Even a failed attempt at a lottery could draw attention to the need for election reform."

"Maybe."

"Come on, Tory. I need your help with this. I've supported your bills. Anyway, if it doesn't go anywhere then we forget about it, but if it does you could go down in history."

"That may not be the way I'd like to be remembered."

"Listen, this could completely stop the financial wars over winning the White House for at least one election. Wouldn't a four-year break be refreshing? Party politics are now lethal. Imagine a president who didn't have to buy, lie and cheat his way into office. Besides that, it would keep the current batch of Republicans out of the White House.

"Could you be doing this because you lost your chance for the presidency?" Thorson said.

"Please give this some serious thought. Ann will be by with the paperwork. In the meantime, see who else you can get to sign on. I know you can do it. While you're at it, get your friends in Texas warmed up to the idea. It won't hurt you to try."

"I'll go along with this only so far as it is feasible. Which, I think, means an early end."

"Thanks, Tory. You know this could be fun." Senator Weinberg returned to his office.

"No, Morris. Don't do this," Ann insisted.

"Sorry Ann I have to. Tory doesn't like the idea either, but I think he's going to help. Let's get started."

Ann knew the procedure. She'd drafted hopeless bills before. Her staff had made a good head start by the end of the week.

CHAPTER 12

By the time Senator Weinberg's bill was complete, Senator Thorson had found two more reluctant senators to sign on. When it came time to introduce it, Senator Weinberg took the podium. He looked at the senators who bothered to be present, and then began to speak. "Someone said recently that by sticking one's finger in a phone book a better president could be found. This comment expresses the frustration we have when none of the presidential candidates are of our choosing. The constant flow of Ivy League alumni and the very rich through American politics, is creating a kind of leadership anemia. What we need, is the hybrid vigor that comes from new people and new ideas. We are now having billion-dollar campaigns as the wealthy and the influential battle for the presidency, only to further disappoint the voters."

Senator Weinberg took a deep breath. "American leadership has become an oligarchy with only the richest Americans buying their way into power. We see this frustration in the all-time low approval ratings of our top elected officials. We in Congress are down to a miserable twelve percent approval rating and the President is below thirty percent. The reasons should be clear—the people are tired of us.

"Years ago, when loggers floated their logs down rivers to sawmills, the logs would sometimes jam up and clog a whole river. When the loggers couldn't clear them away, they turned to dynamite as their last resort. They blasted the logs free. Our government is log jammed. Our dynamite is to select our next president by means of a lottery. By so doing, we will clear away the Byzantine intrigue of power from presidential politics that clogs our government."

Senator Weinberg scanned the expressions of those present. Were they on board with him?

"This bill requires that a constitutional amendment be made," he continued. "One allowing for the one-time selection of a president by lottery, and by setting aside constitutional directives for the election of the President and Vice-president of the United States of America, for one election cycle only. Let's clear away presidential politics in one grand experiment, like a sunny morning clears away fog from the Potomac."

With few objections, the bill was on its way to committee.

The magnitude of recent events overshadowed the Weinberg bill, causing little interest from the press. After all, thousands of bills are dropped every year, many of them nonsensical like a bill requiring all taxi cabs be painted light blue to improve the aesthetics of American streets, or decommissioning the IRS, establishing a J-walking data base, or eliminating presidential term limits. Weinberg's bill fit nicely into this category – forgettable, but not forgotten. Hopeless as this bill may seem, two Republican senators were ready to bend the Weinberg bill to their own advantage.

Senator Bates sat in the office of Senate majority leader Melvin Case. The two men knew each other well and often met to discuss business or just personal matters. Today was business.

"What do you think of Senator Weinberg's lottery bill?" Bates asked.

Case raised a hand that looked something like an old fielder's mitt as his fat lips cracked a crooked grin. "An amusing idea, but don't expect it to go very far." Case shifted his large body in the old-fashioned wooden desk chair. It squeaked under his weight.

Bates picked a truffle from the dish on Case's desk. "You know the President shot himself in the foot too many times to get re-elected," Bates began." It's certain a Democrat can beat him, but consider Weinberg's lottery bill. Whoever wins the White House by lottery would no doubt be some incompetent who won't know politics from pumpkins. When he or maybe she, inevitably screws up, the public will want him out. Impeachment would be easy. But think of this. If we amend the bill to include a Vice-president appointed by the Senate to serve as a backup in case the President can't cut it, then our party would be back in the White House, and this stupid lottery business would be history. That appointment could be me. This lottery is tailor made." Bates continued, "Who would have even dreamed that a stupid California Democrat would set this up for us? When the presidency fails, we will win. It's our chance to retain Republican control."

Senator Case stopped grinning. "There is a chance that someone competent could win. After all, you can expect every politician in the country to buy a lottery ticket along with a lot of prepared citizens."

"Okay there's a chance. Maybe even you or I could win, or even that blockhead Weinberg, but the chances of a competent president coming from a lottery have got to be really small. Maybe some trucker from Texas or a carpenter from Alabama would win. How do you suppose they would handle things? And remember, without the lottery we have little or no chance at all. Business as usual is not in our favor."

"You might be right, but I don't think Weinberg's bill will go anywhere. Who in their right mind would even consider it?

"Listen Mel, I think this lottery thing has merit. Our party is in trouble. It's almost certain that a Democrat will win the next presidential election. But think of this, if the lottery amendment actually happened, not only would the Democrats get aced out of their presidential hopes, but they'd look stupid doing it. All we need do, is get a Republican vice-president. The odds are in our favor. You're the Majority Leader. You name the VP. You know we have a good thing going, our friends in the Middle East are investing millions in our party. With their heavy campaign funding, we're sure to retain a Republican house and senate, but our problem is the President. He's unelectable. Nobody likes him. He was only elected as the least of two evils and he's even more evil than people thought. It's certain that a Democrat will get the White House next term, and you know that with a Democrat president our efforts to appease the caliphate would end, along with our income.

Case eased his oversized body out of his chair and stood. Looking out his window at the Washington monument in the distance, he put one hand in his pocket and began contemplatively rubbing a gold coin between his fingers. The morning sun glistened on his smooth head as he reflected on Lyle's idea. He then turned to Lyle. "They would lose the presidency and we could still win the house and senate, and then the White House as well." The grin returned to his round face as he arched a bushy eyebrow over a droopy brown eye. "Let's see what we can do to make this bill work."

Bates daintily removed another milk chocolate truffle from the candy dish on the Speaker's desk. "I haven't felt this good about our future in a long time.," he smiled. He popped the truffle in his mouth as he exited the room.

Although it was a Democrat bill, Republicans helped it pass both houses to became law. It wasn't until after Congress approved it, that the press and other watchdog organizations woke up to the absurdity of selecting a president by lottery. Most states knew it was coming as a constitutional amendment and were ready to ratify it. This was an experiment people wanted to try. It was like rebellion without an uprising. Cities across the nation held coordinated protests in favor of ratification. States were already involved in lotteries. Hundreds of casinos were popular across the country. The Weinberg bill fit easily into existing practice.

While the lottery bill worked its way toward ratification, Congress passed bills that limited American involvement in the Middle East. American and allied prisoners were exchanged, Guantanamo closed, and most of the combat troops returned home from the Mediterranean region, leaving only advisors and their grounded drones. Congress took all the credit it could for passing antiwar bills. At the same time, the President sent three aircraft carriers to the Sea of Japan followed by more troops in South Korea. Ostensibly to put the North Korean dictator in check. He then got congress to approve the completion of a wall on the Mexican border. These were all efforts to direct attention away from the Middle East, and the forming caliphate.

At the same time, treachery and butchery defined an expanding caliphate. As it grew, faith in the American decision to move out of Middle East affairs declined. Congress argued endlessly about what to do, but did nothing to slow the growth of the caliphate. Appeasement and tolerance kept America free from terrorism. People feared that eventually the caliphate would be too large to control and they would expand into Europe and beyond. It had already reached the borders of Israel and Turkey. Americans became more disillusioned with Washington politics, than ever.

Senator Weinberg and his co-sponsors went from state to state pushing his bill for a lottery president. In capitols across the country, the lottery bill was being ratified. Republicans and Democrats alike supported ratification. Eventually the Supreme Court got involved, saying that congress had the right to make amendments to the constitution, thereby ending any legal maneuvering to derail Weinberg's Bill. After several months, the lottery amendment was ratified. The process of creating the lottery began.

The General Services Administration went to work constructing an on-line lottery website. It would have only one task—select a president. The applicant's name, address, occupation, personal demographics, household names and other pertinent information would be entered online. To qualify, the applicant must be at least 35 years old, a born citizen, have resided in the US for at least fourteen years, be a high school graduate, be in good health, not a felon, and agree to a perjury statement. One hundred dollars would be submitted via credit card to complete the process.

The lottery would open the morning of January twelfth and close at midnight January twenty-second.

Applicants would be screened for accuracy of information. Incomplete or unqualified applications would be purged. Fraudulent applications would be subject to an investigation that could result in fines, imprisonment, or both. No registration fee would be refundable. A proof of purchase receipt would be emailed or, if requested, a paper copy would be mailed.

A preliminary drawing would be held on March fifteenth. Twelve candidates would be selected, using an in-system random number generator to choose finalists from a database of all lottery ticket holders. A thorough background check would be made on each finalist selected. Anyone found unqualified would be eliminated from the lottery and a new finalist would be randomly selected. On October 15th, a random selection of one of the remaining preliminary candidates would determine the winner who would be called, President Select. The winner's name would be announced at eight p.m. Eastern time, on Election Day in November.

The Senate Majority Leader would have two weeks in which to appoint a vice-president from the United States Senate. The President Select would go to Washington to undergo a transitional training period and receive the first intelligence briefing. The lottery president would be made ready by Inauguration Day.

The midterm elections were heating up simultaneously with the progress of the presidential lottery. Sol busied himself providing promised campaign money to those Republicans whose sins were hidden under the cover of wealth. An earlier Supreme Court decision allowed political action committees, Super PACs, to spend unlimited amounts of money on their preferred presidential candidate, without being required to fully disclose the names of their contributors. This is how much of the billion-dollar presidential campaigns were funded.

With the presidential election being skipped, Sol used his fundraising skills to get the PACs to divert some of that money to his corrupt candidates. Many donations came indirectly from the caliphate. Ibrahim's small British oil company was a major contributor. Sol's fundraisers attracted generous donors with some of Ibrahim's money in their pockets.

The money provided better advertising and better venues, resulting in all of Sol's candidates winning re-election. Representative Bireley didn't even have to cheat.

CHAPTER 13

On the morning the presidential lottery went live, four mechanics in the city of Centralia in Washington State, spent their morning break drinking coffee and soaking in the heat from a homemade stove. It burned used drain oil from their auto repair shop. The black smoke from the stove pipe disappeared into a low gray sky. The weather report warned of strong winds and rain on the way from the Pacific Ocean.

Slouching on an old car seat, Mark Pierce took a gulp of coffee and washed down the last bite of a homemade cinnamon roll. He looked over the top of his newspaper at the other three mechanics. "It says here that about all you have to do to buy a presidential lottery ticket, is satisfy the constitutional qualifications for president and not be a felon."

"Is that it?" Al asked. Alan Goodwin owned Al's Automotive.

"Well there's some kind of questionnaire to fill out, and of course they want a hundred bucks. There's a time limit too – eleven days. That's it," Mark said.

"Think you'd like to buy a lottery ticket?" Al asked.

"I'm not that crazy." Mark replied as he licked the last bit of frosting from his fingers.

Leo, Al's young apprentice, interrupted. "You should buy one. Think of all the cool things you could do. They'd fly you around in Air Force One and take you places in bullet proof limousines. You wouldn't even need money. What's more you could do something great for America.

If I were old enough, I'd buy a ticket and hope to win." He smiled broadly at the prospect.

Leo Mendez was the youngest member of one of the few Mexican families in Centralia, and the only American born member of his family.

"I know what I would do." Mark added, "I'd scrape off all the slow bumps in the country and recycle them to fill potholes."

The last to join the conversation was Tran Nguyen, Al's lead mechanic. "I think I would liberalize our immigration laws. We are, after all, the land of the free and the home of the brave. People everywhere want to be free."

Tran escaped Vietnam as a child during the seventies. His family ducked bullets as they ran across The Tan Son Nhut Air Base to one of the last flights out of Saigon. His kids were born in America, and now worked as professionals in the Puget Sound area. "What would you do, Al?" he asked. "

"Probably the same thing I do now. Get up early and put in a good day's work."

Leo got up and walked away from the warm stove. He pulled open a garage door and drove a Chrysler minivan with a bad transmission into the garage. It would keep Tran busy for the rest of the day. He pulled the door shut, closing out the building storm. Back at the oil stove, he told Tran. "Your van is ready." Then sat down to finish his break.

Tran cast an eye at the old minivan. "That thing doesn't look like it's worth a transmission repair." he got up and walked toward it.

Mark stood up, ready to go back to work on an alternator replacement on a Ford Explorer that he called a Ford Exploder. "I can't imagine anyone in his right mind blowing a hundred bucks on this lottery."

"Well, somebody will. It should be fun to watch," Al said. He ducked into his office and called his wife.

"I'll be home early. I want to make sure we're ready for the storm."

"Don't wait too long. The weatherman says it will be on us this afternoon."

Where they lived in the hills east of town, power often went out during windstorms. In the worst ones, trees fell, and roads flooded over. Al hopped into his restored and tricked out old Ford pickup and headed for the wrecking yard to pick up a carburetor for a restoration job Mark was doing on a '68 Camaro.

Although it had appeared that Al was disinterested in the lottery, the presidential lottery captured his imagination. So, on the way he pulled into a parking lot, took out his phone and went to the LotteryPresident.gov website. Then he completed the electronic form and paid his one-hundred-dollars. This would be his secret. He pulled back onto the rain-soaked street.

By the time he got home, wind ripped through the huge Douglas firs, sending limbs through the air with deadly force. Wind whistled around the corners of the Goodwin house, keeping everyone indoors.

The weatherman called it an atmospheric river, but in this part of Western Washington, everybody called it a Pineapple Express, because they blow through in a straight line from the Hawaiian Islands. Like a water hose pouring inches of windblown rain onto the continent, it raises temperatures and causes power outages and flooding.

Al was worried. "Tracy, do you know where Josh is?" Joshua was the second oldest of their three children. At fifteen, he already rode around in other kid's cars, and defied his parents. His school had counseled him for an attention deficit disorder.

"All I know is he came home from school, looked in the refrigerator and took off. When I asked where he was going, he said, 'see ya later.' He left with Cole, who has a car, now."

"It's time to put an end to that."

Later that evening, Al sank into a recliner to watch television. At ten o'clock he switched to the Night Show. It opened with host Archie MacArthur walking to the front of his stage to quiet the audience and shush the band, so he could begin his monologue.

"This morning, the presidential lottery went live. People all over the country were logging in. In congress, C-SPAN video panned the house floor showing several monitors displaying the presidential Lottery website." The large screen behind Archie showed a video of the Senate floor. "Some congressmen even joked that they were running for president. Well, I paid my hundred bucks and, no joke, I'd love to hold office at the source of the richest comedy material on earth."

Archie went on, "It didn't take long for trouble to start. NSA officials announced they nabbed a suspect with three outstanding warrants who signed up for the lottery. But NSA denied having access to lottery data, saying they were tipped off by the IRS. All afternoon tax attorneys were seen rushing to Capitol Hill.

"Let's take a poll. Who here has logged into the lottery website? Raise your hand." Several hands went up, including Archie's.

"Okay now, how many of you actually bought a ticket? Leave your hand up," Archie's hand and a few others remained up.

"I count only twelve including mine. So, what makes you feel qualified to be president? The man in the Hawaiian shirt, what makes you qualified?"

"I don't think I am, but I'd like to give it a shot."

"How about the lady in paisley, are you qualified?"

"I'm a woman. That's how I'm qualified. If I get in the White House, there will be some serious changes made around here."

After the cheering stopped Archie went on, "How about you in the blue polo shirt, why do you think you're qualified?"

"I'm a Berkeley graduate with a master's degree in political science and I think I could do a lot for my country."

"Good luck to all of you. Let's have a big hand for our presidential candidates."

The Night Show band played a jazzy version of Hail to the Chief as Archie walked to his desk.

The lights at Al's house flickered. He could hear the wind whip rain against the side of the house. He hoped the TV would not fail.

Archie continued. "Tonight, our first guest is the man behind the lottery, Senator Morris Weinberg of California. Let's give him a warm welcome."

The audience roared and cheered as the Senator sat down in the guest seat.

"I haven't had a welcome like this in a long time. It really makes me feel good."

"Did you by a lottery ticket?"

"I did," the Senator said, "as soon as I got up this morning."

"Most people are stoked about this lottery, but what are the downsides to it?"

"A real concern is that people won't bother to vote when they have no choice for a president, but what we have to remember is that others are running for office in national, state and local elections that need your vote. Please vote in the Fall elections. The obvious risk is that the new president won't be able to hack it. We are hoping the screening process will reduce this possibility, but not many Americans are prepared to take on the responsibility of president. The lottery president will have a vice-president appointed from the US Senate to ensure a competent backup. On the bright side, the lottery president could be a breath of fresh air in Washington, and not part of the Washington political machine," Weinberg concluded.

Archie went on, "The idea of the lottery was to put corrupt campaigning on hold. Do you think this will work?"

"You can't stop a politician's ambition for office. I expect those eager for office will continue to ..."

Suddenly the lights went out, leaving Al sitting in the dark.

The family spent the night warmed only by a fire in the old wood burning kitchen stove.

Al woke early and checked for damage. He was especially worried about his mom whose small mobile home sat near the barn. But nothing was damaged, only branches and leaves blown around by the wind. The electricity was still out. Next to his pickup stood Cole's green Volkswagen Jetta. Al laid his hand on the hood. It felt warm. The car belonged to Josh's friend Cole. In the house, Tracy had the wood stove fired up as she fried a pan of scrambled eggs and fixed coffee in an aluminum percolator. The Goodwins were used to going without electricity.

Al walked into Josh's room. The two boys were asleep. Al shook Josh awake. "Where have you been?"

"Nowhere, just riding around."

"I went to bed at midnight and you weren't home yet. So, when did you come in?"

"Just after midnight."

"The engine in Cole's car is still warm. Would you like to tell me the truth?"

"Okay, it was a lot after midnight."

"I want you up and ready for school — now. For the next month You will be at school or at home, nowhere else. And you can forget about any allowance. And Cole, I don't want to see your car around here for a month."

Al arrived at his shop early. It too avoided damage, and the lights were on. He entered the office and got the coffee going, then went to the convenience store next door for a newspaper. He returned, unlocked the shop, and poured a cup of coffee. Then he spread his paper on the front counter. The headline read, "Presidential Lottery Sees Millions of Hits on First Day." The article praised the website for having no glitches, then went on to report what some ticket buyers would do if they won. Some would improve our education system or enact stronger gun laws; others would get tough on immigration. It went on to include decriminalizing narcotics, the elimination of welfare, free rent vouchers for homeless people, rainbow striped crosswalks, and several taxation ideas. One guy wanted to get to the bottom of who actually blew up the twin towers. Most respondents said they would reform health care.

Al looked up to see a state patrolman exiting his car. He pulled open the front door. "Morning Al. Just curious about how the roads are out your way. I heard the power was out."

"The power's out and there's limbs all over the road. Other than that, no problems that I know of. But that's not why you dropped in, is it Bill?"

"Not really. During the night, the power went out in town for a while and a convenience store was broken into. A car that looks a lot like the one Cole drives was seen prowling around town. I'm not saying that Josh had anything to do with the break-in. I'm just telling you this as a friend. I think Josh and his buddy Cole may be heading for trouble."

"You might be right. He didn't get in until just before I left for work this morning. Best I know to do, is ground him for a while."

Just then the phone rang. Tran Nguyen said a tree had blown down across his driveway and he would be late for work.

Mark and Leo came in just as Bill left. Mark grabbed a cup of coffee and plopped a bag of four jelly donuts on the counter, then grabbed one. He took a big bite and washed it down with coffee.

"Tran's not coming in so, who wants the extra donut?" Al asked.

"Maybe that state patrolman out there. Cops like donuts."

"State patrolmen aren't exactly cops."

"Oh! I thought all cops liked donuts."

"He's not a cop."

"Who cares? Give me the donut. I'll eat it."

Al picked up the donut and squeezed raspberry jelly into Mark's hand.

CHAPTER 14

Mark Pierce and Al Goodwin were high school buddies, but after graduation Al joined the Army and Mark went away to the University of Washington. Four years later Al returned home, and Mark graduated from the university to begin his carrier as an officer in the Navy. Now, at forty-six years of age, Mark had spent twenty years in the Navy with tactical and combat assignments all over the world. He looked the part, with a close-cropped haircut and a slim, athletic body. He also held his jeans up with his old Navy belt. After retirement, he took up mechanics to fulfill a lifetime love affair with cars that he and Al had shared since their high school auto shop. Especially, the work they did in the restoration shop out back. Custom cars and stock car racing were in their blood. They each had their own stock car that they raced locally. They often competed, and sometimes helped one another win.

Divorced with no children, Mark took a liking to Al's son Josh. It didn't matter that Josh got into trouble. Because of Josh's sensitive and impressionable personality, Mark felt confident that something would come along to turn young Josh around.

Josh spent the winter close to home. If he minded his mom and did well in school, he could expect to have a car in the spring, when he turned sixteen. But Josh couldn't comply. He wasn't disrespectful or angry, he just had to be free. He couldn't sit still in school, and had a hard time regimenting himself to chores at home.

Instead, he spent all the time he could with his friends, adventuring and having fun.

News about the lottery eventually died down. Al seldom thought about it. He busied himself and his little band of mechanics with a pressing work schedule. His lottery ticket receipt lay ignored in his desk drawer.

Late in April, a postal worker walked into Al's Automotive. She asked Al to sign for a registered letter from a government agency. He ripped it open. It began, "You are a finalist in the presidential lottery ..."

The letter explained that his lottery information would be verified, and a background check would be made. At this point, he had the opportunity to withdraw. If he chose to continue, he would move on to the final drawing in October. A form asking for Al's intent to stay in the lottery and a return envelope were provided. It took a moment for Al to absorb what had just happened. Then he filled in the form, sealed the envelope, and left for the post office to mail it.

Should he tell Tracy? There wasn't much of a chance he'd win, why involve her? He didn't know there were only 12 finalists, not hundreds as he imagined. Because of embarrassment, he never told anyone he bought a ticket, but it also excited him to hold out hope of winning. After all, he was a finalist. What if I did win? He thought. He decided it would be best to give Tracy a heads-up, just in case. He pulled off the road and called home.

"Tracy, I didn't tell you earlier, but I bought one of those presidential lottery tickets and today I got notice that I'm a finalist. It's possible that you could be the next First Lady of the United States."

"How much did that cost?"

Al took a deep breath. "I just found out I'm a finalist. I could win! Do you know what that means?"

"How much?"

"A hundred bucks."

Tracy emitted a deep sigh. "I'm sure you're all excited about this, but you shouldn't squander your money on daydreams."

"I probably won't win, but I wanted you to know, just in case."

"That's right, you probably won't. See you at dinner."

Al dropped his registered letter at the post office and went back to work. He couldn't concentrate. He applied too much torque to a valve cover bolt and popped it off. All he could think about was his slim chance to be president, and the hundred bucks he had to admit blowing on the lottery. Now he had let someone else know, ruining his secret. He wasn't going to win anyway so he forced it out of his mind and turned to the task of extracting the broken bolt.

With coaching from Mark, Josh managed to comply enough in school and at home to get the promised car. It wasn't much of a car, but it belonged to him. He couldn't be happier. Josh longed for the coming summer with long warm days of camping, hiking, swimming, and fun with his friends. He could hardly wait.

Tracy busied herself with mountain rescue, leaving Al's mom in charge of the farm.

Al and Mark spent summer nights racking up points at the Speedway. Al's pickleball did well too. The shop office was adorned with trophies and medals. Business couldn't be better. Al hired his oldest son, Connor, as a mechanic for the summer. After Labor Day, Al hired another full-time mechanic. He added another bay to the garage, and a showroom for the restoration shop.

With the coming of November another Pineapple Express drenched Western Washington, however, with business as usual, Al forgot about the lottery. But the lottery didn't forget Al.

On the morning of the first Tuesday in November, two men in dark suits walked into the front office of Al's Auto. Leo greeted them from behind the counter.

"We're looking for Alan Goodwin. Is he here?"

Leo hesitated. Then, "Wait here. He's in the shop."

Al looked up from under the hood of a Chevy Tahoe with a seized serpentine belt tensor, when Leo said, "Hey Boss, there's two guys in suits looking for you. You want to see them?"

"Tell them to wait. I'll be right there."

Leo went back to the two men. He didn't trust what he saw. *Why are these guys wearing sunglasses in November,* he wondered? "Al said wait. He'll be right in." Leo stayed close and watched as the two looked around the office. One started snooping into Al's bookshelves; he even ran a finger down the spine of Al's bible that stood among his shop manuals. They eyed the walls, looking at Al's membership certificates in the Rotary, the Better Business Bureau, some hot rod club, a bunch of mechanic certificates, a business license and a picture of Al's pickle-ball team.

A picture of a Navy combat unit showing Mark Pierce with men dressed in desert combat gear hung on a separate wall. The FBI had done background checks on Al, his family, employees, neighbors, and friends. The Secret Service men in Al's office knew all about Him. They knew about Commander Mark Pierce's Navy record and where the photo was taken. They even knew that Leo's parents were not citizens. Neither of them said anything.

The shop door slid open and Al walked in, vigorously wiping away grease from his hands on a blue shop rag. "I'm Al, what can I do for you?"

The guy with the snoopy finger said, "Mister Goodwin, do you have some place we can talk in private?"

"Who are you and why do you want to talk to me?"

"We have an important message for you."

Must be about Josh, Al thought. "You can tell me right here. Leo, go see if Mark has something for you to do."

Leo left the office uttering a quiet "oh-oh" under his breath.

After showing his Secret Service badge and checking Al's ID, the snoopy agent told Al straight out, "Your name has been selected in the presidential lottery."

"What?"

"That's right. We are here to officially inform you that you are the winner of the Presidential Lottery. "

Al dropped his baseball cap on the counter and ran his dirty fingers through his graying black hair. "I never would have believed it. I thought that by now somebody else won it."

"You're it, mister Goodwin. This is Agent Carlyle. He'll fill you in on some details."

The meeting went on for several minutes. Out in the garage, Leo told Mark about the two men. "They looked like cops," he said.

"Did they say why they're here?" Mark wanted to know.

"No, just something about needing to talk in private."

"Do you think it's about Josh?"

"Maybe. One of Josh's friends got himself arrested for something Friday night," Leo said.

"I wonder if I should go to the school and clue Josh in about this?"

Just then, Al stuck his head in the shop and yelled; "Hey Mark, hold down the fort and have Leo finish that Tahoe for me. The owner wants to pick it up at three. I've got some business to take care of. I'll be gone the rest of the day." Al jumped in his pickup truck and took off with a black government Chevrolet Suburban right behind him.

"Well you heard him, Leo. I guess we'll find out what's going on in the morning."

Al drove home at exactly the speed limit. His hands were cold and sweating. The sky hung gray, and the roads were wet. What is he going tell Tracy? *Hey Tracy, guess what. I'm going to be the President of the United States of America. What am I going to say?* It would be official tonight. His whole family suddenly needed the protection of the Secret Service.

As soon as he pulled in the yard he jumped out of his pickup and ran to the black Chevrolet. "Can you guys give me a couple of minutes to talk to my wife? She only knows I bought a lottery ticket."

"Yes Sir, Mister Goodwin, we'll wait," agent Carlyle said.

Al ran in the front door. "Tracy, we need to talk. Remember that lottery ticket I bought?" As he blurted out everything to his wide-eyed wife, Tracy stood stone still trying to take in what seemed to her like utter madness.

"Why didn't you tell me?"

"I did. Remember, I bought a lottery ticket. I told you I was a finalist. Remember? I had no idea I'd win. You said I wasted money on a daydream."

"What are all these people doing here?"

"They're from the Secret Service. We need their protection."

"Oh no! This can't be happening." The gravity of what Al just said hit her hard. She began walking in circles. "What are we going to do? My hair!"

Outside, more agents arrived in another black Chevrolet Suburban. The chickens ran out of the yard to hide in the tall grass. Tappet, the family's Jack Russell terrier, wouldn't stop barking. The cows stuck their heads through the fence, wondering whether these strangers had brought food.

Al went back out to the Secret Service agents. They wanted to wait for Al's daughter, Hannah to get off the school bus, and for Josh to come home before filling them in on what had happened. Al's older son Conner was called home from college at once.

Shortly after three-thirty, Hannah arrived home, Conner sat in I-5 traffic, and Josh failed to get off his school bus. With Josh missing, an agent had to find him, and soon. At the same time, a large, black motor home pulled into the yard, along with another carload of agents.

The Goodwins were advised that the election announcement would be made at eight p.m. Eastern time, five p.m. on the Pacific coast. In one hour, the world would be introduced to Al and his family. The Secret Service established a guarded perimeter around the little family farm. The telephone company hooked up a phone center in the motorhome. Tracy suddenly realized that none of them could go anywhere; not to the store, not to the shop, not to a friend's house — nowhere. She was stuck. "Al do something. We can't live like this."

Al held Tracy close and apologized. "This is an opportunity like no other. This bit of fortune can benefit us and our family, for generations to come. We have a chance to influence the course of our nation."

Tracy straightened up and faced the window. She ran the home and the farm as well as belonging to a mountain rescue team that kept her in peak condition. Right now, she stared out the window, her soft brown eyes and now-combed brown hair giving no indication of her inner turmoil. She couldn't be more shocked if Martians had landed.

"Hey Carlyle! What's going on with the phones around here?" Al yelled.

"Calls are being intercepted for you Sir."

"Why?"

"In a few minutes, you will get more phone calls than you can handle, same for Tracy and your kids. The transition team will screen all calls and eliminate those you don't need. If you want to make a call, just dial zero and we'll place the call for you. Give me your cell phone. It will be replaced with a secure cell phone."

"Well I want to make a call."

"Then dial zero, Sir," agent Carlyle said. "And don't mention anything about winning the presidency. That will be made clear at five."

Al dialed zero.

"How can I help you, Mister Goodwin?" a young woman asked.

"I want to call my shop."

"I have that number. I'll call it for you."

"Al's auto, Mark here."

"Mark, I want you to drop everything you're doing and close the shop right now. Make sure you, and everyone else, are out of there and in front of a TV for the five-o'clock news."

"Al, there's a couple of cops out front. They said they are here for our protection. What's going on?"

"Never mind, just be sure you are watching the news when it comes on at five, and don't worry, nobody's been hurt. You'll know everything at five."

Somebody from the transition team walked into Al's living room with a couple of guys carrying camera gear. "We need a quick interview for a news release," he said.

"Now?" Tracy said, still completely discombobulated.

"It'll only take a minute. We need this for a press release."

At five o'clock, the very nervous Goodwin family sat staring at the TV waiting for an official announcement.

After reporting details of the lottery, the network switched to Washington D.C. and the Speaker of the House of Representatives, who announced, "We have just learned that the presidential Lottery has selected forty-seven-year-old Alan B Goodwin, a small business owner from Washington State, as the President Select, as he is called. He has a wife Tracy, two sons and a daughter. They live on their family farm east of the little town of Centralia where President Select Goodwin owns an auto repair and restoration business." This was followed by the interview done only moments earlier.

Tracy jumped to her feet with her hands over her face. She ran up the stairs and slammed her bedroom door behind her, then threw herself onto the bed and screamed into the pillow.

"Hey Carlyle, how come you guys sprung this on us without any warning? Can't you see what this is doing to my family?" Al slammed his hand down hard on a countertop. He didn't like to see Tracy upset, and he blamed himself.

"Sorry Sir, we had to do it this way to keep you safe. We didn't know ourselves, until last week. Once the news got out that we had a President Select, we had to be ready. Telling you any sooner could have compromised your safety."

The only other person who knew that Al had bought a lottery ticket was Tracy, and she seemed to have forgotten about it. *How is Mom going to take it?* Today, she was visiting Al's sister in Vancouver. Did they even know? He also wondered what the rest of his family were thinking, and what about friends? He didn't have long to wait.

The phone rang. It was the lady in the motor home. "We are holding calls for you." She named several.

"Give me Conner first, then my sister." He wanted to talk to his mom, but she didn't own a cell phone.

"Dad, what's going on? I heard about you on the radio. Is it true?

"Yes! Come straight home. Don't stop anywhere and don't tell anyone anything."

"It'll be a while. I'm sitting in I-5 traffic."

Al took several more calls, and then instructed that he would only take calls from his family. He then called his friend Mark.

"I suppose you've heard what's going on."

"I'll say. This is so sudden. I had no idea."

"Neither did I. I bought a lottery ticket last winter and forgot all about it. I want you to close the shop until this lottery thing gets straightened out. We'll have time to meet about this later. Sorry Mark. I've got to go. Oh! I almost forgot. You'll have police protection until the shop is closed."

"Hey Dad, there's some sheriff cars down on the road!" Hannah yelled from the front window.

Al went to the window. "Mister Carlyle, do you have any idea why the sheriff is here?"

"They're here to keep the press and curiosity seekers away, Sir."

"Carlyle, if you want to keep an eye on me you might as well help me feed the livestock." A helicopter could be heard above the farm. The whole country watched as Al fed the cows.

CHAPTER 15

Conner arrived home at 6:30. At 9:30 Tracy called out for pizza. At 9:45 Al's mom arrived. Only Josh remained unaccounted for.

On a dark stretch of county road, a deputy sheriff pulled over an old blue Volkswagen Jetta. He tapped on the driver's window, and it rolled down.

"May I see some ID please?" The deputy asked.

A skinny kid with a dyed red explosion of hair handed him his driver's license. A warm, bitter odor drifted out the window. The deputy shined his flashlight at the passenger. "Are you Joshua Goodwin?"

"Yeah! Why?"

"May I see some ID?"

Josh handed over his ID.

"You're wanted at home. I'm supposed to drive you there."

"So, what's the problem?"

"I'll tell you on the way home."

"What if I don't want to go home?"

The deputy shined his flashlight in the back seat. Mixed with the rest of the garbage, he saw an empty beer can. "Both of you get out of the car." The deputy frisked them, then searched the car. He found several empty beer cans behind the seat and some marijuana residue in a cup holder.

"Okay Josh, you want me to drive you home, or should I drive the both of you to jail?"

"I guess I'll go home."

Addressing the driver, the deputy said, "I'm going to let you go, but if I ever catch you with anything like this in your car again, I'll take you straight to jail. You got that? Now go home."

Cole's red hair hung over one eye as he got back in his beat-up car and slowly drove away. Josh slid into the backseat of the deputy's car.

"So why are you picking me up?" Josh asked.

"When you didn't come home from school, the sheriff's department, city police, State Patrol and the Secret Service went looking for you. Even the FBI is looking for you. Looks like I beat them to you."

"That's crap. Nobody gets in that kind of trouble for coming home late."

"It's not what you did, it's what your dad did. He won the presidential lottery."

"The what?"

"The presidential lottery."

"What's that?"

The deputy explained what had happened. By the time the car stopped in the farmyard, Josh knew his life was ruined.

Tracy met Josh at the car Just as a Secret Service car pulled up with the pizza. The Secret Service wasn't about to let some pizza driver anywhere near the farm. The Secret Service now had the whole family together and under their protection for the night.

After an early breakfast, Al met with the transition team in the motor home they set up on the edge of the barn yard. To Al's relief they had everything covered. They provided him with a temporary office in the motor home and a personal assistant, a young woman named Amy, handled his phone calls. Transition money would cover everything he needed until he took office in January.

Phone calls poured in all night. Many were friends, some were government officials, and some were heads of state. Al returned the most important ones. The Prime Minister of Israel was congenial and supportive, the President of Mexico wanted to meet the new President Select, as did some others. Al thanked all the callers, but explained that he couldn't communicate more until after his inauguration. One call came from Senator Lyle Bates. After an abundance of congratulations, Bates cut to the chase. "As you may have been informed, I am your appointed vice-president. I have many years of valuable experience in Washington politics and can be of real service to you and our country. What's important is that you succeed in your presidency. I know how things work here. I have connections and know people who can be of immense service to you and our country."

"Thanks. I'm glad to hear that, but right now I'm kind of busy."

"I understand. We will have plenty of time to talk when you get to Washington." He excused himself and hung up.

"Amy, I don't want any more calls from politicians or any well-wishers."

"Mr. Goodwin, I put through Senator Bates' call because he is your vice-president select. We also have a list of recommended cabinet members and appointments you might want to talk to."

"I appreciate the recommendations. How about we put a hold on that until I get a grasp on what I'm doing."

Agent Carlyle stepped into Al's temporary office. "How's it going, Sir?"

"I want to go to my shop. Can we arrange that?"

"Mister Goodwin, I don't think it would be a good idea to go there."

"Why not?"

"It's a security issue. We have only two cars and we have to order a police escort."

"If the President of the United States can fly jumbo jets all over the world for his pleasure, why can't I go to my place of business in my own truck?"

"That would be far too great a risk for you to take. You can't do that."

Al got up and walked into the yard. He jumped into his pickup and took off for Centralia, pipes roaring down the driveway and onto the county road. Carlyle and two other agents scrambled to their SUV and gave chase. Within a couple of miles, a deputy sheriff joined the chase. Al sped up a bit. His pickup could outrun the Secret Service cars but probably not the deputy's cruiser. He wished he could leave them all in the rainy mist. When he turned on to Harrison Street, a city cruiser cut in front of the Secret Service cars. Al saw blue lights in his rear-view mirror, but he had no intention of stopping. He would do that when he got to his shop, less than a mile ahead.

He skidded to a stop in front of the shop, jumped out of his pickup and dashed through the office door. He locked it behind him. Because the shop was closed, all the garage doors were shut. He could see his pursuers through the windows.

"Hey Mark! We need to talk."

Mark came running from the back of a small moving van parked in the third bay. "Hey man what's going on?" Al gathered his mechanics around the oil stove. They settled into the old car seats. He explained the events of the past twenty-four-hours, while the secret service and other law enforcement people pressed against the garage windows trying get his attention.

Out front, cars pulled up. Several people gathered in the parking lot. A TV news truck pulled up. City cops where were all over.

"I don't know what to do," Al told his mechanics. "The Secret Service has us isolated at home. Nobody can go anywhere or do anything. I have to close up the business for a while, and I didn't want to tell you over the phone. The Secret Service idea of protection feels a whole lot more like house arrest. They even have a no-fly zone over my place."

"Mark, I want you to take complete control of this garage. "Will you do it?"

"Sure, Al. Whatever you want."

"Great. Anything you think you need to do, go ahead and do it. Make sure you get all my personal property out of here. It goes to my barn. Make sure you get the bookkeeper involved. Bills and salaries need to be paid. If you think of anything else just do it. I want you guys to keep the garage closed until I'm out of town. There's a chance this place could become an attraction to curiosity seekers, or worse. You'll have to learn to deal with that. It could be good for business!"

"Sure Al. Do we still call you Al?"

"Yes, I'm Al."

"This visit isn't working the way I thought it would. This place is a circus. It would be better if you guys came out to the house for dinner tonight. We'll have more time to discuss what to do. Right now, I gotta get out of here. We can talk at dinner." Al went to his office. He grabbed the empty trash can from under his desk, opened the drawers, grabbed some personal stuff and put it in the can. There in back of the top drawer, lay a crumpled lottery receipt. He stopped and stared at it. Because of it, life would never be the same again.

Agent Carlyle and his crew were peering inside the garage door windows, while restraining an angry deputy, who didn't seem to know who Al had become. The deputy yelled through door about Al failing to pull over when he turned on his blue lights. Another network TV truck pulled up in the parking lot.

Al's State Patrol friend, Bill, drove up, bringing two motorcycle troopers with him. He banged on the door. "Hey Al, let me in."

Al opened the door for him. Agent Carlyle squeezed in with him, leaving a red-faced deputy kicking the bottom of the door.

"What's up, Bill?"

"We're your escort back to your house."

"Thanks Bill. I have something to attend to first."

"You know Carlyle," he told the agent, "All I wanted to do was talk to my crew and pick up some personal stuff. I didn't think about all these people showing up."

"But overnight, you have become one of the best-known people on the planet. Right now, news agencies are scrambling to learn everything they can about you. We have no idea who might be in that crowd out there. I want you to stay out of sight until we can get you safely out of here. We can't have you risking your life on a whim. It's my responsibility to keep you safe, and I assure you, I'm going to do so whether you object or not, Sir."

"Right now, I think I should talk to those news guys out there,"

"No, no. That's not a good idea."

"Good or bad, that's what I want. Go get the ones you can trust, and bring them in."

"I think you should avoid public contact."

"Fine. Mark, would you and Leo get some reporters in here?"

Carlyle raised his hands palms out, as if to block Mark and Leo. "That's far enough."

Al stepped between Mark and Carlyle, "How do you think it would look if you and your agents got into an altercation with the man you're supposed to protect, and his crew of mechanics?"

With this in mind, Agent Carlyle arranged an impromptu news briefing in an empty garage bay. Three news teams were allowed in as well a local newspaper reporter from Portland. The now better-informed deputy stood with them.

A local reporter started the questioning. "Mister Goodwin, how does it feel to be the next president of the United States?

"It's a big surprise, but I'm good with it."

"Have you decided on any appointments yet?"

"No. It's too early for that. Anyway, I don't have any idea who to appoint. Maybe one of you want an appointment?"

The reporter from Portland pointed at his chest and mouthed a silent, "Me."

Al recognized the next reporter from a national evening news show. "Is it true that Senator Lyle Bates will be your Vice-president?"

"Yes."

"Bates is a Republican. Are you a Republican?"

"I don't really have a party affiliation."

"How do you expect to get anything done in Washington if you don't belong to a party?"

"I don't know. How do people in Washington get anything done if they do belong to a party?"

"What's your position on the Middle East?"

"I can't comment on that."

"What will you do about immigration?"

"I'm sorry, I can't answer those kinds of questions."

"How is your family dealing with all this?"

"I Think they're in shock. How would your family react, if you came home and announced that you were going to be the next president? I just hope my wife will forgive me."

While the press questioned Al, agent Carlyle put together a motorcade, ready for Al's return home.

Leo butted in, "Hey Boss, give me your keys and I'll drive your truck home for you."

Al tossed him the keys. "See you at dinner."

Al talked with reporters for several minutes. At Carlyle's urging, he finally broke off the interview. Several agents flanked Al as he got into a Secret Service car to leave. A mob of people swarmed toward the car but were held back by law enforcement officers. Even the paparazzi were there.

"Is this how it's always going to be?" Al asked Agent Carlyle.

"Only if you decide to run off on your own again. What you saw today is only a sampling. You've got to trust us to protect you. If you want to go somewhere, we need time to plan it."

Al sat quietly for a moment as he contemplated the enormity of what was happening to him and his family. "Sure, Carlyle. I trust you."

As the little caravan wound its way into the hills to the Goodwin farm, agent Carlyle filled Al in on what would happen next.

"The transaction team is waiting for you in Washington. They want you there Monday morning."

"That's pretty short notice."

"Sorry Sir, the transition team wants to get started as soon as possible."

"I'm okay with that. I just worry about my family. I don't think they like what I've gotten them into."

"If you want your family to go with you, we have accommodations."

Back at the farm, the Goodwins were briefed. Housing in Washington DC was ready, and a small jet waited at the Olympia Regional Airport thirty miles away. The Secret Service and the transition team would make all the moving arrangements.

That night at dinner the family and friends had plenty to talk about. Tracy sat TV tables next to the couch and chairs to accommodate everyone. Al and his mechanics sat at the table. After a lot of small talk and reminiscing Al got serious. He looked across the table at Mark. "Would you believe I have to name cabinet members and make appointments? There are more people I have to get on board, too. Usually, presidents know people and have connections. They do paybacks and favors by making appointments. The only people I owe anything to are my few friends and family, and you guys. I hardly know anybody else. Mark, I'd like to have you come along. I need someone I know and trust."

"Sure Al. I'm up for whatever you want."

"I can hire you as a personal assistant or appoint you to something."

"Count me in. Leo and I have already decided that we want to go to Washington DC. You can count on us being there for you."

"Leo, have you talked to your parents about this?"

"Yeah. They're good with it."

"What about your school?"

"I'll worry about that when I get to the other Washington. I already have my mechanic certificate. I don't really need any more education. Anyway, I see this as an opportunity I can't pass up."

Josh had a different opinion, "I'm not going anywhere. All my friends are here and I'm staying."

Al gave him a stern look. "This isn't going to be easy for any of us, but you have to come with us."

"Why can't I just stay here with Mom and Grandma?"

"We are a family, and we are all going."

"We'll see about that." Josh got up and went to his room. Al and Tracy gave each other knowing glances, and thought the same thought, -- *what will become of Josh?*

Agent Carlyle knew trouble when he saw it. If a client were to be protected twenty-four hours a day, it would take a minimum of five agents, and he didn't have extra ones. Also, it appeared that Josh himself, needed full time protection. He would have to make do with one agent who had to keep an eye on all three Goodwin kids until the move to Washington DC. They would have to remain on the farm until then.

Conner would stay on in college until winter break, then move to be with his family. An agent would be assigned to him at school. Hannah couldn't wait to go. Her princess-complex set her mind to imagining her glorious future. Al's mother Carol just said, "I'll be happy wherever you take me. I just don't want to be left alone on the farm."

"Mom, you will be living in the White House with us," Tracy said.

"That'll be just fine, dear. I'll go where I have to go."

By the time dinner ended everything was settled; the shop would be managed by Tran Nguyen, the farm would be cared for by Leo's parents, and the family would all leave together.

Later that night, Josh opened his bedroom window and slipped quietly into the night with a backpack full of his stuff. He sneaked through the orchard away from the floodlights set up in the front yard, then down the fence line to the county road. He followed the ditch right past a deputy sheriff's Ford Explorer and on down the road until he saw a familiar blue Jetta.

CHAPTER 16

Al and Tracy were up early. Everything lay quiet and wet, cool, and foggy. Al sensed this was the last morning of his way of life. He stared into the dark greens and browns of the forest beyond the pasture. He let memories fill his mind, driving the moos of the cows and the clucking of chickens out of his consciousness.

"Get a move on, Al. We've got work to do," Tracy said.

This time there were no helicopters.

Al went to the barn. He snapped open a hay bale and began spreading alfalfa for the cows, then turned his attention to the chickens. Tracey went about waking the rest of the family. She knocked on Josh's door. When he didn't answer, she opened it. The window stood wide open. Tracy ran out of the house yelling, "Al! Josh is gone. He's not in the house."

Al put down a bag of chicken feed and ran toward the house. "What do you mean he's gone?"

"I went to wake him up and saw that his bed wasn't slept in and his widow is wide open."

An agent overheard the commotion and hurried to join the Goodwins. "What's the problem? "

"Josh is gone."

"What do mean gone?"

"His bed hasn't been slept in and his window is open. He's gone," Tracy said.

The agent hustled them to the motor home. "Start a search of the property," Agent Carlyle ordered a subordinate.* Amy, get in touch with the locals and report what's going on. We need their cooperation. Now!"

"I thought you guys were here to protect us," Al snapped.

"I assure you we are, Sir. We just weren't expecting anyone to sneak out."

"Al gave Carlyle a stern look and unloaded. "Josh has issues. He makes poor decisions and has been in trouble around town. His school has him in counseling, and the cops watch him. The circumstances of me winning this lottery confused him. It puts him at risk. I insist that you always keep an eye on him. Furthermore, if he can sneak out, then someone else can sneak in."

"Yes Sir. You're right. We've done a background check on Josh and do know something about him. For what it's worth, Mister and Misses Goodwin, you are far from alone in having a child with a mental condition. Most families like yours never let on that one of their children is bipolar, or has ADD, or is self-destructive. Scratch through the facade of most families, and you'll find that they aren't as normal as they present themselves. I come from a large family and know this from personal experience."

"Mister Carlyle," Amy said, with a phone in her hand. "It's the Sheriff's office. He says he has Josh and another kid in custody at the county jail."

The call was brief.

"Is Josh in trouble?" Al asked.

"Don't worry, Mister Goodwin. Josh is in no trouble. Local law enforcement agencies were given instructions to pick him up and detain him until we can go get him. He has committed no crime. It's for Josh's protection that we are doing this. A deputy saw his friend's car and pulled them over. It's that simple. We'll have him home in no time."

Josh sat in the back seat of a black Secret Service Chevrolet. He had his father's black hair, his wide smile, his tall frame and his strong will, but not his father's mind. He had his mother's blue eyes, which were now glaring at the back of the agent's head. "The next time I take off you'll never find me."

The agent driving explained how dangerous it was for Josh to be out alone. "People could use you to get at your dad. Anything could happen. We just want to go where you go, to make sure you're safe."

Al left Tran to reopen the shop. He would wait a week after the Goodwin's were out of town and the excitement wore off, then reopen. In the meantime, he secured it with cameras, motion sensors, alarms, and plenty of light. He could monitor every bit of the building and grounds on his phone. A federal agent stood guard. It was becoming a tourist attraction. With Al's permission, Tran did some remodeling to accommodate the sightseers. Al's small budget only allowed for an expansion of the front office and a new employee to keep track of who's a customer and who is a tourist. At the farm, a perimeter fence was installed, and two mobile homes were moved in; one for the caretakers and one for the Secret Service.

Once they cleared their belongs out of the shop, Mark and Leo set out together for Washington DC. On the way out of town they saw a new sign, "Welcome to Centralia, home of President Alan B. Goodwin." They took turns driving a rental truck with Mark's Mustang on a trailer. Because they shared the driving, they made the trip in three days.

On their first day in town, Mark found a reasonably priced apartment a half mile from Union Station on E street. As close to the White House as possible, for his budget. It had two bedrooms situated on a corner of the top floor of an older four-story building. A back door opened onto an anemic balcony from which an open staircase descended past more balconies below, to a small gravel parking lot. A row of single car garages faced the parking lot. One went with the apartment. Mark's Mustang fit easily into it. Leo had left his car in the Goodwin's barn.

The President Select and his family had arrived a few days earlier. Mark kept Al informed of the progress of their trip and now called to say that they had arrived.

"Welcome to Washington, Mark. Any luck finding a place to live?"

"It's not what you could call good luck, but we found a cheap two-bedroom apartment. It's closer to the White House than we thought possible, in a kind of rundown neighborhood. Things will take a little getting used to. Right now, we're trying to find a decent espresso shop. This town doesn't seem to have many, And I don't suppose we'll ever get any more of Tracey's cinnamon rolls."

"You think you can't find anything. I'm not even allowed to look. I feel like I'm somebody's property. Everyone is too polite and will bend over backwards for me, but l still have to follow their program, and I can't even step outside. The only places I go are where the transition people take me. The good part is that we're staying in an historical building called the Blair House, the official guest house of the President of the United States. The place is nice."

"Sounds like you're living high on the hog."

"We sure are, but life here isn't easy. Politicians are a real problem. For instance, I'm supposed to be learning the current affairs of our nation, but President Townsend refuses to meet with me. He seems to think I'm part of a plot that has deprived him from running for a second term. He couldn't' get re-elected anyway.

"Would you believe I have to make about four-thousand appointments, one-thousand of them have to be approved by congress?" Al continued. "Right now, I'm interviewing for cabinet members. They can, in turn, find their own subordinates. Many of my prospects are turning me down. I've concluded that the conditions of my so-called selection have made me a political pariah. Nonetheless, I have made a few appointments. One of the sponsors of the lottery bill, Senator Tory Thorson, agreed to Secretary of Defense. I'm sure he'll be good, he's a West Point graduate with combat experience, but a Republican Congress must approve him, and he's a Democrat.

"That could be a problem."

"So, Senator Bates is to be my vice-president. He's a Republican and has several Republican recommendations, but there's something about that guy that I don't trust. He keeps trying to tell me what to do. I know I'm new at all this, but I want to make my own appointments, my own decisions. While we're on the subject, Mark, I'd like you to join my staff as Personal Assistant. You would work with me and my chief of staff directly. It pays a whole lot more than you were getting at the shop. How about it?"

"Sure Al, how can I resist? Have you been following yourself in the news?"

"Some."

"What I hear is that the politicians are confused about you, but the public likes you and wants to know more about you."

"You said it. Publishers want to write about me. They're offering some serious money. Can you believe that? Seems like all you have to do to get rich in this country, is attain high public office. But, I'm not sure I can trust what they might write."

"Don't wait too long, I already read a short biography in a magazine article!"

"Mister Goodwin, someone from the Justice Department wants to talk to you." It was Amy Styles, on Al's intercom. She had stayed on as his personal secretary. She grew up in Maryland and had a degree from Brown University. She knew her way around town. She was a keeper.

"I have to go Mark, email me that biography that you read."

Al switched phones, "This is Alan Goodwin."

"Mister Goodwin, this is Walter Preston, the Attorney General. We want to straighten out a small matter with you that could become problematic. We have learned that the people you hired as caretakers of your farm are illegal aliens. Were you aware of this?"

"No. Not really. Why?"

"We've checked their backgrounds and they are in this country illegally. I suggest you find some other caretakers before the press gets wind of this."

"The Mendez's? How can that be? They've lived in Centralia for years. Their children grew up there. Their son Leo has been in my employ for two years."

"Leo and his siblings were born in this country, but their parents are from Mexico. Immigration and

Customs Enforcement checked it out. They are defiantly illegal. ICE is waiting to deport them."

"I suggest you leave the Mendez family alone. They're good people."

"We can't do that sir. Imagine how it would look if the public hears that you have an illegal in your employ."

"The Mendez family agreed to take care of my place, and you can just leave them alone!"

Al hung up and called Mark back. "Looks like Leo's family is in trouble with immigration. Did you know they are illegal's? The Attorney General just told me. I think he wanted to intimidate me. These people are evil. I think I should appoint a new Attorney General as soon possible, someone that I can trust. We've had a couple good attorneys general back home. I'm going to have Amy set up appointments with them. I don't like the Justice Department digging into my background, and especially Leo's folks. It's all my fault. If I hadn't bought that lottery ticket no one would have done a background check on Leo's family. "

"I'd like you to do me a favor, Mark. Remember our press meeting at the shop? One of the reporters from Oregon pointed to himself, when I joked if one of them would like to be Press Secretary. I took that as an application. Could you find out who that reporter is? If he wants the job, have him call Amy for an interview."

While Al worked with his transition the rest of the family had their own adjustments to make. Al's mom, Dorothy, took charge of household matters, leaving the rest of the family free to make their switch from the farm to the White House. Tracy went school shopping. She found a nearby private school for Hanna, who couldn't wait to start. Conner was recruited by several colleges and had his choice. He chose George Washington University, where he would start after the new year. Josh stood his ground. He insisted on not going to school at all. He already had a school and he wanted to go back to it. Al told him he had no choice. To ease the tension, Tracy hired a tutor. Josh would be home schooled. She also found a psychiatric social worker who would visit him weekly. Josh didn't like any of it. He wanted to go home to Centralia. He holed up in his room or draped himself over the couch spending his free time texting and gaming with his buddies back home.

His boredom paused when some of his text messages were handed to him in print by a secret service agent who explained, "Your text messages are in the public domain. Anyone can read them, especially now that everyone knows who you are. What you are writing reflects poorly on the President Select, and some of it puts you and your family at risk. The rest of it is just nonsense, like calling the Blair House a 'dump'."

Josh's life couldn't be worse. He had no car, no freedom, no friends, and now he learned his phone calls and texts were in the public domain.

"I'm get'n out of this prison," he told the agent. "And not you or anybody can stop me."

The hard work and long hours took a day off for Thanksgiving. Dorothy helped Tracy prepare dinner. They refused to allow anyone else to do it for them.

Al paced around the kitchen. "What am I going to say at the inauguration? I just can't think of anything, except facing a huge crowd. I mean huge. I'm scared stiff. I don't want to do this. How do other people face crowds and not die of heart failure?"

"You should have thought of that before you bought that stupid lottery ticket," Tracy said.

Dorothy had enough. "Alan, I'm your mom and you listen to me. You always worry too much. Have Amy find you a speech writer and a speech coach and keep it short. You'll be just fine. In the meantime, you have plenty of speaking opportunities to practice on. Now why don't you find something better to do, like help with dinner?" She handed him a potato peeler.

The family and their guests, Mark and Leo, enjoyed Thanksgiving dinner safely tucked away in the temporary home. Tappet wagged his tail and ran between the chairs around the table, whining for whatever offerings may come his way. He wasn't disappointed.

They talked mostly about home, but Al wanted to know how Mark and Leo were adjusting to life in DC. "We're doing great, Mark said. "We've seen several of the national monuments and museums. We're getting the hang of traffic too, and we found a decent coffee house. Seems like folks around here aren't really big on coffee, but we got lucky. There's a place over on 12th called the Capital Grind that serves coffee just like back home. They even roast their own beans. I'll bring you a bag next time I'm here, you'll love it."

"Don't bother, Mark. We can't bring in outside food. The kitchen buys all the food. It's for our protection."

"Next you'll be telling me you have a taster."

"The coffee here is any way we want it," Tracy said. "Next time you come over I'll have some homemade cinnamon rolls to go with it."

Leo chimed in. "Listen Boss, I have a problem. I want a job, but every time I give you as a reference, I get turned down. They don't take me seriously. You got any Ideas?"

"How would you like to join the White House Transportation Agency? That's where they keep the President's limos. I'll have Amy look into it for you."

"Thanks, Mister President."

"I'm not president yet and besides, my friends call me Al."

"Right, boss."

"Mark, I took your advice. I gave permission to one of the publishers that wanted to do my biography. I didn't want to do it, but I'm a much richer man for it. Now they want to do one on Tracy. It's insane."

Leo wanted to talk about his mom and dad possibly getting deported. "How can they do that?" he said. "They've been here since they were kids."

"Try not to worry. There's a program for people who came into the county as kids that allows them to become citizens. The current president doesn't like the program, but I assure you, when I take office your folks will become citizens of the only country they've ever known. I hired a lawyer for them. He'll know what to do. I'm not worried and I don't want you to worry either."

Leo felt better.

Tomorrow would be Black Friday. Everyone but Al and Josh would join the crowds looking for bargains. But for one man, it truly was a black Friday.

Early Friday morning after Thanksgiving, a farmer east of Hagerstown Maryland made a phone call.

"911. What's your emergency?"

"I just ran across an abandoned car in the woods behind my place. I thought law enforcement ought to take a look at it."

"Just an abandoned car?"

"Yes ma'am. But it also has what looks like human bones in it."

"We'll send an officer."

On a narrow, wooded path, two deputies arrived to find an abandoned Chrysler. The woods were so remote that the Chrysler could have stayed there for years, had the property owner not decided to use his day off to set up a hunting blind for the upcoming muzzleloader deer season.

An investigative frenzy erupted. Local and federal agents combed the area. Two pistols lay on the floor of the car. Beside the car, several 9mm brass casings were dug out of the grass. Matching slugs were found in the car. Neither of the decomposed victims had any ID, but by afternoon the Sheriff announced that the car was the same one used in the assassination of Congressman Roger Carlson at the Capital Grind two years earlier. The Sherriff speculated that the two bodies must be those of the two assassins. The investigation was turned over to the FBI.

On that same day, Fred Ferguson sat in his car in the Walmart parking lot waiting for his wife and son to get in on some Black Friday deals. He had the radio on when the discovery of the car was announced. " ... the car and the remains of two individuals believed to be the killers of congressmen Roger Carlson have been found in a remote wooded area east of Hagerstown."

Fred believed the dead men in the Chrysler were killed for the same reason that the would-be presidential assassin, Delmar Fawcett, was killed -- to eliminate witnesses and protect an organization.

Fred wanted to learn more. Maybe something about this discovery could lead to the man-in-black. Fred decided to check it out.

The following Monday, Fred went to the sheriff's office and asked for a report. He was told the investigation was in progress and that it had been given to the FBI. They told him nothing else. From county records, Fred found out who owned the property where the car was found, a man named Phillip Turgin. He worked as parts manager for a car dealership in Baltimore.

Fred walked up to the dealership counter and asked for Phillip.

"Is he expecting you?"

"No." Fred laid his business card on the counter.

Phillip came out, motioning toward an alcove with a few chairs and a table.

"I'd like to ask you a few questions about that car you found on your property,"

Fred began. "It was used in a crime that effects a client of mine. I need to know as much as I can. Law enforcement people won't tell me anything. I hope you can help."

"Go for it. Those guys ruined my hunting plans! The cops blocked off the whole area. I can't even use my own property. What's more, they treat me like a suspect."

"Can you describe what you found?"

"I can do better than that. I photographed everything while I was waiting for the deputies to show up."

Fred left the dealership with several pictures in his Dropbox and a list of the questions investigators had asked Phillip. He called Marion with the new information. He could hardly contain himself. "I finally have some new information for you. As you probably know, the FBI has the car used in the Carlson murder. They also have two skeletons and two pistols, money from the holdup and other evidence. I'm sure they know who these guys were. The property owner said the license plates and the VIN number were missing, but since he works for a new car dealership he knew where to look in the engine compartment for a copy of the VIN. He photographed it.

"Slow down," Marion said.

"Anyway, I used that information to find out who the car was registered to, and where it was purchased. That led to a visit with a used car dealer. He told me that the FBI had already been there. The buyer of the car never registered it. He paid cash and used a phony driver's license. The dealer did say the buyer told him he won a Silver Star in Iraq. Does that sound familiar? When I asked for a description, he described Delmar Fawcett. The same guy who winged the President, also bought the car used in Carlson's assassination. The FBI has already reported that Fawcett worked for a Washington real estate broker as a handy man."

"Where are you going with this?"

"I went to see the real estate broker. The FBI had already been there. I learned pretty much the same thing as the FBI. Fawcett was a hard worker and a devoted employee, but people on staff didn't like him. He had no friends at work. I hung around at closing time and questioned the broker's administrative assistant. She volunteered that her boss, the broker, really liked Delmar and came to depend on him. 'Too bad' she said, 'about what his friend did to him.' I asked what that was. She told me that only days before Delmar's death, her boss and Delmar had a private meeting with another broker. She said that her boss gave her five-hundred dollars to give to Delmar, when the other broker said he liked the car he bought. When she gave the money to him, she asked what the meeting was about. He said he bought a car and had been given a chance to earn some real money. I asked if she told the FBI, and she said, 'No. They never talked to me. Just my boss.' The other broker was a man named Sol Solomon."

CHAPTER 17

Except for a small group of select congressmen, Washington politicians cautiously avoided President Select Alan Goodwin. Few would accept appointments, and many of those already in office under the current President vowed to leave in January. The Secretary of Health and Human Services summed it up when he said he couldn't "... effectively serve under some grease monkey from the land of lumberjacks and fishermen." Washington State's congressional delegation immediately rebuked him. They offered Al some nominees.

This flight from office by qualified personnel could weaken Al's already precarious beginnings. Thousands of appointed personnel held a corporate memory. They held the level of professionalism needed to manage the executive branch of government. After a conversation with Senator Weinberg, Al decided to de-layer the executive branch. That meant he would remove all unnecessary layers of management between his appointees, and people who actually did the work.

Reducing the number of political appointments could significantly improve management. Cuts in appointed positions would allow him to fill the top levels of the executive branch more quickly. Reducing the layers of authority between cabinet secretaries and the operational levels of government would speed up efficiency. Keeping the bottom layers intact would preserve institutional memory and improve the promotional aspirations of career executives.

Because Al didn't have more than one friend interested in a government appointment, cronyism was out. Also, appointees must be well qualified. So, he went beyond personal friends and asked for resumés. An adequate number of applications were submitted, especially from western states.

The transition team did all it could to bring their new president up to speed, but Al was in over his head. After one particularly trying day, he admitted to his mother that he regretted what he had done. "Mom, I'm overwhelmed. I wish I had never bought that lottery ticket."

"Remember when you started your business? You didn't know what you were doing then either, but you learned. This can't be all that much different. I don't think past presidents always knew what they were doing either. Take it one day at a time. You'll get the hang of it."

Toward the end of December, Al was contacted by both the Democratic National Committee and the Republican National Committee. Both wanted his membership. Not to be outdone, several lesser party committees also approached him. They had plenty to gain if the president became their party leader. To put an end to what looked like an on ongoing problem, Al publicly announced that he would join the Republican party, but added that he owed nothing to any political party. This played into what Senator Case and Vice-president Select Bates had hoped for. They were going to have a Republican White House. Al's party affiliation and independent attitude immediately increased the number of candidates interested in executive appointments.

While Al got ready to assume the presidency, his family warmed up to becoming the first family. They gave interviews and appeared on television. But not Josh. He wanted none of it. He was treated well, had nice things, could go places – under supervision and protection — but he was homesick. He spent most of his time talking with, texting, and gaming his friends back home. He stayed mostly in his room, longing for the little town where he and his friends had so many good times. He knew that the day he turned eighteen he could go home, and no one could stop him. A few more months seemed like an eternity, in his troubled mind. He wanted out now. All he had ever known filled his little corner of the world back home. He had lived in the same house his whole life, and his friends were from childhood. Now this. It did help that Mark and Leo found time to take Him on drives around Washington and the Virginia countryside, but Josh only complained that it wasn't home.

Josh's social worker warned Al that Josh was not adapting well to so many changes in his routine. She explained Josh's mental state caused him to be adversely affected by change. He was in danger of some kind of break, the consequences of which could be catastrophic. She wanted to know if the Goodwins could find a place for him to live back home. It could stabilize him.

"No," Al said. "His place is with his family. These are trying times for all of us. He has to live through them. Avoidance would just make things worse. What he needs to do, is accustom himself to his new way of life with something to look forward to. You're here to help him achieve that."

"I am, and my recommendation is to put him back in his established and familiar environment."

"That environment vanished the day I won the lottery. If he goes back home now, he won't find the home that he left. That could be worse for him than what he faces here. Can you imagine him out cruising the Main Street of town with a Secret Service agent in the car?"

"Mister Goodwin, I think Josh will run away and try to get back home on his own."

"He can't retreat into what was. There simply is no future in it."

The best Al could promise was a visit home next year — maybe August. The whole family could fly home together in Air Force One. It would be an adventure. Then he could see how different things had become at home.

Christmas break was welcome in Washington. Most bureaucrats stayed on the job, but elected officials had an extended vacation to return home to be with family and to meet with their constituents. They got out from under foot, giving Washington some time to relax. Al would keep his nose to the grindstone right up to his inauguration.

For Sol Solomon, there could be no better time to head for the Cayman Islands. Sol invited Senator Lyle Bates to come along. Bates would soon become the vice-president and needed to be convinced to follow Senator Case's lead in dealing with the caliphate. Case led Sol's legislative efforts. He needed to have Bates and Case working together. A day of deep-sea fishing and a night on the town would go a long way toward making Bates a team player.

A pleasant eighty-four-degree day greeted the two men when they deplaned on Grand Cayman, and met Sol's caretaker, Marla, at the airport. He knew, by now, that someone had to keep an eye on the place. The job was simple enough, just watch the place and do any needed maintenance, except when he visited. Then, she provided meals and did housework. He might be absent for weeks at a time. It was a good arrangement, as Marla and her husband had full access to the house and could use the boat as a perk.

The house itself, spread out above the garage on a narrow lot. Large windows gave a sweeping view of the marina and Sol's boat, the Double Eagle, moored below the deck.

Marla served the two men sandwich's and beer on a small table in a shaded corner of the deck. The two men sat down to eat and watch the sun go down.

"So, what do you think of my little Island hideaway?" Sol said.

"Nice. Where did you find the housekeeper?"

"Don't get any ideas. Her husband works for the marina and takes care of my boat. He'll be here in the morning to make sure the boat is ready for us to go fishing. He's the one who showed me how to fish these waters, and how to operate my boat."

"So, when did you take up fishing?"

"I've done a little freshwater fishing, but a couple of years ago I went on a fishing charter out of Miami. I caught this big old King fish. I had the most exhilarating experience imaginable! Every time I go out I long to relive that moment. Maybe you'll find out what it's like tomorrow."

The sun goes down early in December and even though the days-were warm, the nights were long and cool. As dark invaded the marina, lights came on around the water's edge and on several of the boats. A cool breeze moved across the deck, coxing the two conspirators to go into the house. There, Sol lead Lyle to a large picture of his boat, the Double Eagle. He lifted it from the wall, exposing a wall safe. Sol opened it. In it, Lyle saw money, gold coins, and other valuables. Sol displayed the rewards of supporting the caliphate.

"That's rather a lot to keep in your house. Aren't you worried someone might steal it?"

"This is my emergency reserve. Influencing congress and supporting the caliphate is risky business. If anything goes wrong, I have this to fall back on."

From where she stood at the kitchen counter, Marla was able to catch a glimpse of the safe. What she saw astounded her. *These men must be criminals, who else would hide such wealth,* she thought. She ducked just out of sight of the two men. She had no idea that a US Senator stood in the living room, and she didn't like him. It was the way he looked at her. But she stood still and quiet, listening to what the two men were saying. *They really are crooks,* she thought.

Sol reached into the safe. "Our benefactor has authorized me to award you with a bonus, for getting yourself into a better position to help the caliphate," he explained. He took out a bank deposit slip for one-million dollars deposited in Lyle's Cayman Island account. "This is for being selected as vice-president and the cleaver way you got there. When we get rid of Al Goodwin, and you assume the presidency, there will be a much larger deposit. You will even be introduced personally to our benefactor."

"Omigosh!" Lyle put the slip in his wallet.

"Don't thank me. Thank our benefactor." Sol then removed five one-ounce American Eagle gold coins. He placed them in Lyle's hand, saying, "Use these to show your appreciation toward those who can help us achieve our goals."

"I hear you."

Marla excused herself. "Mister Bishop, if you don't need me anymore, I'd like leave for the night."

"Sure. Take off."

"I'll be back early to get your breakfast."

Lyle and Sol looked across the marina, sipping martinis and puffing on their cigars.

"You are the only one who knows what I have here, on Grand Cayman. People here don't even know my real name. Everyone here thinks I'm Author Bishop. I'm showing you this as an example of what you could do. If I need to disappear, this is the place to do it. I have enough money and securities in that safe to keep me living in style for years. I suggest you find your own hideaway, just in case."

"I don't need to hide. You're a pessimist, Sol. When I make president, this whole caliphate thing will be settled in short order and we can get on with business as usual."

"Maybe, but it doesn't hurt to have a little hideaway. In case you ever need a place to get away to. You'll always be welcome here."

At dawn, Sol and Lyle boarded the Double Eagle. Once past the breakwater, Sol throttled back to an easy ten knots for the ride out to where he hoped to do some real fishing. On the way, Sol handed Lyle the coffee thermos. "There isn't much time before the President Select takes office. We need to plan ahead. Senator Case is coordinating our congressmen. We now have nearly thirty members who will vote as Case directs, and we're still recruiting more." He frowned, slightly. "We'll also need insiders in the DOJ and the FBI to give us a heads up on anything that affects us legally. And we'll need the immigration people to help us stick it to Al Goodwin over his hiring of illegal aliens. We also need a mole inside the executive branch. That's you."

"Has Goodwin been approached about cooperating with us?" Lyle asked.

"No. I haven't yet found a way to approach him. Finding his vulnerabilities will be your job. Once he's overwhelmed by the responsibilities of the Presidency, he may decide to resign. If he doesn't, we have to find a way to impeach him. As soon as he displays his ineptitudes, we can get him out quick and easy. So far, we have his employment of illegals to hold against him. He was told to get rid of them by the attorney general. He said he wouldn't. That shows intent.

"Senator Case is crafting a bill that would recognize the caliphate. Written clever enough, to pass both houses - which is almost a certainty - but no one knows what the new president will do. Our benefactor wants Goodwin to either cooperate or be gotten rid of. Hopefully, we can get rid of Goodwin before that bill reaches the White House."

"As his Vice-president Select, I'm beginning to know this guy, Goodwin. He's a hard worker and a fast study. Does he have any behaviors that can be used against him? Honestly, I don't think he's done anything wrong in his whole life. His army record earned him the rank of sergeant in his four-year enlistment as a mechanic in an airborne unit. He was honorably discharged with a good conduct medal. He had a good reputation in school, and there is no police record on him, save a couple speeding tickets. This guy is a straight arrow."

"All we need to do, is watch him until he screws up. He's never directed anything larger an auto repair shop. Can you imagine how he will behave in a national crisis? How is he going to react when he has to stand face to face with the likes of the Russian President or some prime minister? His incompetency will doom his presidency. You'll take over, and we will continue to receive support from the caliphate and our nation will remain free of terrorism."

Sol took the thermos back and poured some coffee. The boat cut through a smooth sea under a still sky, making it easy for Sol to encourage Bates. "I know I'm going on and on, but this is the best time to explain some things. Congressman who have joined our cause know people who can help us. Some are on important committees that could help us get inside the DOJ or ICE. Maybe, even, the FBI. These agencies can help us. Such as, finding evidence to impeach the new president."

As the two talked, a breeze came up from the South, building ripples on the water. The boat began to rise and fall, on long lazy swells. They had reached their fishing grounds. Sol set the throttle to idle. The two men continued their conversation as they as they got their fishing gear ready.

"The most important goal we have, right now," Sol said as he attached lures to his and Lyle's lines, "is to either intimidate the new president into cooperating or get him impeached. He might even be convinced to quit on his own. There's money in it for us. There's also money for congressman who influence l bureaucrats."

"How much money are we talking about?"

"I can't tell you that, but it's a lot. Our benefactor said it's cheaper and more effective to buy congress than to wage war."

"Who is this benefactor?"

"I can't tell you that either, but once you achieve the presidency, you'll know. For now, all you need to know is that an agent of the caliphate will pay to influence congress, and I am his only intermediator between congress and the caliphate." Lyle's expression appeared doubtful.

"Surely, you can't do this all by yourself?"

"Caliphate operatives are available to help me."

"But how many?"

"I don't know, but they're a large organization. They are responsible for managing our offshore accounts, providing campaign financing, organizing speaking engagements and all the rest. Just between you and me, these operatives can enter or leave the US anytime they want without passports or visas."

"Are you serious?"

"You already know more than anyone else. I just want you to know that these guys are large and well organized. If we hold up our end of the bargain, we'll have it made, but if we don't, the consequences could be dire."

"Okay. Okay. But how much do you really know?"

"Like I said, I'm their confidential intermediary. I know both ends from the middle."

Lyle glanced at a darkening sky, where clouds filled the western horizon. The ripples had become white caps, topping each wave.

"Do you think we should go back?"

Rough weather fishing was not something Sol had trained for. He and Lyle pulled in their lines and dropped the poles on the deck. Sol pulled back on the throttle and steered the Double Eagle toward the distant shore. The swells grew larger and the wind increased. It began to rain. As the storm became ugly, talk switched from corrupt politics, to the weather. The fun ended before it started. Now the challenge was getting home. Sol worked to keep the bow heading into the waves and didn't allow any to hit the boat broadside. He welcomed the experience of navigating rough seas. Lyle stared through round, scared eyes toward the island beyond the horizon. The Double Eagle slid down a breaking swell, and sent water crashing onto the deck. Water poured into the engine compartment. The engine sputtered to a stop.

Sol sent an SOS message to the Cayman Islands Coast Guard. Lyle panicked watching the wind tossed waves. Sol reassured him. "We'll be okay. The Coast Guard will tow us in." Both men hunkered down in the cabin, unable to do anything but wait.

"I don't care about that. What's it going to look like when the news gets out that a US Senator had to be rescued, and on your boat?"

"Around here, I'm known as Arthur Bishop. What's your middle name?"

"Martin. Why?"

"If the Coast Guard asks, tell them your name is Martin Bates. If anybody asks for ID, Which I doubt, it will say Lyle Martin Bates. Problem solved. No one cares about any Martin Bates getting rescued, and I doubt anyone around here knows who you are anyway."

Lyle relaxed a little and went back to worrying about the boat sinking. Then he got seasick. Sol turned on the bilge pumps.

The Coast Guard towed the Double Eagle to safety, while Lyle hung over the side vomiting into the sea.

By the time they got back to the marina the squall had passed, leaving a sky full of dark clouds. Sol and a very pale Lyle Bates stepped onto the dock. Marla greeted them. "I was worried about you."

"I guess I should have checked the weather forecast," Sol said.

For Lyle, the adventure had ended. He had enough of Sol and his Island. The next morning, Marla drove him to the airport. He went home early, to a wife disappointed that he hadn't stayed longer. Sol didn't return to Washington until the holiday break was over.

Like snowbirds to Arizona, swallows to Capistrano, and buzzards to a carcass, Congress returned to Washington.

CHAPTER 18

The January sky dawned a chilly light blue. Washington was shut down, as streets were blocked off and businesses closed. The Capitol grounds filled with people eager to witness this most memorable inauguration. Spectators poured in from everywhere, dressed in their warmest winter clothes. Some had blankets and comforters wrapped about them. Horse-mounted park police maneuvered through the crowds. Thousands of portable toilets stood at the ready. By mid-morning nearly two million spectators crowded the National Mall. A full day of ceremonies, parades, protests, demonstrations, balls and a massive security operation made Washington the busiest city in the world.

The Capitol's West Front was fitted with a large stage adorned with flags and buntings, chairs and equipment, ready to consummate the selection of an American president by lottery.

Although DC officials spent a year and millions of dollars gearing up to deal with this event, the ceremony itself would last less than an hour.

At twelve-o'clock noon, with his family at his side, Al laid his hand on the little bible he took with him from his shop. The Chief Justice of the United States swore him in. Alan B. Goodwin uttered the oath of office, fulfilling the only inauguration element mandated by the United States Constitution. The United States Marine Band performed four ruffles and flourishes. After that, a twenty-one gun artillery salute sounded north of the Capitol, followed by the playing of Hail, Columbia.

Al stiffened with fear. His palms were cold and sweaty as he clutched his wife's hand and moved toward the podium. "Stay close to me. I've got to get through this."

"You can do it, Al. Breathe slow and deep and don't lock your knees."

Just then Al glanced at a network TV camera – in fact, a whole tower of them were aimed at him. His spine muscles tightened until his head quivered under the tension. He took a deep breath, rocked back and forth on his feet, and then gripped each side of the podium for support, making him look in control. He remembered the fear and excitement he felt when he first began stock car racing, then the thrill of victory. The thought of his first parachute jump. After a few jumps all fear was gone. He could do this. Millions of people were looking at him. He stood tall, in his black, off-the-rack, suit and red tie. He lifted his eyes above the crowd to the top of the Washington monument, then slowly followed it back down to the crowd. He could see the words of his speech in the prompters. He had only to read them, like he and his speech coach had done several times. Then a tight smile crossed his lips as he began.

"Like many of you I paid my hundred dollars and registered for the lottery." Al paused, listening to his own voice reverberating from the distance. He took a long, deep breath before continuing.

"I wanted to be part of this experiment. It was exciting to think that I, or anyone, could be picked from the masses of Americans to become president of the United States of America just by chance alone.

"I've bought lottery tickets before and won nothing. I had no expectation of winning the presidential lottery, but owning a ticket spurred my imagination. What if I did win? What then? The tinge of fear that engulfed me faded away, as I realized that the odds were impossible. I had nothing to worry about. Yet, I found myself wondering what I would do as president. The thought festered in my mind until I began studying what the job of president is about. I realized that I wasn't alone in this. Ticket holders across the country were paying closer attention to politics. If this lottery succeeds at nothing else, it has already succeeded in causing Americans to be better informed about our government. But for the luck of the draw, any one of thousands of you could be standing on this platform today.

"People think it's crazy to choose a president by lottery. Maybe it is, but is it any crazier than what our elected officials have done?

"Is it crazy to spend billions of dollars bailing out failing and fraudulant corporations?

"Is it crazy to finance countries who want to annihilate us?

"Is it crazy to spend fifty thousand dollars apiece for paintings of high ranking government officials?

"Is it crazy that politicians spend billions of dollars to get elected?

"Is it crazy for America to spend more money than it recieves? Our national debt is so immense that to measure it in cash would require a stack of dollar bills that would reach to the moon four times.

"It seems craziness decends into madness, when we consider some of the things government can't afford to spend its borrowed trillions on.

"We can't afford to secure our southern border. Around the world people are waiting years and paying thousands of dollars to fullfil their dreams of becoming Americans, while others sneak accross our boarder and wait for amnisty.

"We can't afford to keep our highways safe. Across the nation bridges are collapsing into rivers and canyons for lack of maintenance.

"We can't afford to care for our wounded and sick veterans, but we can afford to send them into battle.

"We can't afford to treat people who are mentally ill. So they go untreated and forgotten. Some sleep on the heat vents along Washington's sidewalks or under bridges in cities across the country. Some of you are sitting today where some them will be sleeping tonight. When one such individual becomes delusional and kills, we pass more gun laws, that have nothing at all to do with treating the base cause.

"We can't afford to provide for people with disabilities. Those who rely on us for their very lives are being denied life-sustaining treatment and housing, without which they perish.

"Idealogues who have become slaves to established notions, are sentencing those who are intelectually disabled to live in isolation and those who are mentally Ill to sleep outdoors.

"Whether you are a Democrat, a Republican or anything else, ask yourself, 'Is this what I voted for?' How crazy is it then, to select your president by lottery?"

Mark and Leonardo sat in their assigned seats as guests of the President. They listened to each word their boss and friend said, as he stood before the world making his first major speech. Mark was nervous for him, afraid that at any moment Al would falter. He pushed away a Bag of Skittles that Leo pulled out of his backpack.

Just below the inauguration platform sat Al's pickle-ball team, a handful of mechanics and their families from Centralia, Washington, and a good many of Al and Tracy's family and friends. Not far away sat a man in a black overcoat and matching fedora. Farther back in the crowd sat Ibrahim Bin Jabar and several of his countryman who arrived by way of Ibrahim's Midnight Express, just for this occasion.

Al's speech went on. "Now, I find myself standing before you as President of the United States. I've been a mechanic, a farmer, a soldier, a husband and a father. These experiences, together with the love of my country, are what I can bring to this awesome office. I have no political aspirations and no experience in government, but most importantly I owe no one for this office. Not one of you.

"Back home I managed a small business. To stay in business, I knew that the customer had to be satisfied. Here in Washington I will continue with that credo, knowing the customer is you and the customer is always right.

"But this presidency is not about me, it's about all of us. It's about an America that has decided to experiment with the election of a president. Most Americans believe in the Constitution of the United States and the principals that brought it into being. I have just sworn to uphold that constitution, and that's what I will do. With your help, we must bring honor and integrity to our nation and to this office that I barely understand. Now the experiment must play out.

"Thank you and may God bless America."

The crowd broke into applause as President Goodwin lifted one hand into the air and waved at the crowd, then turned away to begin the festivities that would consume the rest of the day.

"I did it," he whispered to Tracy, as his body quivered with unwinding tension.

The President and his family were escorted a short distance away to enjoy the traditional inaugural luncheon in Statuary Hall. Josh wished he could hide somewhere, but he went along avoiding eye contact with everyone until he saw the beautiful statues that surrounded the room. Figures he could look at that couldn't see him.

Reporters busied themselves interpreting one of the shortest inaugural speeches ever given. One reporter called President Goodwin hopelessly inexperienced; another called his speech "Crazy. One we could not afford to take seriously." Another said, "it was honest and heartfelt." Yet another simply said, "He didn't have much to say." Al's little bit of grist was ample to flood the mills of reporters and pundits of every stripe.

It was a long day. After parades, balls, and receptions it was finally over. Al and his family were at last alone in the presidential residence, tucked into the heart of the White House.

Tracy slipped off her shoes and leaned back into the plush couch, "Look at this Al, our home for the next four years."

All their personal items were put in place during the inauguration. Their clothes were hung, their pictures placed. They felt like the only guests in an opulent illusion that would vanish upon waking.

At six a.m., Al awoke. This was it.

At 7:00 sharp, the same time Al went to work in the auto shop, President Al Goodwin walked into the Oval Office as the nation's chief executive. For the next few minutes, he sat alone, savoring a moment of silence. He studied the Oval Office. Some of his treasures from his shop were placed around the room; his stock car and pickleball trophies sat on the mantel, a picture of the auto shop and his mechanics sat on the credenza along with photos of his family. Beyond curved walls, the West Wing bustled with confusion and excitement like the first day of school. A beam of thin morning sunshine poured across his desk, welcoming the first full day of the Goodwin administration.

The first lady stuck her head into the Oval Office, breaking Al's solitude. "Well there you are, sitting at the most important desk in the world. Do you have any idea what you're doing?"

"Not really, but we are going to a prayer service at the Washington National Cathedral in a little while. Did you know new presidents have been starting their administration this way since George Washington? After that it's lunch in the White House Mess." Business started when the White House Chief of Staff walked in with Al's schedule for the day.

After lunch, President Goodwin's first official act ordered his Chief of Staff to put a hold on all activities of the outgoing president.

"I'll approve of nothing until I see it first," he said. In Al's mind, nothing former President Townsend did could be trusted. He also had a new appointment for the Attorney General waiting to be vetted by congress, along with several others. Al sat with amazement at the power the pen could wield. He signed his first executive order, asking that an alternative be found for the millions of tons of salt being dumped on American roads. He already knew that taxpayers spent billions trying to mitigate corrosive damage that eats into vehicles and bridges. As a mechanic, Al knew how dangerous a rusted-out vehicle could be. The order included the phasing out of studded tires that were destroying the Interstate Highway system in northern states. He did this purposely, to signal that his presidency would address a failing highway infrastructure and the needless loss of life on the American highway.

He followed that, by signing another executive order that would delayer the executive branch, thereby reducing the number of layers of administration. In the briefing room the newshounds had something to chew on. He also set in motion orders to convert the tennis court to a pickleball court with spectator amenities — the sooner the better.

At two o'clock, President Goodwin sat down with the National Security Council to be briefed. After some small talk and a discussion of current events, the President took charge of the course of the meeting. He addressed General Carter, the chairman of the Joint Chiefs of Staff, "What are our greatest concerns from the military point of view?"

"The Middle East. Our lack of involvement and troop drawbacks have allowed every kind of terrorist to advance their agenda. They are now in control of enough territory to constitute a small nation."

Vice-president Bates spoke next. "We haven't had a single act of terrorism in this county in two years. Even Internet chatter is down. Military pullbacks allow the Middle East to normalize in a way that works best for them. Even Israel is having fewer problems, and there's no problem with oil supply. No, General, the Middle East is not our biggest problem. What we should worry about is North Korea and illegal entries across the Mexican border."

The general shot back. "Of course, North Korea is worrisome, so are some other places, but the Middle East is the bigger threat. Their goal is a caliphate. Then what?"

NSA Director Edward Langford, broke in. "Just because terrorism is down doesn't mean we're safe. Once a caliphate is established, I think we'll be in for it."

"So, what are we going to do about it?" Al said.

Secretary of State Ida Barns quickly answered. "Mister President, we are having ongoing negotiations with several of the leaders of Middle Eastern nations. What you must understand is the complex nature of their culture, and alliances. I have met many times with my counterparts in the region. They worry as much about protocol and tradition, as they do about politics. We have to be sensitive of these conditions if we expect to continue peaceful relationships."

President Goodwin considered his response, carefully. "I understand we are sending money and other supports to Iraq, Afghanistan, Syria, and so on, yet the caliphate continues to expand into their territories. Even with military assistance from outside of the region they still expand. Has anyone met with these caliphate guys?

"No. We don't deal with terrorists," Secretary Barnes said.

"Our best policy is hands off," Bates said.

"No," Al said. "Even my mechanics know better than that. I want each of your written advice on my desk no later than tomorrow morning. Title it, 'What to do about the caliphate' and keep it short."

The rest of the meeting was spent advising Al of a myriad of security concerns.

Later that afternoon, Vice-president Bates cracked open the door of Senator Majority Leader Melvin Case's office.

"Come on in Lyle. Pull up a chair and tell me about your first day as Vice-president.

"I can't believe this guy. He gave the Security Council homework. He wants briefs on how to contain a caliphate and he wants them tomorrow morning. He even implied that his mechanics know better than I do, about Middle East policy."

"Don't let it bother you. He's just trying to figure out what's going on. He needs to be convinced that messing with the caliphate will bring back terrorism. Anyway, we have some time to see what he does."

"Other than that, he wants to see the Dream Act instituted, and he said, 'as soon as possible.' I think he's trying to protect the illegals he's harboring on his farm."

Speaker Case reached his big hand over and grabbed Lyle's wrist. "Listen Lyle, I want to know the minute he does anything to jeopardize our security." "Our Security" had become code with Bates and Case and their co-conspirators, to protect their newfound wealth.

"Don't worry, you'll be the first to know. He asked a lot of naive questions today. He's not exactly hitting the ground running. I just wonder how long it will take for him screw things up so bad that we can start an impeachment investigation. He's already in violation of the law regarding the illegals at his farm."

"Be patient and enjoy your homework. I'll get some material for you."

"Thanks, Mel." Bates left.

Case pulled out his phone and called his Chief of Staff. "This is Case. Looks like our new president is getting interested in Middle Eastern affairs. He asked the Security Council members to each give him a written brief on the subject in the morning. The topic is, what should we do about the caliphate? I'd like you to gather some of our reasoning for staying out of the Middle East for the Vice-president's report. I want it ASAP. Lyle has to hand it over in the morning."

Al decided to spend the last hour of the day exploring the West Wing. What a marvel to see the historic paintings, woodwork and honorariums of this great office building. He walked alone into the press briefing room. Once a swimming pool for FDR, it was covered over and filled with comfortable chairs like a small rectangular theater. Lots of equipment hung from the ceiling and more gadgets were scattered around the room. There were a few people in the room, all of whom stopped what they were doing when the President walked in.

"Continue with what you were doing," Al said. "Don't pay any attention to me, I'm just looking around."

Nobody moved.

A reporter from one of the major networks spoke up. "Mister President, how's your first day going?" He continued speaking without waiting for a response. "Think your executive order to get rid of road salt is going to do the job?"

"It's not what I think that matters. Researchers across the country are looking for alternatives. I'm just trying to bring their concern to the forefront. As a mechanic, I've seen the damage salt does to vehicles. I've seen major parts rusted through, like broken frames and separating tire rims. It does the same thing to bridges and other metal infrastructure."

"What do studded tires have to do with all of this?"

"Those little metal studs grind away pavement. In heavily trafficked areas they form ruts in the road that pull against tires. This would be a dangerous condition for autonomous vehicles. Replacing rutted pavement is expensive. There are alternatives to studs. It's been nice talking to you. I gotta go."

"Do you miss your garage?"

"Sure, I do, but that's in the past. I have other things to do these days. See ya later."

"Past presidents have added facilities to the White House. Nixon put in a bowling alley, and FDR put in a swimming pool. You could add a garage."

"I don't need any wise cracks about my career as a mechanic. Remember, I already have a garage. We keep all the limousines there. But you can expect to see a pickleball court."

Al left the room to continue his walk. He peeked into his secretary's office, "Hi Amy. How was your first day?"

"I'm glad it's over. I'm still trying to get my arms around all that is going on around here."

"Me too. I feel somewhat lost."

"By the way, congress approved your Attorney General. He's been invited to tomorrow's cabinet meeting."

After his first full day, Al finally relaxed with the whole family in their new home. Josh was the only one missing. He hid in his new bedroom. Tomorrow he would go shopping for video equipment. Neither Al nor Tracy liked having the Secret Service babysitting their son. Al had to find something more positive for Josh to do.

Tracy thought she knew. "Josh needs to identify with something. Maybe it would be good for him if we shipped his car out here?"

"That's a good idea, but it would be cheaper to buy one here. Car hunting might be good for him. I'll have Mark arrange that tomorrow. We can keep it out at Camp David." Al wondered if there was a garage at Camp David.

CHAPTER 19

Lying in bed, Al turned on the Night Show to see Archie MacArthur's monologue. A lot of it had to do Al's first day in the Oval Office.

"We have it on good authority," Archie said, "that President Goodwin was seen wandering through the West Wing today looking for the garage. When asked if he thought he could find it, he said he already had. Then he said he was going to install a pickleball court. We know that unlike past presidents, President Goodwin does not play golf. He races stock cars and plays pickleball. Some of you are probably asking, 'what the heck is pickleball?' It's played on a dummied down tennis court where the players use big ping pong paddles to whack around a lightweight ball. The game is named after some dead senator's dog, 'Pickles.' With the first redneck president in office, what can we expect next? How about a salt tax? That's right. Today our mechanic-in-chief signed an executive order asking for a study of alternatives to salt on our highways. When Senate Majority Leader Melvin Case heard about it, he said, 'there is no alternative to salt. It keeps ice off the roads and saves lives. 'But,' he said, 'we can always impose a salt tax if that will make him happy.'"

Al disgustedly turned off the TV.

The next morning the Security Council came prepared with their reports. President Goodwin gathered them into a little stack that he carried back to the Oval Office. He spent the next hour reading through them.

They showed great contrast in the opinions of members. The Chairman of the joint chiefs of Staff gave a firm warning, that Congress wanted to tie the hands of the armed forces. Vice-president Bates, on the other hand, saw no reason to interfere at all in Middle East affairs. He argued that the caliphate would grow to encompass the region and then stop with the formation of a new nation, like the Ottoman Empire that the British broke up a long time ago. Besides that, he argued, there has been no terrorist activity in America.

Al wasn't buying it. He asked Amy to arrange a meeting with the New Secretary of Defense, Tory Thorson.

Secretary Thorson arrived in the Oval Office late that afternoon. After some pleasantries, they settled in for a private meeting. The President leaned forward in his chair. "Have you ever been in this office before?

"No, I haven't"

"Me neither, and that's the point of our visit. I'm so new at this that I still have grease in the callouses of my hands. I'm afraid I will be manipulated and out maneuvered by clever politicians who think they can control me or want to see me fail. I have here a stack of reports given to me this morning. They vary from one another far too much to be the best advice of the Security Council. Right now, what I need to know is what our real policies are in the Middle East. I also need to know what we will do if Israel is attacked, or terrorists strike us here at home. Don't we have scenarios about this?"

Thorson studied the sincerity of the President's demeanor. "I'm sure there are contingency plans. I'll get them for you. More worrisome, are bills that have been going through congress. Congressmen have the idea that Americans are tired of Middle East involvement. For the last couple of years bills have passed that tie the hands of our military. There is currently a bill being drafted that would recognize the legitimacy of a caliphate state in the areas held by radicals in several nations."

"If I see a bill like that, I'll veto it. The US has never recognized a maverick state and we're not going to start under my watch."

"There are certain congressmen who like to portray you in a certain way, how shall I say this?"

"Never mind. I've seen the cartoons. Most of them have wrenches sticking out of my pockets. Just last night, that guy MacArthur on the Night show called me a redneck and said I was walking around the White House looking for the garage."

"You're right. Certain congressmen think you will be easy to manipulate."

"That's just what I'm afraid of, but I have bigger concerns. While you're coming up with scenarios, come up with one that rescues the caliphate's persecuted minorities. We must put a stop to the persecution in the occupied areas of the Middle East. As a nation, we cannot stand by while individual freedoms are being snuffed out and lives ended. I've already told the Secretary of State. Soon I will tell everyone. This is an emergency. Everything else can wait. We've ignored the Middle East far too long."

Later that week, Al gave his first address to the nation from the Oval Office. He wanted to tell everyone his vision. "I have three long term priorities. First, something must be done about the Electoral College. It's obsolete. A popular vote is what people want. In addition to that, all primary voting should occur on the same day.

Choosing candidates state by state causes some states to have no say at all, in who the primaries put forward. Had we been electing presidents according to the people's wishes, no one would ever have thought of such a thing as a lottery. Two; medical care and pharmaceuticals should be made available to all Americans. Surely our medical community can come up with a way to do this, even if our politicians can't. And three; we must rescue refugees from the wars in the Middle East. These are problems that affect all Americans."

After his address, Senate Majority Leader Case called Al. He said that Congress was eager to work with the President but cautioned that getting involved with anything in the Middle East was a bad idea. Al didn't think so.

"Mister President, since we've been pulling away from the Middle East, we have had no terrorism from any foreign source — none."

"It's just a matter of time Senator. I think the movement for a religious caliphate is cancerous. We need to be concerned about the wellbeing of Americans, not sanctioning a revolutionary state in the Middle East."

"These people have a right to their own destiny. A caliphate is what they want. Once that's established, they will have no further need for terrorism," Senator Case replied.

"Can you tell me where you think their borders will stop?"

Over the next weeks the President worked congress for their cooperation. They dragged their feet. He tasked the Secretaries of State and Defense to seek solutions that the President could enact unilaterally. He was exploring the limits of presidential power.

Al had only a couple of days off since arriving in Washington, and none, since he entered the presidency. He decided to schedule some trips. He got in touch with Agent Carlyle. He knew the secret service had to have plenty of time to plan. He checked the NASCAR calendar for nearby races and the Indianapolis 500. He also scheduled a visit to the Pacific Northwest and to the Atlantic regional pickleball tournaments. If other presidents could spend time on golf courses, he could play pickleball and go to the races. He also wanted to go home for a week. He didn't plan beyond that. His more immediate schedule included a weekend at Camp David and a tour of the Air and Space museum with the family. Carlyle said no to the Air and Space museum. "I'd rather not have to arrange that," Was Carlyle's response.

For his week at home, Al told the Secret Service that his son and two of his friends would accompany him while he toured his hometown and attended other business and a speaking engagement.

"We know the two boys," Agent Carlyle said. "They are known to be involved with drinking, cruising, marijuana, driving without insurance and other infractions and misdemeanors. We routinely discourage any proximity to such people."

"My main purpose in taking this trip is so my son can have some time at home with his friends or anyone else he wants to be with. I don't see a problem. He will see them. Period."

Al tried to get Josh interested in doing something, but his social worker insisted he was depressed and reclusive. He needed more time to adjust to his new surroundings. Mark and Leo helped a lot by taking him places were Al just couldn't go. On one trip Josh purchased a used Honda Civic. It was a fixer-upper that Al hoped would brighten his son's spirits. Al could use that car to teach mechanics, as well as a focal point for him and his son to do things together. Josh hoped to escape in it. They took the car to Camp David where they found a spacious garage. Mark bought a set of mechanic tools for Josh.

For their week at home, Josh would go along with his dad, mother, grandmother, and sister who were also getting homesick. Josh's social worker said no. She wasn't ready to give Josh that much freedom just yet. It would be like dangling his freedom just out of reach. But Al thought a family visit home would be good for everyone, especially Josh. Carlyle started planning.

Before Al could take any personal trips, he had to go to Brussels for a meeting with European Union leaders. The topic would be international trade — not something Al knew a lot about. He spent several days being tutored on current trade agreements and protocol. Al knew that European automakers built cars in the United States to avoid tariffs, but many replacement parts still came from Europe at high cost. Parts made in Mexico were cheaper than parts made in Europe. Al wanted to do something to even out the costs, because auto repair shops made less money fixing cars with European parts because they wanted to keep the costs of repairs down. This would be his first trip on official business. He and Tracey left for a two-day affair.

This would be the new president's first test to see if he could handle such responsibilities. News agencies worldwide watched him closely. In Washington, Vice-president Bates and Senator Case were especially attentive. They watched all the televised reports only to be disappointed by the President's ease dealing with heads of state. Al was well coached ahead of time and followed his instructions. The closed doors agreements included international cooperation in offering relief for Middle Eastern refugees. Trade agreements lifting tariffs on European auto parts, the EU even agreed to lift tariffs on American wine.

While Al met with his peers, the First Lady found an opportunity to visit a mission where she stated, "No one in the world should ever go hungry. Hunger is the result of war, poor politics, and poverty, not lack of food." being seen on TV serving the hungry, launched the First Lady's debut as an advocate for the poor.

The next day, the President and his entourage visited the world's largest automobile manufacturer in Wolfsburg Germany, where hundreds of Volkswagen mechanics cheered his arrival. Sol's cadre of corrupted congressmen were livid.

On arrival back in Washington, the Goodwin's went to Camp David. Al and Josh worked on Josh's Honda. Al enjoyed doing mechanical work. Josh pitched in and showed real pleasure for the first time in months, but as he dreamed of driving back home, he knew that every cop in the country would be looking for him. For now, driving around Camp David would have to do. Conner did his part by doing runs to the parts store. All three test drove the Honda. Camp David officials became concerned when Al and Mark showed Josh how to do a high-speed drift though a tight curve. By the time Josh had the maneuver figured out, security at Camp David were running along the road, waving their arms and trying to get him stop. Josh hadn't felt better in months. He and Conner spent the evening researching stereo systems online. His car would have all the stereo he could pack into it.

Al left the family at Camp David. He had an early morning walk scheduled from the White House to Senator Case's office. They would meet about Case's caliphate recognition bill. Al planned this event to bring media attention to the crisis in the Middle East. He couldn't just walk, he had to bring along a bunch of Secret Service agents, motorcycles, cops and street closures. A helicopter hovered above. They looked like a gang of Blues Brothers with plastic cords hanging out of their ears, and those were just the ones Al could see.

Agent Carlyle was in a bad mood. Only Al had a smile on his face. Al's procession used the middle of the street. Several pedestrians watched. Rather than walk in the middle the street with black suited agents surrounding him, Al moved to the edge of the street, and started giving high-fives. Carlyle urged him to return to the middle. Instead, Al broke into a run. He outran two thirds of the Blues Brothers, including agent Carlyle. Josh saw it on TV and forgot his funky attitude for a while.

Al was blown away by the opulence and history of the Senator's magnificent office complex. From where Al sat, he could see the Washington monument, the Mall and the great buildings that flanked it. It seemed the office was more important than the man. Senator Case offered snacks while they discussed the Senate bill that would recognize a caliphate state. Case tried to sell the virtues of such a recognition, but Al wasn't buying it. "I'm not signing it," he said, "and I doubt you have the votes to override my veto."

"Don't be so sure. Americans want to put Middle East problems behind them. We can do that for them."

"I don't think so. What we should be doing is rescuing the victims of the caliphate. I want congress's help to find a means of doing so."

"I think that could happen once you sign the bill."

"If I sign the bill, then we would be recognizing the caliphate as a sovereign nation and there'd be no rescuing of the innocent victims. Forget it."

Al remembered seeing Case play football. That same powerful man now stood behind his desk, leaning on his knuckles; a lopsided, liver lipped scowl on his face. Al was intimidated. He thanked Case for seeing him and left the Senator's office.

Carlyle, still angry over the President's run to the Capitol, had a motorcade ready for Al's trip back to the White House.

That evening Al entertained the leaders of major automobile manufacturers with music and dinner. He also invited the administrator of the National Highway Traffic Safety Administration, and the leader of a private safety watchdog group, as well as prominent members of hotrod clubs and other automobile interests. It was time for Al to start pushing for highway safety.

After dinner, Al started a debate by suggesting that car makers get rid of distractive dashboard controls. "The fewer gadgets you guys put on cars, the safer we'll be." Al told them. A polite argument followed. Manufacturers insisted that their vehicles were safer than ever. That it was the customers who required such conveniences. Al stirred the pot by suggesting that he could sign an executive order requiring safer dashboard controls. The evening ended with well entertained and well-fed manufacturers agreeing to study the level of distraction caused by dashboard devices.

That night, Al settled in to watch the Night Show. Archie was in his usual form. This time he had a skit set up showing Al outrunning the Secret Service. Except it was done on a wall sized film clip of the keystone cops trying to catch a chicken thief.

Al caught an elbow in his side from Tracy. "Shut it off, Al."

CHAPTER 20

There are four-hundred-thirty-five representatives and one-hundred senators in congress. Of them, Fred found thirty-one worth reporting to Marion West. But now, it looked like the well was running dry. He hadn't reported any congressmen to Marion in over three months. Then, as he sat drinking coffee at the Capital Grind, he saw it; a small news article in the local pages of his newspaper. It reported FBI Deputy Director Arnold Rankin broadsided a car at one o'clock Sunday morning. His blood alcohol level exceeded the legal limit. He was cited for DUI, and reckless driving. In the car with him, was Senator Maxine Byte of South Dakota. Fred investigated Byte a year earlier and found no wrongdoing. Now he had to wonder, *what were they doing in the same car in the wee hours of Sunday morning?*

After coffee, Fred left for the metropolitan police station where he read the police report. It said both were drunk. Senator Byte had a broken arm that required a trip the ER. Rankin tried to excuse himself by saying he was taking Senator Byte home because she had too much to drink and didn't want to drive. He didn't realize he was intoxicated. Fred knew that both had families and lived in the district.

Why were these two together and where were they drinking? Fred picked up his investigation of Byte where he left off last year. The Senator lived in a two-story colonial, separated from the sidewalk by a small lawn.

Her car sat in the driveway next to the house. Fred placed a magnetized GPS tracker under it. He then set up a surveillance camera a half block away from the house. He could monitor comings and goings from his cell phone. Rankin's condo building presented a problem. It had cameras everywhere. The parking garage had a pass-coded gate. Fred had to keep his distance from those cameras.

Staking out a residence can be the most boring of jobs, but it helped that he could watch both residences at the same time. So, he staked out the condo building in person and watched Byte's place on his cell phone. His first action came on Friday evening, Byte left home alone. Fred tracked her movements on his phone. Her car stopped a few blocks away. Fred drove to the location. She left it parked it on a quiet neighborhood street. Fred parked under a large oak tree a few car lengths away. He waited. Shortly after one a. m., a new Chevy Impala pulled in front of her car and parked. Arnold Rankin got out and walked around to other side of his car. He opened door for Senator Byte. They walked to Byte's car and embraced for a long goodnight kiss. Rankin returned to his car and drove away. Fred followed. Rankin stopped in front of an all-night convenience store. As soon as he entered the store Fred pulled in beside him, jumped out of his car and stuck a GPS tracker under his car. Now he could track both vehicles remotely, in real time, and streamed from the cloud. Fred went home.

Over the next two weeks, Fred mapped the travels of both cars. A pattern developed from each for each car; daily commutes to grocery stores, restaurants, and other destinations. Two stood out as unusual. One was a hotel where Rankin's car parked for a few hours on two nights while Bytes car sat on a quiet neighborhood street. The other was a restaurant near the Capitol, where both cars stopped on Wednesday nights at eight. Fred showed up at the restaurant the following Wednesday at a quarter to eight. He waited in the reception area for Rankin and Byte to arrive. When they did, they were escorted to a table where a man in an expensive looking pinstriped suit greeted them. Fred asked to be seated close by. He ordered coffee and pie and listened. He heard the man addressed as Michael. Fred returned to his car and waited for Michael to come out. When he did, Fred got the license number of his car. So far, Fred had a photo of Senator Byte and Arnold Rankin in each other's arms and the address of the hotel where they spent time together. Fred wondered what their families thought about them being gone late at night, but Congress often burned the midnight oil.

Fred imposed on a buddy in his old Military Police unit to run the license number. It came back registered to Michael Pancost with an address in Herndon, Virginia, some twenty-five miles away. Fred learned he was the chief financial officer for Piedmont Software, a large technology company headquartered in Reston, Virginia.

It didn't take Fred long to learn that Congress was interested in passing legislation to limit Piedmont Software's digital surveillance network. Piedmont Software could track any individual who had a cell phone with GPS active. The company knew what stores, gas stations, hotels or any other destinations were visited. This information targeted advertising to be sold to other tech companies. Congress feared it could be used by foreign governments to harm Americans and their interests. Testimony on Capitol Hill stalled as cagey tech geeks took full advantage of the technological illiteracy of Congress. As the hearings progressed, Piedmont Software stock fell.

Marion West's phone rang. It was Fred. "I have another corrupt senator for you. Can we meet somewhere?"

"Sure. How about lunch at Napoleon's?

"See you then."

Fred arrived early and ordered a Rueben sandwich. He had it half eaten when Marion finally arrived. Fred handed her a flash drive. "I have some pretty damning information on Senator Maxine Byte and her paramour FBI Deputy Director Arnold Rankin. I spotted them in a news article involving a DUI. Since then I learned they are in a romantic affair. But worse than that, they're involved with congressional hearings looking into the Piedmont Software information network. Senator Byte sits on that committee. She and Rankin are having clandestine meetings with the CFO of Piedmont Software. Your client should be highly interested. I can't prove it, but I think they may be taking bribes from Piedmont Software. In addition to that, If Piedmont Software can prevent Congress from limiting their activities their stock will go up significantly. I think Byte and Rankin expect to take advantage of insider trading. It's all on the flash drive.

"You think there are more congressmen involved?"

"Probably not. Because of their romantic relationship I'd say they are operating alone."

"I thought we were running out of suspects!"

"I don't think we'll ever run out of crooked congressmen."

Fred wrapped the last half of his sandwich in a napkin and shoved it into his coat pocket. With the

Senator handed off, he went back to more legitimate investigations, like looking into hidden properties important to a divorce lawsuit.

Sol's phone vibrated in his pocket. The caller ID showed Marion West. "Good morning Mister Bishop. We have another corrupt congressman for you."

Sol immediately translated that to a possible million dollars. "That's great. When can I stop by for the details?"

"Anytime. I'll be here all day."

Sol walked out of his new Chevy Chase real estate office along with his driver. He went home for a quick change into his sky-blue suit. His sleek Mercedes Maybach soon pulled up in front of Marion's office. In Marion's conference room, She gave Sol a folder of information and very little conversation. Sol wanted to get started on his new prospect. Back at his office, he studied the information Marion gave him. A narrative provided all the details. Pictures said the rest. Sol remembered Senator Byte from a fundraiser he and Senator Case sponsored two years earlier. He had never heard of Arnold Rankin, but a corruptible FBI insider could be valuable to Sol's cause. Since Sol was a fundraiser for the RNC he had no trouble arranging a meeting with Senator Byte the following morning.

The walls of Senator Byte's office barely had room for the tastefully framed degrees, awards and honors that celebrated her career in law and politics. She greeted Sol with a gentle smile. "Please be seated, Mister Solomon." She motioned toward a soft chair. "Can I get you some coffee or tea?"

Sol never felt intimidated by people in power. In fact, he enjoyed their company, until this moment. The Senator's sparkling green eyes sized Sol up in the moment it took for him to answer. "Thank you. Yes, I would appreciate a cup of coffee." Sol made it a point to accept what people offered, especially if he expected them to receive his offer.

Byte turned to her Keurig coffee maker on the credenza. "How may I help you, Mister Solomon?"

"Like I said on the phone, there is a Republican Party contributor who may have campaign funding sources for you, but it's conditional. It involves ending terrorism in America.

"Sugar or cream?"

"No thanks."

Byte handed Sol a large white cup with red cursive lettering that read, "I'm the Boss." She continued her warm smile, as she sat on the corner of her desk with one shapely leg crossed over the other. She wore a form fitting red dress. Sitting or standing, she was taller than Sol. The cast on her arm showed some notable signatures, including that of the Vice-president. "Please explain," she said.

Sol began as he had with so many others. "How would you like to run your next campaign on the reputation of having stopped terrorism in America?"

"Why would I want to? There hasn't been a terrorist threat in this country in two years."

"The reason for that is because we have scaled back our Middle East involvement. Because of that, several others in congress have been receiving plenty of funding for their campaigns. You could do the same."

"I have no trouble getting elected. I would, of course, appreciate extra funding, but with no strings attached."

Wrong approach. This woman radiated self-confidence. She didn't need anything, but Sol believed she took bribes from a major software company. "Would you be interested in one-million dollars tax free to help the US government stay out of the Middle East?"

"What does that have to do with campaign financing?"

"It doesn't, but it has the same effect. There is a benefactor willing to pay, to have congress pass laws that would keep America out of the Middle East."

Byte rose to her feet. "How dare you come to a United States Senator with a bribe of one-million dollars. Are you nuts? I could have you arrested right now."

"I only asked you if you were interested."

"I most certainly am not." Although her face had a serious cast to it, a smile remained.

"Even if you're not interested in money, your help is still needed to keep terrorism out of America, and America out of the Middle East. It's a noble cause," Sol reasoned.

"You came here to discuss campaign financing, not bribery. If you have no more on that topic, then our meeting is over."

"I have one more thing." Sol opened his briefcase. He took out a picture of Byte with FBI Deputy Director Arnold Rankin and the CFO of Piedmont Software at a restaurant table. He handed it to Byte. "If you are not interested in money, what are you doing with these people?"

"It's none of your business who I dine with." She glared down at Sol. Her smile slipped away. If Sol hadn't helped her find funding years ago, she would have kicked him out at that moment.

"I think you're right when you say you don't need money. You're getting it from Piedmont Software. I don't think you want people to know about these meetings, or your affair with Arnold Rankin." Sol handed over the

Picture of Byte arm in arm and lip to lip with FBI Deputy Director Arnold Rankin next to Byte's car.

"Are you blackmailing me?"

"I don't care about your personal life and I don't care anything about Piedmont Software. All I care about is getting you on board with staying out of the Middle East. All you have to do is vote in favor of bills that would affect that end. You may even want to get creative and daft your own bills. There's a million bucks in it for you, tax free, available right now, and bonuses for work done. I know you're looking for money, or you wouldn't be meeting with Piedmont Software, and you wouldn't be the only one doing this. There are thirty others in congress devoted to keeping us out of the Middle East. All of them have something to hide and all of them sincerely want to be free of terrorism and out of wars in the Middle East. You could be working with these people to achieve that end. All of them have received a considerable amount of money for their efforts."

"I don't like that you have information about my personal life. What else do know about me?"

"That's it."

"Where'd you get it?"

"A private investigator gathered it. Don't worry. No one will ever see this."

"You mean no one will see it unless I don't cooperate. You are on thin ice. What you're doing could ruin your life, maybe even get you killed."

"Yes, I'm putting myself at risk, but the end justifies the means. Such risks have given us a Republican White House, and no terrorism for the last two years. But we continue to need votes in Congress, like yours."

"Where is all this money coming from?"

"A silent benefactor in the Middle East."

Senator Byte leaned against her desk and stared at a spot on the carpet. Sol took a tube of 20 Gold Eagles from his briefcase. He stacked nineteen of them neatly, and surreptitiously, on the side table next to his cup, placed his business card on top, and held it down with the twentieth coin. "There are other benefits to this offer, like bonuses and well-paid speaking engagements. I'm going to leave now. I want you to call me when you've thought over my offer."

Over at the J. Edger Hoover building the Deputy Director's phone vibrated.

"Arnold, I just had a visit from a Republican National Community fundraiser who knows about our affair and our dealings with Piedmont Software. He wants to buy my votes in the Senate."

"Bribing a US Senator can put him in prison for a long time."

"I said he knows all about us. He can ruin us. I think if we crossed this guy, we'd be the ones going to jail not him."

"How much is the bribe?"

"Plenty. Plus, more later."

"What's his name?"

"Not now, Arnold. We need to talk."

The talking took place, mid-afternoon, at an out of the way cafe near Alexandria. These two didn't want to be seen together, even though they couldn't resist each other. They slid into an out of the way booth. A waitress in blue jeans offered a menu, then returned to filling saltshakers and topping off catchup bottles. The lunch crowd was gone, and the dinner customers wouldn't start showing up for another hour. After a while, the waitress sauntered back to the booth with coffee. After taking their orders, she gathered menus from the tables and sat down at the far end of the counter by the front door. She took her time replacing the lunch special with the dinner special in each menu. Left alone under the cover of cocktail music flowing from the Muzak system, Maxine told Arnold about her visit from Sol.

"A million dollars! Blackmail and extortion, pure and simple," Arnold said.

"He knows too much. If I accept his offer, he keeps quiet about us and Piedmont Software and I get a lot of money."

"He's a criminal. Even if you accept his offer how do you know you can trust him to keep quiet?"

"Problem is, we're criminals too. I'm already receiving money for votes and you're already subverting an FBI investigation into Piedmont Software, and we're both inside traders. I think I should take Sol's offer."

"Once you accept, he'll be back asking for more. I think you should tell him no. What can he do? He can get busted bad for bribing a member of congress."

"He has photographs, Arnold — you and me in a rather passionate embrace. I saw it. I couldn't stand the disgrace of us being found out."

"It's possible, you know, to have him eliminated."

"I've got to accept Sol's offer. He has good reason to keep his mouth shut and we'll get lots of money. I'll split everything right down middle with you, just like we're doing with the Piedmont money. Maxine reached into her purse and pulled out a one-once gold coin. She handed it to Arnold. "He left a whole stack of these things in my office — twenty of them." She fished out nine more of the coins, making a neat stack in front of Arnold. "That little stack is worth maybe fifteen-thousand dollars. That's your half. You can have them."

Arnold hesitated until he saw the waitress coming with their lunch, then he quickly grabbed the coins and dropped them into his coat pocket.

Senator Case answered his phone. "I'm happy to inform you that Senator Maxine Byte has joined us."

"Good work, Sol said. "She has a lot of influence among senators. We'll need her if we have to override a presidential veto."

CHAPTER 21

After years of wanting to see a NASCAR race, tonight Al would see one. The President left the Oval Office early Friday afternoon. He and Mark wasted no time getting to the residence where Leo, Josh, and Conner were waiting for them.

This small event put several government agencies in gear studying and planning every moment of the outing. They covered security, communications, the press, medical, and military, all to protect the President. Even such mundane things as access to drinking water and restrooms, had to be considered. Advance personnel made everything ready for Al's night at the racetrack. This would be a news-making event that would only be announced once the President was in route.

The President's helicopter took off for the hundred-mile flight to the speedway. High above, an F-16 fighter patrolled the sky. Mark was experienced in helicopter flight, but the others weren't. They stared out the window, pointing and talking, as they flew low over the city. Forty-five minutes later, they touched down in the parking lot behind the racetrack. Al's group went straight from the helicopter to a private suite at the top of the grandstands. They had a sweeping view of the track between the first and second turns.

Back on Capitol Hill, Vice-president Bates stood in Senator Case's office nibbling on a truffle. "Do you know where our mechanic-in-chief is?"

"How am I supposed to know?"

"At a stock car race."

"So?"

"Those places are associated with white supremacy, and other redneck activities. It just might be possible to paint the President as a bigot."

Case furrowed his forehead into a washboard of wrinkles. "NASCAR isn't the good old boy network it used to be. It's just as mainstream as the NFL. I don't see how going to a stock car race can sully the President's reputation. Other presidents have been to NASCAR events without any problems."

"All we have on this guy, so far, is the illegal alien thing. We need more. I intend to make this president look like a bigot. It would tinge his character in an impeachment trial. Right now, I have people at the racetrack taking pictures and getting whatever information they can."

"Okay that's fine. Since you have people at the racetrack, make sure the President is photographed with the son of that illegal who works for him. That's what will get him impeached."

Al and his crew ordered the track specialty, hot dogs. They had a whole suite to themselves, along with the ubiquitous Secret Service staff. By now everyone knew the President was at the track. It was announced that he would hand off the winner's trophy at the end of the race.

While waiting for the race to get started, Al took the opportunity to ask Leo how his folks were doing.

"Great," Leo said. "They're taking good care of the farm, and Papá is doing pretty good at his job too. Being friends with the President doesn't hurt."

"I'm not doing him any favors. There are people in congress who would like to see your mom and dad arrested, just to get to me. So far, our attorney has found ways to prevent that, but there's no guarantee that they are safe. The Attorney General is also helping."

"One more thing, your folks are on a watch list. If they cross an international border they will be arrested. Not only that, the border patrol has authority to stop anyone they want, within a hundred miles of the border, if they suspect an illegal. Remember, the Canadian border isn't far from home.

"Can't you just grant them citizenship, and get all this over with?"

"I just don't have the authority to grant citizenship to individuals. Congress does give me discretionary power to delay deportation of certain groups of people. I'm exercising that power now, not just for your family, but for others like them as well.

"There are people in Congress who want to use the fact that I hired your parents as a reason to seek my impeachment. The President of the United States isn't supposed to break the law by hiring illegal aliens."

"You're going get impeached?"

"Maybe. It seems like there are certain congressmen who want to get rid of me."

The race began. Everyone's attention turned to the track except for those sent by Vice-president Bates. Josh wasn't watching either. Bate's people were scattered around searching for any sign of bigotry or white supremacy. Josh searched for a way out.

Once the race got started, Josh could see that all eyes concentrated on the track. Even the Secret Service agents were into it. He excused himself and left for the restroom. He passed two Secret Service agents on the way. Once inside the restroom, he pulled out his cell phone and texted his friend Cole in Centralia, "I'm at the racetrack. I'm going to get lost in the crowd. Then, if I'm lucky, get out of here and catch a bus home. I'll text you when I'm free."

Josh left the restroom and headed for the stairs. There were Secret Service agents blocking his way.

"Excuse me," Josh said."

The agents stepped aside, and Josh trotted down the stairs. So far so good, he thought. At each landing were two more agents. Another two were waiting on the ground level. He excused himself, and once again the agents stepped aside. *Piece of cake.*

Josh walked out of the entrance. The parking lot was full, the Marine One helicopter stood where they left it, protected by a handful of agents. Josh walked straight toward the edge of the lot, some distance away. He looked back to see one of the Secret Service agents walking toward him. He looked ahead where another agent stepped into view. He had to ditch these guys. He turned and ran between the cars heading toward the distant fence and freedom.

At school he had turned out for track and lettered in long distance running. He knew he could run for a few miles and leave these guys, with their dark suits and ties, well behind. He soon reached a six-foot chain link fence. In one bound he grabbed the top and pulled himself over. He didn't think about landing. He hit the ground flat on his back, knocking the wind out of him. He looked up to see the agent coming fast, wingtips, necktie, and all. As soon as Josh caught his breath, he took off running again. The agent wasn't keeping up. Josh came out of the park onto a city street. A black Secret Service Chevrolet Suburban came speeding toward him. He dodged to one side but the Suburban cut him off. They had him.

"Why can't you guys just leave me alone?" Josh panted.

"Why do you keep trying to run off?"

"Why do I have to be treated like a convict?"

"Sorry, son, it's for your own good."

"Don't be calling me son. Why don't you just call me prisoner." Josh hauled off and slugged the agent in the gut and broke away. Immediately he had two agents on him. One agent pinned him down with a knee in his back. He was read his Miranda rights.

"Assault is a crime, son. You're under arrest."

Al's full attention was on the track until a car went up against a wall. A yellow flag came out slowing the race. Al noticed Josh's half eaten hotdog and no Josh. "Hey Mark, don't you think Josh has been gone to the can too long?"

"I'll go check."

Agent Carlyle, standing one tier behind Al's window seat, had the agents holding Josh on the phone. "Hold it Mark. A couple of Agents have him. He tried to run off. When he got caught, he assaulted an agent who arrested him."

Al popped to his feet. "He what?"

"Don't worry," Carlyle said. "We can work this out. We don't like to interfere with one's freedom to move about, but it seemed Josh took off at a run. He's being held in the back of a car. He was never out of our sight."

"We've been down this road before, Mister Carlyle. Josh wants to run off. It's your job to see that he doesn't. What are you going to do with him?"

"I expect he'll be charged with third degree assault and taken back to the residence."

"Take your time. Let him stew for a while. He's has to learn something."

"Yes sir." Carlyle was embarrassed and angry, but glad to see Josh get some discipline.

Al ordered a fresh hotdog and settled in to watch the rest of the race.

After the checkered flag, Al's group was escorted through the pedestrian tunnel to Victory Lane where the winning driver, and a mass of jubilant others partied. Al joined the driver and his crew for photographs. Al and the winning stock car driver held the trophy above their heads and poured champagne on each other. The winner gave Al the checkered flag as a memento. The crowd went wild. Al invited the winner, his crew and their families to dinner at the White House. Al hung around talking to drivers until Carlyle urged him to leave.

The President and his company were escorted through the maze of vehicles toward the Marine One helicopter. Along the way a cell phone photographer caught Al walking next to a pickup truck with a stars and bars rebel license plate replacement bolted to the front bumper. NASCAR frowns on such things but there it was. Just what the Vice-president hoped for — the President next to some redneck's truck.

In the excitement of the moment, Al's thoughts never left what Josh had done. They hung onto him, causing a blemish over what should have been a special time.

Vice-president Bate's phone sounded. A text had arrived with a photo. He forwarded it to Senator Case with the message, "This is it, a photo of the President next to a truck with a rebel flag, and for frosting on the cake, he's with the son of his illegal caretaker. Can you get this to your press connections?"

Al got home in time for the Night Show with Archie MacArthur. He smelled of cheap champagne. The First

Lady got up and left the room as the program started. Archie trotted on stage with a happy smile and a question. "Did you know that our mechanic-in-chief, Al Goodwin, went to a stock car race?" The wall sized screen behind Archie suddenly projected a picture of Al and Leo next to a Chevy pickup. "What we have here is a picture of President Goodwin hanging out at a stock car race. Could that be a white–supremacists' pickup he's next to? Look at the stars and bars on the front bumper. It happens that the President employs an illegal alien on his farm in Washington State, and that's the illegal's son right there next to the President. And look how they're dressed. Aren't jeans and sleeveless tee shirts the way rednecks usually dress? What are you doing Mister President?"

Al's mom walked in. "So, what are you doing, Mister President?"

"How can they get this stuff on TV so fast, and why do they keep calling me a redneck?"

"What you should be asking, is what to do about Leo's parents."

Al had a new attorney general and a lawyer working to resolve this problem. "I'm on top of it, Mom."

"No, you're not. You need to find new caretakers for the farm and make a statement that you didn't know they were in the country illegally."

"Mom!"

"Don't Mom me. This is best for all of us including the Mendes family. They are the interest of every imagination agent in the country, just because of you."

Although it was almost midnight in Washington DC, it was still early enough on the West Coast to call his caretaker. He explained the situation to Mister Mendes, who understood. Tomorrow he would call a real estate manager in Centralia to find a caretaker for his farm.

Josh never got home until he could be arraigned on Monday morning. Assaulting a federal officer got him a court date.

CHAPTER 22

First thing Monday morning, The White House press secretary made a public announcement that the President's caretakers were dismissed, as they may have been illegal aliens. He then met with the Secretary of Defense and the Joint Chiefs of Staff. This set in motion a feasibility study, and scenarios for rescuing innocent victims in the caliphate occupied territory. He also instructed the Secretary of State to gather support among America's allies. Al knew what he wanted to do was an up-hill battle, but he went ahead with his plans, knowing that the persecuted minorities in the Middle East must be rescued.

During lunch, Secret Service agents brought Josh home. Angry and humiliated, he vowed to escape at any opportunity, Realizing that just running off wasn't working, he needed a better plan and had plenty of time to think of one. His old man jerked his phone for a month and stopped his allowance.

The news people got ahold of the juvenile court proceedings and learned that the President's son was arraigned for assaulting a federal officer. They used the incident to further paint Al as a read neck. One major network asked, "What kind of people do we have in the White House, who would attack a Secret Service agent?"

Al was learning the pitfalls of being a public figure. He sought the council of his staff and experienced politicians. He was learning fast. He noticed that some Republican members of congress acted like they were afraid to talk about anything Middle Eastern and liked to talk down to him. This proved especially true during a meeting with Senator Maxine Byte who grilled him on his competency.

"Why would an automobile mechanic want to be president?" Byte asked.

"I have an aptitude for mechanics and enjoy all things automotive. I only bought into the lottery so I could feel like I had a stake in it. I never imagined I would win. In fact, my family is upset about the changes that are affecting their lives. I wish I hadn't bought that lottery ticket. But since I did, I'm going to make the best of it."

"No one would fault you, if you admitted the job was beyond your abilities. You could resign honorably under those circumstances and leave the office of the presidency in the competent hands of Lyle Bates."

"I am not a quitter. I took an oath and I'm sticking to it. You are here to educate me on the activities of your committees, not to tell me I'm incompetent."

Byte echoed Vice-president Lyle Bates who also advised Al that resignation could be an honorable exit, any time the responsibilities became too heavy.

Al wasn't having any of it. He set up a committee to screen individuals from outside of government who wanted to advice the President. He would talk to one every day. He enjoyed hearing suggestions and chatting with regular people. One gave some solid advice that Al put into practice. "Don't take any crap from Washington insiders. They want to eat you alive." Al wasn't about to be on their menu. He went to work every day, all day, just like back at the auto shop. He wasn't going to miss the opportunity to guide his nation in a way that most everyday citizens hoped for and asked for.

Before his meeting with Senator Byte ended, Al said. "I'm here to stay, and you'd better get used to it."

Later that day, Senator Byte met with Senator Case and Vice-president Bates in Case's office.

"Seems Like our lottery president is more resilient than we thought," Case said. "According to what he told you, he has no intention of resigning his office, and according to Lyle, he is adapting. It doesn't look like we can get rid of him for incompetency."

"I know someone in the FBI who might expand his background check," offered Byte. "There could be something overlooked. For example, his son Joshua and his friends were researched. The FBI found that two of them have Juvenile offenses. One offense was committed in a car registered to the President."

You're wasting your time," Sol said. "Our benefactor wants the President to comply or leave office. So far all you have against him is hiring an illegal. We need to con him, frame him, or put the fear death in him."

Amy stepped into Al's private office, to deliver the news that Al's pickleball court was ready. He grabbed Mark, and they went to see it. As they walked along the edge of the South Lawn, Al called Tracy. "I just found out the pickleball court is ready. Can you bring my pickleball bag to the court? I'd like to try it out."

"I'm helping Josh with home schooling."

"Bring him with you. He doesn't like school anyway. The fresh air will do him good."

The tennis court was more than converted, Trees were removed, and concrete poured to accommodate viewing seats. Restrooms, dressing rooms, lockers, and a snack bar were added, all covered by a stark white canopy with bright LED lighting. Even court-side tables were added. New trees and landscaping shielded it from public view. When Tracy and Josh showed up, they tried it out.

"We need to do this when we have more time," Al said as he adjusted his necktie.

Al and Mark went back to work with fresh excitement about having a pickleball court for the next three years.

That night, Al spent a warm evening on the Truman balcony outside his bedroom, preparing for a meeting with the Speaker of the House and other represent-atives. Tracy broke his solitude when she called through the open living room door. "Hey Al. Are you coming to bed?"

"Come on out here. It's a lovely evening and the view is perfect."

Tracy dragged a chair next to Al and sat down. "Al, I don't see much of you anymore. What with all the meetings, dinners, and dignitaries, I feel more like a formal acquaintance than a wife."

"You're a great First Lady, Tracy. Every time you are with me, things go better. You have a way with people that puts them at ease." Al moved his chair a little closer and held Tracy's hand. "Three more years and we can go home."

"Can't we take a vacation somewhere, just you and me?"

"Anywhere your heart desires."

"I want to go home."

"Sure. So do the rest of us. I've arranged it. I was waiting to tell you when I found the right week. Maybe next month when Congress is on break."

"There's something else I want to talk to you about. It's the Feed the Hunger program I'm starting. It now has a name, Universal Diner. Senator Weinberg has agreed to help. He owns a large farm in Salinas, California, where he knows people who have agriculture interests. There should be plenty of food available. Hunger is not caused by the scarcity of food, you know. We plan to collect surplus meat and produce, then distribute it to the diners like chain restaurants do. Just like any other restaurant, there will be a menu and prices. The difference will be that payment is optional. A pilot program will open in Salinas. For publicity, I will be serving food at the Gospel Outreach Mission here in Washington, but it needs funding. Do you think you could convince Congress to budget it?"

"You provide the details, and I'll ask."

Josh stepped through the living room door. "What are you guys doing out here?"

"Just talking."

Josh grabbed a chair and sat down. "About what?"

"You would be interested to know that we are planning a trip home for a week."

"When?"

"Not sure, but soon. I came out here to plan a presentation to Congress tomorrow, but I keep thinking instead about the limousine convoy that will take me there. It's a waste of money. I know it's for my protection, but still ..."

"You've got to get used to it, Al," Tracey said.

"Why don't you use the tunnel?" Josh said.

"What tunnel?"

"There's a tunnel that goes from the White House to the Capitol."

"I never heard of one. What makes you think so?"

"There's all kind of tunnels. One goes over to the Treasury building, too. There are tunnels all over Washington. You should check them out."

"Where are you getting your information?"

"My teacher likes to talk about Washington history. He says tunnels were built to provide safe places, in case we get attacked, and to allow secret passage in and out of the White House. Who knows, how many? To hear him talk, it sounds like the ground under Washington has more holes than a Swiss cheese."

"I know of some of the tunnels, and so do you. How about the bunker under the White House and the tunnel connecting it to my office? But I've never heard of a tunnel to the Capitol."

"My teacher says there's one. You ought to check it out." Josh had high interest in tunnels. He knew of more tunnels than he cared to mention, like the one that connects the White House with an ally on H Street. Josh did his homework. He might be able to use a tunnel to sneak out. So far in his explorations around the White House, he found only the tunnel to the Treasury building, but it was locked.

"I'll look into it. If such a tunnel exists, I'd like to use it."

Next morning, the presidential motorcade pulled up to the Capitol. Al hustled off to a conference room.

A congressional committee greeted him. They politely rose to their feet. Once greetings ended, Al took a seat and was welcomed by the Speaker of the House. Al wasn't interested in formalities. He had a mission. "You know why I'm here; it's about rescuing the victims of the caliphate." He explained that the military was studying how to do it, and that the Secretary of State was raising international interest. What he needed was Congressional approval.

"We don't think it would be good for America to have a military presence in the Mediterranean," The Speaker said.

"All I'm asking for is a rescue mission. Surely, you understand the human suffering of minorities in that region."

"We are about to recognize the caliphate as a sovereign nation. How do you think it would look if we recognized their nationality, then at the same time, invaded their territory?"

"Mister President," Representative Bireley said, "I serve at the pleasure of my constituents. They want nothing to do with the Middle East, and neither do I. Let them have their caliphate. Once we recognize them, we will have a trading partner instead of an enemy."

"I think Representative Bireley has spoken for all of us. We will not support your plan," the Speaker said.

"Senator Case told me if I signed the caliphate recognition bill, he would support a rescue mission. Do you feel the same way?"

"When you sign the bill, the caliphate will allow us to remove anyone who wants to leave the caliphate."

"How do you know all this unless someone in Congress is negotiating with the caliphate? I get the impression that members of both the Senate and the House are engaged in clandestine negotiations with the caliphate. Is that true?"

"No one is doing any such thing. All we want is peace in the Middle East, and we intend to have it."

"I think you should scrap the caliphate bill and look to providing relief for its victims instead. Have you no compassion?

"Why can't you just leave well enough alone?" Bireley said.

Al didn't like the tone of his voice. He also saw the Speaker shoot an angry glance at him. It was time to change subjects. "As you know, I am trying to promote automobile safety. I've asked for an alternative to using salt, and I've asked for fewer distractions on dashboards and steering wheels. This requires a change in law. I would like to work with you on this."

Representative Bireley wasn't the only one in the room who had received gold from Sol Solomon. He spoke for the rest of them when he said, "sign the caliphate bill and then we can talk about traffic safety."

"No."

The Speaker of the House looked at Bireley, "Let me handle this." He then turned his attention to the President. "As I'm sure you've heard, we are drafting articles of impeachment. You have committed a felony by hiring illegal aliens, and you are usurping the authority of Congress by sending armed forces into harm's way. We are in no mood to entertain any requests for legislation from the office of the President, until after your trial."

"I can declare an emergency to get the rescue done, and I can issue an executive order to get the salt off the roads. I also intend to open an unused tunnel that connects the White House with the Capitol. That will save money and add more security. It will also allow me more frequent visits."

No one spoke.

"I had hoped we would be in a better mood. I wanted to invite any of you who play pickleball to join me for a round or two. I will commemorate the new court with a cookout and refreshments. I've invited some of the top players in the country for an exposition. You are all invited to come. This is not politics. This is good will. You will receive a formal invitation."

Al scanned the room looking at each congressman in the delegation. Only the Speaker, and Representative Bireley looked him in the eye. Al left without another word. Bireley got up and followed him out of the room. He caught up with the President and said, "I play pickleball."

"How about tonight after work. Say six?"

"Sure."

At six, Mark had a half dozen staff members learning the sport of pickleball. Al and Bireley talked and ate ham sandwiches while waiting their turn.

"Why can't you sign the caliphate bill?" Bireley asked.

"They are a rouge, terrorist movement that in no way resembles a sovereign nation. The United States has never, nor will ever, recognize such an entity, and it's my job to see that we don't."

"You know the last president would have done it."

"The last president was the worst president the union ever had."

"He would have done it because his life was in danger."

"How's that?"

"The caliphate had him in their pocket. Cooperate or else. I'm telling you this because I think you're in danger, if you don't sign the bill. These caliphate guys are serious. Don't mess with them. They'll try to corrupt you with offers of money and threats of blackmail."

"How do you know?"

"Let's just say I've been approached."

"I've taken risks before. I served in the Army in Iraq. I've seen the horror of war. I didn't like what I saw then, and don't like what I see now."

It was time for Al and Bireley to play.

The next day, formal invitations went out to members of the House and Senate, inviting them and their families to attend the first annual Presidential Pickleball Exposition.

CHAPTER 23

On a muggy Friday afternoon, the First Family boarded the Marine One helicopter for a short ride to Andrews Air Force base. The Goodwin family was finally going to have a week at home. This was the first time the kids and Al's mom had been on Air Force One. They took a quick tour of the plane, then settled into the trip to Joint Base Lewis McChord in Washington State, which would be followed by another helicopter ride fifty miles South to the farm.

When they reached home, Tracy stepped onto the helipad shocked by what she saw. "Al, they've turned our home into a concentration camp!"

The farm wasn't what they remembered; the barnyard was paved over with a heliport, a portable building stood ready for the Secret Service, a mobile home housed the new caretakers, the driveway was paved double-wide all the way to an automatic steel gate at the county road, a chain link fence surrounded the property, and a standard American flag flew above it all.

"I'm sorry Tracy, but we need the security," Al said, expecting to see a guard tower with machine-guns sticking out. "You know they're calling this the Northwest White House, don't you?"

"Don't rub it in."

The house remained as they left it. The Goodwin's were home. Even though it was late, Tracy put some frozen pizza's in the oven. Al reclined in his chair, soaking in the familiarity of his home. He turned on the

TV. After a while the Night Show with Archie MacArthur came on. Josh walked over to his dad. "Can I have some friends over?"

"Sure. Who do you want to invite?"

"Cole and Noah."

"Okay. How about tomorrow morning?"

"Can We go pick them up?"

"No. You'll have to stay on the farm until we all go out tomorrow. They can come here. Just because we're home, doesn't mean we can do things like we used to."

"Maybe ... "

"Not now Josh. I want to hear what Archie has to say."

After picking on some other politicians Archie got around to Al. "We all know that our mechanic in chief hasn't been home since leaving for Washington last fall. But, are the folks in his hometown happy to see him come back? We decided to visit the little town of Centralia, Washington to learn more about the President's hometown. We also thought it would be fun to ask people on the street what they thought of our new president." the big screen behind Archie showed the main drag in the older downtown area with Archie standing on the sidewalk, microphone in hand. A young man in jeans and a plaid shirt walked by. "Excuse me. Did you know that President Goodwin is coming to town?"

"No."

"What do you think of the new president?"

"I don't know. I guess he's okay."

"Do you know the President's first name?"

"Ah, is it Lyle or something?"

Archie walked over to a man with long hair sitting on a blanket leaning against a brick wall, and asked,

"Excuse me. Did you know that President Goodwin is coming to town?"

"No."

"What do you think of the new President?"

"Great guy. He served me dinner at the mission."

"What do you mean?"

"The President used to help out at the mission. He would serve dinner some nights."

"Do you know the President's first name?"

"Sure. It's Al. Alan B. Goodwin. You don't suppose you could spare a couple bucks do ya?"

"Archie pulled out a five-dollar bill and dropped it on him.

A schoolgirl walked by. "Excuse me. Did you know that President Goodwin is coming to town?"

"Yeah."

"What do you think of the new President?"

"I don't know, but I went to school with his son Josh. He's hot."

"What do you mean by hot?"

"Well, he's good looking."

"What else?"

"Am I going to be on TV?"

"Maybe."

"Then I better not tell you what else, if you know what I mean."

At the end of the video Archie said, "There you have it, folks. A girl who is happy the President is coming to town — with his son, that is."

The closing picture showed an old tavern with a lot of pickup trucks parked in front. "In that building are some of the rednecks in Goodwin's lily-white corner of the Northwest.

What wasn't shown, were interviews recorded inside the tavern. Archie reasoned that since fewer than one percent of the population of Centralia was black, there must be some white supremacists around. Maybe they all were. A local tavern might be a good place to find out. He chose the Maple Leaf Tavern, a log building with a low shake roof. It sat on a gravel parking lot next to a huge Big Leaf maple tree, its windows filled with neon beer signs. The inside walls displayed pictures of old-time loggers showing off gigantic trees. The wall behind the shuffleboard featured pictures and yellowed news articles about the infamous D. B. Cooper, who hijacked a plane in Seattle and parachuted out somewhere south of Centralia. He vanished into the night with two-hundred-thousand extorted dollars, never to be seen again. A picture of President Goodwin hung among them.

Archie felt like he had struck gold. He and his cameraman attracted attention. He got friendly by buying beer for everyone, then asking, "what's good to eat?" He ordered a Bigfoot Burger and a bottle of Olympia beer. He started schmoozing with the locals. After a while he edged in some questions trying to see if anyone could identify Goodwin as a white supremacist. He wasn't making much progress until he asked one inebriate the wrong question. "Do you think it possible that Al Goodwin is a racist or a white supremacist?"

"Hell no. What do you think you're doing asking stupid questions like that for?"

"Well, I thought since this town seems to be pretty much all white, that it could be possible."

"Listen, you dumb idiot. You don't go calling our president names." He grabbed the microphone away from Archie and hit him in the head with it, knocking him down. The bartender threw the drunk out. Archie packed up and left for LA. All the way home he plotted how he could use his show to get even with the President, but the tavern experience couldn't be shown on the Night Show.

Al had it. It was one thing for MacArthur to pick on him, but now he impugned Josh's reputation, using the televised remarks of an underage girl. He didn't know what to do about it, maybe call the Attorney General. Josh and Cole were on the phone talking about what they just saw on TV. Both boys knew the girl, very well.

In the morning, Josh's two friends came for breakfast with the family, then joined the President in his limousine. They traveled by motorcade to Al's Automotive. Local police guarded the cleared parking lot. The manager, Tran Nguyen, and six employees stood in a row waving at the motorcade. Al got out and walked toward them. He looked up and noticed that under the big Al's Automotive sign a new line read: "Owner President Alan B. Goodwin".

Al shook Tran's hand. "Looks like you've made a lot of changes."

"Had to. Business is booming. We're a tourist attracttion."

Tran led Al into the font office. Tran's twelve new employees followed behind with two Secret Service agents. They entered a gift shop that replaced the front office. Several copies of Al's biography, The Lottery President, filled one shelf next to some gift books. Al opened one. He flipped through pictures of himself in the Oval Office, Speaking to Congress, and entertaining heads of state, as well as pictures of his farm and business. The gift shop offered; paper weights, belt buckles, baseball caps, and all the usual souvenirs. Al saw a refrigerator magnet he had to have. It was a cutout of the White House over which was written, "Mechanic on duty 24/7." A row of President Goodwin bobbleheads sat on a countertop.

Al pointed at them. "What's that all about?"

"Those are President Goodwin bobbleheads. We give one away with each service. They sell like hotcakes." Tran handed one to Al.

"Do you guys still take breaks around the old oil stove?

"Let me show you."

They stepped into the first bay. Red velvet ropes surrounded the brake area. A sign read, "Here is where President Goodwin decided to enter the Presidential Lottery." A copy of the newspaper that announced the lottery lay on one of the car seats. On the antique twenty-gallon Richfield oil drum the mechanics used for a coffee table, were four coffee mugs and four imitation cinnamon rolls. Everything was restored to that fateful moment in time.

Tran continued. "We are now making as much money from the gift shop as we are from the auto shop. On top of that, one of the mechanics in the restoration shop has a customer who wants his custom hot rod signed by the President. It turns out that people would pay considerably more for a signed car. We have a car magazine ready to do a feature about it. What do you think?"

"That's amazing. You go ahead and do whatever you want. The business is in your hands. I can't get involved."

"Could you sign a couple cars while you're here?"

"Show me the cars."

Tran took Al to the restoration shop where Mark once worked. In the window sat two cars; a 1932 Ford highboy and a fully tricked out 1965 Chevy pickup. Both had printed just forward of the driver's door, 'Built by Al's Automotive'. Tran handed Al a paint pen. Al crouched down and signed each car.

After a little more looking around Al got back into the limo. Next, he would speak at the high school in support of local Republicans. He entered through a side door to the gymnasium. The public entered through the main entrance and a metal detector. Josh and his two friends were seated in the middle of a bevy of Lewis County Republicans, one of whom hoped to be a United States Senator. Part way into Al's speech he invited the senatorial candidate and some other politicians to the stage. The crowd rose and applauded. Josh also got to his feet and used the commotion to sneak out of the auditorium, unnoticed. His friends sat grinning as he walked up the aisle and out the door.

Back home in his own high school, Josh knew where to go. He ran straight for the woods, free and on his home turf at last. The trail twisted through the dense Douglas Fir forest. Josh took a narrow side trail into a grove of vine maple. He scanned the area for a hiding place. Just as he ducked under a brush-covered log, a hand grasped his color. "Hold it Joshua."

Josh jerked to a stop, spun around glaring at the agent, then bolted for freedom, but the agent never released his grip. Josh wanted to fight his way free, but already learned that hitting one these guys would get him in trouble. He still had a court date pending from the last time he tried that. He had to submit to his capture. The agent held his arm and guided him back to the auditorium. On the way, the agent gave Josh a short lecture. "You've got to stop trying to run away. All you're doing is embarrassing you mom and dad. You'll be eighteen next year, then you can be like your brother Connor and come and go as you please."

"Stick it!"

The agent led Josh back to his seat. "I tried," he said to his friends. No one on stage even missed him.

"The next morning, the Secret Service showed up at Al's favorite restaurant, the Country Cousin. Al and his family joined regular patrons for breakfast. It was Sunday morning; the place was packed.

When Al's family arrived, they were escorted to an inside booth away from the windows. He ordered his regular, bacon and eggs with a buttermilk biscuit and apple butter.

Except for the secret service and a bunch of curious patrons, it was just like old times. Al, Tracy, Josh, and Hannah were at the table. Conner stayed in the other Washington and Leo was with his parents.

"How come Leo can go where he wants, and I can't," Josh said.

"Because you can't be trusted not to run away and Leo is an adult. I heard about your dash for the woods yesterday. Don't you know that if you run off, you'll be recognized and brought home? You also put yourself in danger. People might want to use you for evil purposes, maybe to get to me. When will you understand that there is nothing to runaway to?"

"It's not my fault you bought that stupid lottery ticket. Nobody asked me if I wanted to be the President's son." He turned to his mother, "Mom. If you're not going to eat that bacon, can I have it?"

"Sure."

Josh figured it was time to change the subject.

"Dad, did you find that tunnel I told you about?"

"As a matter of fact, I did. There is an old tunnel that goes from the White House to the Capitol but it's narrow and blocked off. It can't be used."

"You're the President, order it fixed."

"I wish I could. I would much prefer walking instead of those extravagant motorcades."

After breakfast, the Secret Service agents parted the crowd like Moses parting the Red Sea. Al's company walked straight through. Along the way questions were shouted to the President.

"Are you sending troops to the Middle East?"

"I don't know."

"Do you think you'll be impeached?"

"No."

"How does it feel to be back home?"

All stopped. "Weird. I can't do the things I used to do. All I want to do is manage my business and farm. Instead, I'll have to manage the affairs of our whole nation. Be careful what kind of lottery ticket you buy."

"Where are you going now?"

"Home. I have to service my pickup truck."

When Al found out that Archie MacArthur had been assaulted at the Maple Leaf tavern, he arranged to meet a television reporter there.

"No. Absolutely not. You can't visit that tavern," Carlyle said.

"It's what I want to do."

"It's too risky. That tavern is dangerous."

"I'm going. If you won't protect me, my crew of mechanics will. They are all invited."

On Tuesday afternoon, Al and three of his mechanics sat at the bar in the Big Leaf Tavern, talking with the bartender about Archie MacArthur's incident. Al drank a beer from the bottle. On a sunny weekday afternoon, there were only a few costumers. Over by the pool table a large, grey bearded, man in a black, sleeveless t-shirt lay down his pool cue. He pulled out his cellphone and raised his voice. "Hey Al, you want to see some pictures of MacArthur gettin' his head knocked in?"

Al recognized him as a costumer of his auto shop. "Sure. What ya got?"

The big man walked up to Al and showed him photos of MacArthur's unfortunate encounter with a drunk. The reporter eagerly snapped them up. It was Al's turn to stick it to MacArthur and do it on national television. Al ordered another beer and curly fries with cheese. He spent the next half hour shooting the breeze with anyone who wanted to talk. He finished the visit playing pool with the big man in the black t-shirt. Al felt normal for the first time since leaving home.

Tracey had friends to visit, and some hiking to do. Hannah went to a friend's house. Josh wanted to stay with friends too, but he couldn't be trusted, so Al and Josh were left alone on the farm. The caretakers had everything in ship shape except the vehicles. Al and Josh spent the next day servicing the cars they left behind. He got Tran to deliver the needed parts from the shop. After that, they went to work on the old Ferguson tractor that had been on the farm for the past sixty years.

The whole family was back together on the farm Thursday afternoon in time to watch Al and Josh grill hamburgers on the back deck. When the burgers were gone, Al and Tracy sat on lawn chairs drinking cold pop. They were home together, at least for now.

"Al, I have a favor to ask," Tracy said, "I'd like to help serve breakfast at the mission tomorrow. I've already gotten the go-ahead from them; I just want to be sure it's okay with you and the Secret Service guys."

"Fine with me. I'll check with Carlyle."

"Not only do I want to help, but I have an ulterior motive. It will help me publicize my Universal Diner program."

Friday night, Tracey helped serve dinner at the mission. In her interview with television reporters, she made a pitch for her Diner program saying the first Diner would open in Salinas, California the day after Labor Day

Everyone wanted to stay home just as bad as Josh did, but on Saturday morning the family returned to the other Washington.

The motorcade vehicles followed in their own planes as did the helicopters in its planes, and all the agents in their planes. The vacation cost the taxpayers close to four million dollars.

CHAPTER 24

After the President's daily briefing, Al had a question for the Attorney General. "Have you ever watched the Night Show?

"A few times. Why?"

"Did you happen to watch it a couple of Fridays ago?"

"No. But I saw a news segment about MacArthur getting assaulted in some redneck tavern.

"Archie MacArthur likes to pick on me. That's okay, but last week he showed an interview with an underage girl in our hometown who said things about my son, like, "he's hot." Isn't there some law being broken?"

"These guys have an understanding that they are not to involve the families of elected officials, but there is no law forbidding it. The only thing he may have done wrong, is illegally videotape a minor without proper consent."

"Could you get somebody to contact the Night Show and get them to knock it off? My kids are none of their business."

"Yes, sir. But it may not do much good."

"Just so they know I don't like it."

That afternoon Al met with Josh's social worker. He updated her on his son's escape.

"He doesn't seem to get the picture that he can't run off. The Secret Service watches him pretty close, and besides everybody knows who he is. Where would he run to?"

"If he keeps trying, he will eventually succeed. Besides that, it gives him a goal to work toward and a source of excitement. His various attempts to run off have made him a sort of cultural hero. It plays into his ego."

"I don't know what to do."

"Like I've suggested before, send him to live with someone back home. That's what he's trying to do on his own anyway."

"You might be right, but his place is with his family."

"He told me that if he stays here until he turns eighteen, he can walk out of here and no one can stop him. Then what will you do?"

"If he wants to leave when he turns eighteen, then that's his business. In the meantime, he's my responsibility and I will take care of him. He may change his mind before then."

That night the President hosted dinner for several senators including Senator Case. They enjoyed an all Northwest meal with Sockeye salmon, Olympia oysters, scalloped Idaho russets, Columbia Basin asparagus, wild blackberry pie, and Columbia river wines. The after-dinner conversation started amicably. Senator Byte wanted to know how Al's vacation went. Someone else mentioned the Night Show events. Al steered the discourse toward the Middle East. He learned that Case's bill to recognize the caliphate was in committee.

"I just don't understand why it is so important to recognize the caliphate." Al locked eyes with Senator Case.

"By America staying out of their affairs they have been able to focus on nation building, instead of terrorizing the western world. While they're doing that, we have saved billions of defense dollars to use elsewhere," Case replied.

"What about the persecuted minorities under their control? What's going to happen to them?"

"We've added a refugee program to the bill. We have set aside enough money from military savings to construct refugee camps in countries close to, but not affected by, the caliphate. We are doing this in part to compromise with you and have a bill we can all agree on."

Several of the senators at the table had solid gold reasons to agree with Senator Case. They nodded and murmured assent to everything Case said.

"Who's going to rescue the minorities?" Al said.

"They don't need to be rescued. The caliphate doesn't want them included. Our bill has money to help them relocate."

Al took a deep breath. Maybe his reasoning hadn't been clear enough. "The Joint Chiefs of Staff and Secretary of Defense don't agree with you. They think that once a caliphate is in place they will expand. Just because we recognize them as a sovereignty, doesn't mean they will honor any of our agreements. Those people have been fighting each other for centuries. I don't think anything we do will change that. Try to imagine a caliphate encompassing the entire Middle East with access to Pakistan's nuclear weapons. And one more thing, who's been negotiating with the caliphate? Our Secretary of State hasn't been. How do you know what the caliphate wants in our legislation? Has there been clandestine communications?"

"The caliphate has been reaching out to all nations asking for recognition. Don't you read the newspaper?"

"I find it hard to believe that such legislation would be based solely on what's in the news. Somebody is in communication with the caliphate, and I want know who it is."

"You don't understand. This is a gesture of good will from our nation to theirs that will allow a peaceful coexistence with a forming nation."

"You expect me to believe that? I keep telling you I'll veto it and I mean it."

Vice-president Bates spoke up. "Mister President, a lot of time and energy has gone into this bill. It will allow the people of the Middle East to be united and at peace for the first time in modern history."

"I don't think so. I ask that you give me the power to deploy our armed forces to rescue minorities being persecuted in the Middle East."

"No Mister President, we can't do that," Case said.

"I'll do it anyway. Tomorrow I shall officially notify Congress that I will send our armed forces on a rescue mission to the Middle East."

"That would be in violation of the War Powers Resolution," Case said.

"I have the emergency authority to send troops into combat as long as I notify congress, which I will do tomorrow."

True to his word, the next morning Al handed his official intent on White House letterhead to the President of the Senate, Lyle Bates. Bates turned red with rage as he went looking for Senator Case. Al sent a copy to the Speaker of the House. Then he called The Secretary of Defense, Tory Thorson. The rescue mission had begun.

Vice-president Bates walked on to the Senate floor and showed Senator Case the President's letter. Both men hurried off to Case's office.

"The President just stepped out of line. He can't declare an emergency unless an attack, or the-imminent threat of an attack, is made against the US," Bates said. "He's breaking the law by doing it. Add this to his hiring of illegals, and that should synch winning an impeachment. Also, add to that the fact that his business in Washington State is making money from his presidency."

"I'll get in touch with the Speaker of the House and see if we can get him to start the articles of Impeachment.

"Another thing." Bates said. "It may take a while to get through an impeachment. In the meantime, we need to get Sol to have his operatives cook up a way to get Goodwin to start agreeing with us."

Sol's phone rang. It was Senator Case.

"Sol, we need to talk. Can you come to my office?"

"Sure."

Senator Case wasted no time telling Sol what was on his mind. "Congress is about to start the impeachment process against Goodwin, but we don't have time to wait for that. We have to find a way to convince him to leave the caliphate alone."

Sol reached for the truffle dish. "You got any ideas?"

"Well, someone shot the last president on a golf course. That changed his attitude a lot."

Sol didn't like what he was hearing. "But that President was already receiving benefits from the caliphate. Goodwin is not."

Case rubbed his head and shifted his weight in his squeaky chair. "What if we rough up someone in his family, like his college kid. Then warn him that if he doesn't cooperate something worse will happen?"

"Maybe. Someone could follow his college boy around for a while and set up an ambush. When it comes close to time to sign the bill, we'll work him over and go from there."

"As a last resort, we could assassinate him. That would put Lyle in office and seal the deal for the caliphate."

Sol grabbed another truffle on his way out.

Sol sunk his fork into a spinach quiche at the Le Diplomate Restaurant on 14th, just as a man took the other chair at his table. A certain gold coin lay in his hand. Sol extracted his fork and listened.

"Mister Jabar has a task for you. He wants you to arrange financial incentives for the President. He needs to be offered opportunities to acquire wealth that would cause him to support the caliphate. Maybe a charity would be good. One that would receive large donations from nations and organizations that support the caliphate. His wife's charity might be a good place to start. If he put one of his family in charge as executive director a large salary could be paid. Ibrahim has agents setting up speaking opportunities and other means of acquiring wealth for President Goodwin. He wants you to approach the President about these matters as a Republican National Committee fundraiser. You can talk about raising money for his eventual presidential museum, and other endeavors that he cannot afford on his salary. Talk about how much he will need to fund his re-election. The important thing is that he succumbs to our efforts, to keep him away from our caliphate."

"Okay. I also have a request for you. We need help intimidating the President."

Sol explained the plans he and Senator Case had made regarding working over the President's son

Conner. The coin bearer agreed that if other means of incentives failed, threats of violence would be appropriate. He would make arrangements with Ibrahim to send special personnel to watch Conner.

As the coin bearer politely excused himself. Sol summoned a waiter to heat his quiche. While he waited, he called the Republican National Committee, volunteering to approach the President about funding for a future presidential library. His manager at the RNC agreed. They would discuss procedures in his office. In addition to what the RNC had to offer Sol had his own offerings, including an offshore bank account and Ibrahim's many donors.

CHAPTER 25

Earlier in the year, Connor Goodwin transferred to George Washington University as a senior. He felt privileged to study political science in the nation's capital, and in the fall, he would intern in the White House. With the university being only three blocks from the White House, it took Conner longer to cross the campus than to walk home at night. He marveled at the good fortune his father's lottery ticket had brought him. He could not have guessed what lay ahead.

In the pre-dawn of a Monday morning, two men parked a blue Ford Escape near the campus. They dressed like typical students, backpacks, and all. They watched Connor for a full week; they knew his class schedule, his routes between classes, and where he walked between the White House and the University. They also noted the behavior of the Secret Service agent. The men where professional assassins dispatched via the Midnight Express by Ibrahim Bin Jabar.

After that week, between Connor's first and second class, the two assassins fell in behind him and his agent as they walked to Connor's Comparative Politics class. With lightning speed, tasers were jammed into the sides of both Connor and the agent. Immediately, they were pulled under a bush next to a building, gagged, zip-tied, and left squirming on the ground. One of the assailants kicked Connor in face while the other shoved a note in the agent's pocket. It took less than thirty seconds. The two attackers casually walked out from behind the bushes and disappeared into the between-class foot traffic.

The agent and Connor rolled out as fast as they could. Passing students freed them. The campus went on lockdown as a hoard of campus cops, municipal police, the Secret Service, and others, converged to search for the attackers.

Agent Carlyle stepped into Amy's office. "I need to see the President immediately. There's been an incident involving his son Connor."

"Follow me, he's in a meeting." Amy headed for the Cabinet room and opened the door to a room full of people. "Mr. President, agent Carlyle wants to see you. It's urgent."

Al excused himself and left the room. Carlyle explained what had just happened.

"Is he okay?"

"He's fine but has a contusion on his right cheek. Secret Service agents are talking to him now."

Just then, Al's phone buzzed in his pocket. It was Conner. He gave his dad a quick rundown of what had happened, then said, "The Secret Service thinks I should go home, but I can't miss classes. I already missed one. I won't miss any more."

"But, are you okay, son?"

"Yeah. I'm okay. I'll be fine."

Al turned his attention to Carlyle, "How is it possible for your agent to let this happen?

I thought you guys were protecting Connor!"

"This was a professional job. I Don't know how we could have anticipated it. There's one more thing. The assailants left a note on my agent. It read, 'Keep out of the Middle East or else'"

"Great. So, my family is being threatened. Now what?"

"It would be best if Conner stayed away from school, until this matter is resolved.

"He told me he wasn't going miss another class over this. What he needs is extra protection."

"We can't provide him with more agents."

"I don't want to hear what you can't do. This is what you're going to do: assign two agents to be with him at school and provide secure transportation to and from the University. I'm sure this attack has to do with the caliphate bill. Once that gets settled, things should get back to normal."

"Sir, can we negotiate your request?"

"It's not a request, it's an order. Right now, I'm sending my assistant, Mark, to stay with Connor until you assign the extra agent. Mark has experience dealing with terrorists, and he's armed. It's not Connor's fault that he needs protection. It's my fault for buying that stupid lottery ticket."

As Mark arrived on campus, the two assailants stepped aboard a Salt Breeze fishing boat moored at the lodge. They were on their way out of the country.

Al received a telephone briefing from the Deputy Director of the FBI letting him know that they were on top of every aspect of this crime.

"What do you know so far?" Al asked.

"We know that there were two of them. They seemed to be well trained for what they did."

"Anything else?"

"We know they have eluded capture and have disappeared somewhere in the city. We're devoting a lot of resources to track them down."

"In other words, you don't have any idea who they are or where they went."

The next day, the Deputy Director of the FBI and his entourage arrived in the Oval Office for a show and tell. Several cabinet members were there, as well as the Director of the CIA. They set up a small TV, on which they showed campus security videos of the two assailants. They appeared on several videos taken the week prior to the crime, as well as the day it happened.

The images were given to Homeland Security for facial recognition. One was recognized as a Syrian National named Mustafa Hajjar, but no record was found of him entering the United States. His image was obtained from Turkey, where he was a suspect in a car bombing in Ankara.

Al addressed the Director of the CIA. "Can't we send agents after this guy?"

"We already have."

"So, how's that going?"

"Quite well."

"How, quite well? I want details."

"Mister President, the actions of the CIA are confidential. We have to protect the safety of our agents."

"I'm your boss, my son is a victim, and I want to know details. Everyone in this room has a top-secret clearance, Now tell me."

"Hajjar showed up at the airport in Dubai with another man. We have agents on the ground looking for them. That's everything we know."

"Thank you. I want to be notified of any updates. My family is being targeted by terrorists, and it has got to stop."

After the meeting Al called Carlyle to his office.

"Connor's attack was an act of terrorism. I've been warned to lay off the Middle East or something bad will happen. Anyone in my family could be the target of further aggression. I have requested more funding for the Secret Service. I want every member of my family and my close friends protected, including my sister's family in Vancouver, Washington."

"We'll get on this as soon as the funds arrive."

"You'll get on it today. The funds will follow."

"You want me to send a contingent of agents to Vancouver, Washington?"

"I've put everyone I know in danger. Senator Weinberg told me that he conceived of the lottery to end big money interests and crime at the highest level of government. I'm what he and a lot of others are counting on. Yes, Carlyle, send a contingent to Vancouver. We need protection.

Al's phone rang. The Director of the CIA had some news. "We've located the two assailants that assaulted your son Connor. They're in a primitive village on the Coast of Syria. We're working on a plan to extract them, but because it requires military intervention, we'll need your cooperation."

"A Navy task force is on the way to the Mediterranean. I'll direct the Secretary of Defense to contact you.", Al replied."

"When should we expect the Navy task force to be in place?"

"Three days. Don't lose those terrorists. I want to see them locked up."

At midnight of the third day, the task force positioned itself of the Syrian coast. At one a.m. Syrian time two Black Hawk helicopters lifted off from an aircraft carrier deck. One contained a Navy Seal team, the other acted as a backup. They flew just above the waves in a direct line toward the village. A reconnaissance drone sent visual data from where it circled the small town where Connor's attackers thought they were safe. When the helicopters arrived, the little community of dirt streets and concrete block houses was dark. A CIA agent waited in an open area several houses away, to provide landing support. The helicopters were muffled for quiet operation.

The team sprang into action immediately on landing. They ran, as practiced, to the little house holding their targets. On reaching the house, the team smashed in the door, grabbed two very surprised men, bound and gagged them, and carried them back to the helicopter. The operation from touch down to take off took less than ten minutes.

In the White House Situation Room, President Goodwin, the Secretary of Defense, the Secretary of State, and other cabinet members received updates of the abduction in real time. When the helicopters lifted off, Mark stood up and cheered. He knew from firsthand experience what had happened on the ground.

Back on the aircraft carrier, the two captured men were separated and questioned extensively. They soon admitted they were part of the caliphate movement and worked as professional assassins.

"Why did you attack the President's son?" The interrogator asked one of the assassins.

"I was following orders."

"What orders?"

We were to rough up the kid up to show the President we could harm him or his family anytime we felt like it."

"Who's orders?"

"A guy named Jameel."

"What's the rest of his name?"

"I don't know." Both assassins could have said a lot more but clammed up tight.

Amy answered her phone. It was the Chairman of the Republican National Committee. He wanted to arrange a meeting between one of his fundraisers and the President. Amy calendared Sol Solomon for the next Tuesday at 11:00 a.m. for fifteen minutes, topic: Raise money for a presidential library.

At the appointed time, Sol sat in the lobby of the West Wing. He couldn't be happier. All his life he wanted be around important people. Today he would visit the Oval Office. The West Wing receptionist rose from her chair. "Mister Solomon. The President will see you now. Please come with me."

Sol nervously walked beside the receptionist for the short distance to the Oval Office. He told himself, you can handle this. He's just an ordinary mechanic.

"Mister President, Mister Solomon is here." The receptionist announced.

The President greeted Sol and pointed to a chair.

"I understand you want to talk about raising money for a presidential library. This is something that never crossed my mind," Al said.

"When you leave office, the American public will expect you to have a presidential library. They cost millions of dollars which is not provided by the government. Only private donations can build it. The private money can be raised from any source, and there is no limit to the amount. Even foreign governments can contribute. So can people or corporations who seek government favors. Best of all, there are no disclosure requirements. The donors' identities can remain confidential. That means you can receive all the money you want, no questions asked."

"I see," Al said.

"It's important for you to form a library committee to plan your library and to raise funds for it."

"Okay. I guess I can do that."

"I have a donor who runs a small oil company who wants to give the first million, and yes he has a governmental issue he'd like some help with. But it's a small favor and well worth providing."

"First things first. I'll find a museum chairperson and that person can take care of donations and will be your contact in such matters."

Sol felt encouraged. He pulled out a gold coin and laid it on the President's desk. "This is an example of how wealth can be attracted to your causes when you allow people a few favors. The gold in this coin is worth we'll over a thousand dollars, but because it's a rare coin, it's worth many times that. You can keep it as a token of friendship from the oil company donor. There's more where that came from. The same donor is willing to provide you with some personal wealth. So would some other donors."

"I can't take gifts. If I'm given something of value, it is interpreted to be a gift to the American people. I'll see that this coin is included in that library that you're talking about. Tell your friend I appreciate his gift." Al didn't like what he was hearing. "Let me inform you that every transaction made in this office will see the light of day. No unknown donors. No secrets. Besides that, I don't need money, personally.

"Thanks for reminding me that I need a library. As soon as I appoint a chairperson, you'll be the first to

know. I have another appointment, now. The reception-
tionist will see you out."

Sol left the Oval Office disappointed. Now he had to
deal with a museum fund chairperson, plus he just gave
away a valuable coin for nothing. It looked to him like a
threat to the President's family remained as the only
option.

Several Republican senators waited for their turn to
see the President. Sol recognized a few of them as he
walked through the reception room. He nodded at
Senators Case and Byte, as they were invited into the
Oval Office.

It was difficult for Al to take his mind off this current
threat to his family, but he must remain at work and in
charge. He needed to talk with influential congressmen
who might help him push some of his ideas through
congress. He addressed the Senators, "A while back, I
met with major automobile manufacturers regarding
distractions built into their vehicles. They agreed to
study the topic. I now have their report. Any perceived
distractions like video displays or all those little buttons
that have to be attended to while driving, have been
deemed safe. The conclusion of the report finds no need
to change anything. Well, I don't buy it. There are too
many distractions and too many fatalities on our
highways. I'd like to see Congress study the problem
with an eye toward regulating and standardizing such
conveniences."

Senator Case respond first. "How are you doing with
getting the salt and studded tires off the road?"

"Automobile safety should be everyone's top priority.
That would include banning salt and studded tires. In
addition to that, people drive worn out cars, drive drunk
or loaded, have a cell phone or a cup of coffee in their

hand, and many drive with no insurance. When my tow truck is called to pull vehicles apart, we see it all. It's gruesome. Forty-thousand people died on our highways last year. Four-and-a-half-million more were seriously injured. That's unacceptable. Can you imagine the uproar if those numbers were from airline crashes?"

"We already have people attending to those issues, Mister President," Case said.

"Doesn't seem like it."

Senator Maxine Byte said, "I think you should take these issues up with the National Highway Traffic Safety Administration. Not congress." Several present agreed.

I am taking it up with Congress. You're going to hear more about this."

Al switched topics to rescuing persecuted minorities in the Middle East. "As you know, I have set in motion a task force that is already in the Mediterranean Sea to rescue persecuted minorities. I would like to do this with your blessing."

"If you sign the caliphate recognition bill, we will rescue the minorities. We may even consider your automobile safety issues. I recommend you sign the bill," Case said.

"I don't want to hear any more about signing that bill, and those persecuted minorities are going to get rescued."

Senator Byte shot back. "We will override your veto."

Al upped the ante. "Yesterday, the CIA caught the men who attacked my son Connor. They were captured during a night raid inside caliphate territory. I must conclude that the attack on my son resulted from my plan to send a rescue task force to the Middle East and my intent to veto the caliphate recognition bill. Terrorism is again being directed at the American people. What I don't understand is why congress wants to recognize a terrorist state when we have proof that they sent terrorists into our land to do harm.

After the meeting, Senator Case called Sol. "We're getting nowhere with the President. The task force is on its way and Goodwin says the Navy has the men who attacked his son. The good news is the Speaker of the House has started impeachment proceedings. The Articles of Impeachment have just received a passing vote in committee. The Senate can start its trial in a matter of weeks. We're about to put the President out of office."

When Sol stepped out of the elevator of his condo, he saw the coin bearer seated on a couch. The man rose to meet him. He motioned toward the chairs by the fireplace. Once seated he said, "There is a military force in the Mediterranean Sea. Why is this?"

"Our congressmen couldn't stop him. The President is acting unilaterally and illegally by sending a task force. But there's some good news. I just learned the articles of impeachment have been voted on in the house and the President's trial in the Senate will follow shortly after. He is certain to be removed from office. That will put an end to any more threats to your movement."

"That will take too long. We need to stop him now. You told me you could stop his task force in congress, and you failed. Now you must prevent the task force from acting. Do it by any means possible but do it. If you don't stop that task force, we will be forced to assassinate the President."

CHAPTER 26

Josh's friend Cole walked out of Centralia High School, as soon as the last bell rang. The school had excused Cole for what he said was a family affair out of town. His folks thought he was spending a week with Noah. Instead, he had a several days trip ahead of him to rescue his friend Josh. So, instead of his usual cruise through town, his old blue Jetta headed straight to I-5. It was Friday night.

His bicycle and guitar were in the pawnshop and he had sold his laptop. Every dollar he could get his hands on were in his wallet. A Styrofoam cooler full of Coke and Red Bull, sat on the passenger seat. The backseat of his ratty old car held camping gear and snack food taken from home. Once settled into the heavy afternoon traffic he pulled out his cell phone and texted Josh. "C U soon."

By midnight, he had reached Boise, Idaho, where he saw a Walmart just off the freeway. Cole took the next off-ramp. He knew from experience that driving around town late at night attracted cops. Even more so, with out-of-state license plates. He had to keep telling himself he wasn't doing anything wrong. He pulled up near an old motorhome at the edge of the parking lot, got out of his car, and headed for the store.

He cleaned up, bought a few things and went back to his car. He ran the engine long enough to heat himself up, then curled up under his sleeping bag and went to sleep. Dawn began slowly, as the sun crept through a grey horizon. Cole tossed his sleeping bag in the back seat. While the car engine idled to warm the car, a police cruiser drove close to the few vehicles in the parking lot, checking for overnighters. Cole pulled out of the parking lot, drove to the McDonald's next door, ordered a large coffee and an Egg McMuffin, and got back on I-84 heading East.

By noon, Cole had reached Salt Lake City and was looking for a place to sleep. He pulled into a Home Depot. A bright sunny sky warmed his car. Exhausted, it didn't take long for him to drift into a long nap, well past sunset. When he awoke, he opened a bag of Doritos and a can of Coke and aimed his car toward the freeway. Well rested, he decided to drive all night. While ascending the Wasatch Mountains on I-80, his phone rang. It was his friend Noah, who he was supposed to be spending the week with.

"Where you at?" Noah asked.

"Somewhere in Utah on I-80. They have a seventy-five-mile-an-hour speed limit here, but most everybody is going eighty or ninety. Anybody been asking about me?"

"No. Why should they?"

"If anybody asks, you don't know anything. You're the only one who knows what I'm doing. Let's keep it that way."

"What if your parents call?"

"They never check on me, but if they do just say I went somewhere."

"Where?"

"Anywhere. Make up something. I expect to be back next weekend."

They talked for a long time as Cole continued through the mountains.

Sitting in his White House bedroom, Josh paused his Hulu rerun to answer a call from Cole. "I'm in Wyoming."

Josh responded, "Stop calling me. The White House has spies."

"Go to Walmart. Get a throwaway phone."

"Good idea, if I can get to Walmart. Don't text me either. I'll let you know when I have a safe phone. I gotta go."

Being held in this old mansion is a solvable problem, thought Josh. His dad was generous with money, this would help. He expected Cole would be in town in a couple of days. In the meantime, escape dominated Josh's thoughts. So far, his attempts to run away failed, but this time he had a plan.

As much as Josh hated being stuck in the White House, it had some good points. The best part was the food. He ate great hamburgers, good pizza, even homemade French fries, and milkshakes. Around the residence, as they called the living quarters of the White House, were people who took care of everything. If he tossed a potato chip bag on the floor it would disappear. If he left cookie crumbs on the couch they vanished. His clothes were ironed, folded, and put away. These caretakers seemed to sneak around and clean everything while no one was looking. Also, he could watch just about anything he wanted on TV, except for some programming his old man had blocked.

However, Josh couldn't stand the part of the White House outside of the residence. There were too many people, including celebrities, tourists, and guards. Josh just couldn't deal with it. He tried to explain this to his social worker, who seemed to understand, but could only talk about therapy, treatment, and medications. He told her life wasn't worth living. He wanted to end it all. Not really. He just liked exciting the social worker. He never swallowed his meds. He held them in his cheek and spit them out later.

His tutor liked him and seemed to understand Josh's problems. He sometimes took him for rides to places educational. A secret service guy always came along. They didn't trust him.

Josh felt trapped ever since the Deputy Sheriff told him his dad would become the next president. All he wanted was to be with his friends like before. In his mind, he relived some of his best times, like the all-night party on the Chehalis River on a moonlit summer night. He and his friends sat on the bank talking about great things and forecasting how life would be in the future, while tossing cigarette butts and beer cans into the river. This summer would soon be over. He missed all the fun. He wanted to go home.

Josh found some happiness hiding out in his room talking or playing games with his friends. Sometimes, he'd Face Time with them, but that made him even more homesick. He now found contentment reviewing his escape. He had a plan, and this time the plan was simple. No more waiting for a chance to run for it.

He would ask his grandma to take him out to buy some normal clothes. He knew she and the Secret Service agent would go for it, because everyone had been on his case about his pants hanging so low that his underwear showed. He was an embarrassment to the entire White House. Then, when they got to the department store, he would ditch Grandma and the agent.

The next morning Josh, his grandma, and the agent, left to go shopping. They would go to a large store where it would be easier for Josh to allude his company. He wore two sets of clothes: his usual brightly colored clothes on the outside with jeans, and a black sweatshirt underneath.

Just after sunrise, Cole pulled into McDonalds off I-80 near Omaha, Nebraska. He washed up and ordered hotcakes and coffee. As he leaned against the wall of his small booth, his eyes slowly closed.

While Cole napped, Josh, his grandmother, and the Secret Service agent, were in Nordstrom's. He sorted through slacks and sports coats, shirts, and ties, with a delighted Grandma at his side. The Secret Service agent kept a respectable distance. Josh went into the fitting room with an armload of clothing.

"This might take a few minutes, Grandma."

"That's okay. Take your time."

The agent scanned the nearly empty men's department, then looked inside each fitting room. Meanwhile, Josh took off his outer layer of clothing and peeked through the door. "Grandma, would you get the darker brown sports coat? I think I like that one better."

"Okay." The sport coats were on the other side of the room.

Josh watched his grandma walk away, with the agent close behind her. This was it. He sneaked around the corner of the fitting room and briskly walked out into the street. He walked along L Street looking at every building for a hiding place. His Levi's were pulled up to a respectable height and the black sweatshirt fit snuggly. They would be looking for him in green cargo pants worn low, with a red shirt and leather jacket. Those were now bundled under his arm. He saw a JVC drug store straight ahead. He chucked his bundle of clothes into the garbage receptacle by the entrance. Now he had only to get to Walmart for a new phone, then hang out somewhere until Cole got to town.

One of the unfortunate symptoms of Josh's condition, was the inability to anticipate the consequences of one's actions. Some, like him, might spend all their money at the mall and then have no money for bus fare home. So, although Josh's escape had worked just as planned, he now needed to figure what to do next. By now, people would be looking for him. He left the drugstore with dark rimed reading glasses, and his hair was combed flat under a new Washington Senators baseball cap.

Cole woke to a hand on his shoulder, "Hey man, are you okay?"

"Yeah, I'm just tired." Cole walked out of McDonalds to his car where he fell back to sleep.

Halfway across the country, Josh walked a couple of blocks beyond the drugstore and went into a Subway sandwich shop. He ordered a Coke and had the cashier call a cab. At Walmart, he bought a warm tan jacket, a black backpack, sleeping bag, extra clothes, and a cheap phone. He then headed for Pennsylvania Avenue where he would hang with the homeless people until Cole arrived.

A bearded guy and his black Labrador sat on a park bench. Josh took the other end of the bench, placing his backpack between himself and the homeless guy. With his new supplies and clean clothes, he didn't look much like the usual street person, but he didn't look much like himself ether. He got out his new phone.

Cole awoke to his phone ringing. It was Josh. "I'm free. I ditched the Secret Service guy and went to Walmart for a phone. When are you going to get here?"

"Great! I'm in Omaha, Nebraska. What are you going to do until I get there?"

"I'm hanging with the street people on Pennsylvania Avenue. When do you think you'll be here?"

"I've still got a thousand miles to go, maybe sometime tomorrow night, if I can stay awake."

"That long? I thought you'd be here by now."

"Maybe you don't know it, but it's almost three thousand miles from Washington State to Washington DC. And I have to sleep."

"Call me just as soon as you get here."

Cole went back to sleep. By mid-afternoon he was rested and back on I-80, driving toward the night.

President Goodwin stepped out of a staff meeting. Agent Carlyle stopped him in the hall. "Mister President. I need to tell you something in private. May I have a minute?"

Al motioned for Carlyle to follow him into his Office.

"Mister President. Josh ditched his security agent and your mother at Nordstrom's this morning. We don't know where he went."

"What? How did that happen?"

Carlyle got a piece of Al's mind before he could respond. "We're searching for him with help from the police and the FBI. I assure you we are doing all we can to find him. He can't be far off."

"What do you know, so far?"

"We know what he was wearing, and from which door he left Nordstrom's. There are agents fanning out from there, the local authorities and the press have been notified. We expect to find him quickly."

"In other words, you don't know anything, and the press knows all about it."

"I'm sorry, Mister President. We're doing our best."

As soon as Carlyle left the Oval Office, Al went into Amy's office. "Get me the Director of the FBI, then find Mark. Josh finally did it. He ran off and nobody knows were his is. I'll be in my residence."

Halfway to the residence his phone rang. It was the Director of the FBI. Al's first question was, "What are you doing to find my son Josh?"

CHAPTER 27

The Secret Service agent who lost Josh received a harsh grilling but could only describe Josh's appearance, and what time he left the building. Josh's Grandmother and a store associate were also questioned, confirming the agent's description, but were unable to add anything more. Officials collected surveillance videos from Nordstrom's and surrounding businesses. At first, they failed to recognize him because of his radical change of clothes, giving Josh a head start. Al would be kept up to date.

As soon as the FBI director said goodbye, Al's phone rang again. It was Mark. Al filled him in on Josh's disappearance.

"I heard about it on the news. He might have a plan. If we can figure out what it is, we might have a chance of finding him. I'm driving around looking him right now."

Al left his office with his phone pressed to his ear. He had to get home fast. He stopped abruptly face to face with a White House tour. "Mark, I'll call you back." He slipped his phone into his pocket, forced a smile, and said, "How are all of you doing?"

A pleasant older woman said, "Have they found your son?"

"You'll excuse me, I have to go be with the family."

Cole held a Hostess pie in his hand with a Red Bull in the cup holder. The car radio was cranked up loud.

He began noticing a certain rhythm to the road. By speeding up, he got the repetitive rhythm to match the beat of the radio. It occurred at exactly eighty-three miles per hour. He took a long drink of Red Bull, and a bite of pie, while steering with his knee. Blue and red lights flashed in his rear-view mirror.

The State Policeman asked some questions to which Cole said he was going to visit his friend in Washington. With stern admonition, the policeman wrote a warning ticket. Cole was back on the freeway in ten minutes. He called Josh. "You're big news dude. They're talking about you on the radio."

"I know. Even my dad's friend Mark is looking for me. I saw his car drive right past me. I'm sitting on a park bench next to some homeless guy with a dog. You wouldn't believe what he's been telling me. He's some kind of disabled vet. As long as I stay close to him, I'll look homeless too, but these homeless people have a look to them that I just don't have."

I-80 became I-90 as the two Interstates merged to pass South of Lake Superior and Chicago. Cole slowed down to throw change into a toll booth basket. The Interstate was several lanes wide. Semi-trucks seemed to outnumber cars, so that Cole couldn't see much ahead of or around them. When he approached his fourth toll gate he was out of change. He was also stuck between trucks and couldn't change lanes to the booth with an attendant. He soon sat at the toll gate with no change. *Now what?* He stepped on the gas. The toll barrier slid up the hood and scraped across the top of the car. He sped off, watching his rear-view mirror. Running a toll booth in Illinois is a simple misdemeanor. Cole's license number was read, his address found, and a letter sent to his home. All automated.

Once in Indiana he calmed down. By the time he hit Ohio, fatigue overtook him. He pulled into a rest stop and fell asleep.

Josh spent hours on the park bench, sometimes chatting with the bearded veteran. As darkness came, the veteran asked if Josh wanted to go with him to a safe place to sleep for the night. As they walked the veteran asked. "Where you from kid?"

"The West."

"You run away from home?"

"What makes you say that?"

"You don't exactly look like street people. How far West?"

"Way West. What do you mean, I don't look like street people?"

"Everything about you is brand new. Including your shiny pink face. I don't think you've been on the street all day."

"I'm waiting for a ride home. A friend is coming to get me, he won't be here until sometime tomorrow."

"I still think you're a runaway. Let me give you some good advice. Stay clear of street people."

Josh sized up the veteran. A long stick of a man with a shaggy salt and pepper beard, wearing layers of clothing covered with a thick, hooded coat. "Does that include you?" Josh said.

"There are hundreds of homeless people around here. They're not necessarily bad people, but they could be bad for you. They can hurt you in ways you never dreamed of. And, don't touch any of them. Close contact is how the cooties get on you. You know, fleas, scabies, lice. The homeless can give you diseases too, like TB, hepatitis, the flu, and all kinds of other diseases. Most don't have doctors or take medicine. In the morning, the cops will find the bodies of the ones who died during the night, not just from disease, but from drugs, alcohol and murder. Stay away from where they hang out."

"What are you doing hanging around with them?"

"I don't! I just happen to use the same space. I have a small pension that I get because I'm a disabled veteran. When I get my check at the first of the month, I rent a cheap motel room for a few days, then spend the rest of the month on the street.

The veteran continued to fill Josh in on the dangers of being on the street. "It's not always easy to find a place to go to the bathroom around here. Oh sure, you look clean and tidy. You can use a restroom someplace. Real street people can't. Businesses won't let them in. The street people often just use the ground. They also leave needles behind. In the morning tourists will walk the mall where the homeless relieved themselves during the night. They'll sit on benches where someone slept or did drugs."

Josh was surprised at the amount of detail being offered him. Maybe this guy had a son his age. In any event, the advice continued, nonstop.

"Here's something for you to chew on: where you have filth, rats are multiplying. They carry disease. You ever hear of Bubonic Plague, Typhus or Typhoid Fever? Well, rats carry those diseases from the homeless encampments to neighborhoods where the fleas get on nice little kitties and lap dogs. They, in turn, can infect regular people. What do you think will happen when ordinary people show up in the ER with Bubonic Plague?"

"It can't be all that bad."

"It's that bad. I'll show you an encampment. It's not far from where we're going."

When they got there, they walked past blue tarp tents, camp tents, cardboard shelters, and heaps of refuse. Like a suburban home might have a pickup truck in the driveway, there were loaded shopping carts pushed into the sides of shelters. Where a suburbanite might have a gas grill on the patio, a fire burned on the street. Everything was so close together it looked like one continuous mess. The homes of the homeless.

They walked several more blocks to an unlighted building where two people leaned against a wall near a large rhododendron. Their gear lay on the ground. An overhanging roof protected them from a drizzling rain. The few people Josh saw covered themselves with whatever they had. One guy had a piece of plastic tarp, another had blankets, covered by a large leather coat. Josh's temporary companion and his dog were both squeezed into a green plastic-covered sleeping bag. Josh wrapped himself in his sleeping bag and leaned against his backpack next to the building. Two guys and a very skinny chick were sitting behind the rhododendron, shooting meth. Another clutched a whiskey bottle.

Josh asked the veteran, "where do these guys get money for drugs?"

"Panhandling, car prowling, burglary, prostitution, whatever it takes to feed their addictions. But not all street people are users. A lot of them are mentally ill, unwanted by their families and everybody else. If one of these guys wants to talk to you just say, 'Not now man. I'm sick.' Most of them don't want to be around sick people."

The little cluster of street people Josh was embedded with, were copies of other such groupings and encampments scattered all over town. The more established homeless had tents and makeshift huts as semipermanent shelters. Some lived under bridges and in parks, some slept in doorways. Occasionally cops would relocate them or just run them off. Temporary encampments were provided by the city, but most street people avoided them. Thousands of such people live in the shadow of the opulence of a great society. One could, on a single street, find the poorest and the most powerful separated only by the thickness of a wall and the whims of fortune.

Everything Josh saw repulsed him. He wished he had waited one more day to run away, escaping this whole experience. He sat cold, hungry, and tired on the wet ground. Eventually he fell asleep.

Dawn arrived slowly through the clouds, as Cole pulled back onto I-76.

Josh awoke cold and damp. He called Cole. "Where are you?"

"I'm almost to Cleveland. I figure I can pick you up about three o'clock."

"Well hurry up. I can't talk anymore my battery is low. Text me when you get here."

Josh talked some more with the veteran. Turned out he was an army medic who received a brain injury in Iraq years earlier. The trauma resulted in psychological issues that made him unemployable.

As they talked, a large brown beetle landed on the corner of Josh's backpack. It felt around the edges and then backed away a little, checking with its back feet that all was safe. Satisfied, it raised its tiny head and gazed at the morning sky. Josh wondered about this marvelous work of creation. This little being can fly and land wherever it wants and even secure its safety, free to do just as it wished, he thought. There they sat, two free spirits gazing toward the horizon and greeting the promise of a new day. Then it opened its wing covers and furled its transparent wings. Effortlessly, it flew in a perfect arc to land on the veteran's knee.

"Aah," he yelled, "a bug!" He brushed it off and crushed it beneath his foot. The dog leaned over and ate it.

Josh, his stomach empty, marveled at how easily some are fed and how quickly one's fortunes can change.

The veteran knew of a place that serves a free breakfast. He invited Josh to go with him. They gathered their stuff and walked to the Gospel Outreach Mission. In a large room filled with folding tables and chairs, they helped themselves to a very welcome and warm cup of thin coffee. They sat at a table in the back of the room, avoiding others as best they could.

Before long, a man dressed in jeans and a black shirt with a white collar stepped in among the tables. He opened a bible and began to preach. Josh's companion said, "You have to listen to this before you get anything to eat."

The pastor began, "Have you ever prayed for anything? Did you know that God hears your quietest innermost payer? The Bible says God knew you from when He knit you together in your mother's womb. He wants to hear from you." He went on for a while, then said a prayer for the food. Josh got in line with the veteran and waited for their tray of breakfast.

A cameraman came into the room. His camera focused on the serving line.

"This isn't good," the veteran said, "A lot of these people are paranoid about being photographed."

Sure enough, some turned away from the camera. A few more exited the building. The pastor came out from behind the serving line. He had an announcement. "We are privileged today to have with us on our serving line, the First Lady of the United States, Tracy Goodwin. She is here to kick off a program that will help feed the poor across the nation."

In shock, Josh turned his back toward his mother and sneaked out the door. He hoped he hadn't been seen. He wondered, as he walked back to the park bench on Pennsylvania Avenue, doesn't Mom know I'm missing? What is she doing at the mission? Maybe nobody's looking for me. He sat on the bench analyzing his thoughts until the veteran showed up.

"What happened to you? The veteran asked. "Afraid of cameras?"

"It's worse than that. I just had to get out of there."

Another paranoid runaway thought the veteran. "What's the matter? afraid you're going to get caught?"

"Something like that."

"Here. I brought you a banana. It was handed to me by the First Lady. What do think of that?"

It made him tearful to realize that his mom had somehow provided for him, even as he hid from her. He remembered her saying, "food tastes better, seasoned with hunger." That banana tasted better than any he had ever eaten.

Homelessness was far too boring. How could the veteran just sit all the time? Josh ached to be doing something besides sitting and waiting. Cole would arrive soon.

When the President's kid goes missing the entire world hears about it. Newspapers from Washington to London to Moscow and Tel Aviv had Josh's face on their front pages. The Internet had even more. Social media was filled with ideas and even imagined sightings. Josh became as well-known as any celebrity. The entire country searched for him and everybody knew what he looked like. He browsed his name on his phone. He found his image everywhere, including his new disguise with black rimmed glasses and baseball cap. He took off the glasses, turned his cap around backwards, and opened his soggy sleeping bag over his lap. He looked around. No one noticed him, but Just a few blocks away evil minds discussed his fate.

In an opulent private dining room at the Jefferson Hotel on DuPont Circle, Sol Solomon and several congressmen were having lunch. Also, at the table, was the Vice-president. All fourteen walnut and leather chairs were occupied at a long wooden table. The room was finished in dark woods with inset, sparkling, glass doored wine cabinets displaying hundreds of fine wines from floor to ceiling. The ceiling consisted of two cream colored domed sections from which hung crystal chandeliers. Under it all, a floor of curly maple beautified the room. A huge painting of Thomas Jefferson's vineyard filled the end wall. Luxury would be an understatement. The opulence of the dining was important to Sol. He loved being rich.

The topic of conversation was President Goodwin's promise to veto the caliphate recognition bill that would pull all remaining military presence out of the Middle East and establish diplomatic relations. This represented a huge cash deal for these congressmen. The President mustn't veto this bill. But how could they stop him? They didn't know how to intimidate or bribe him like they did the last president.

However, the President's missing son became a glimmer of hope. Maybe it could distract him. The caliphate Recognition bill had just arrived on the President's desk ready for his approval or his promised veto.

Jim Tubbs, the Senator thought to have embezzled his mother-in-law's inheritance and keeping a bigamous second wife somewhere said, "He has four more days to sign the bill or return it to congress. If he doesn't, it is automatically passed," he said as he sunk his fork into a fillet of Dover Sole Almandine.

William Kirk, the Senator seen with child pornography, added "I think this is an opportunity we should exploit," never taking his eyes off his barbecued oysters.

Vice-president Bates, known to cheat on his wife, had an idea. "What if I suggested to the President that as Vice-president, I can handle presidential business, while he attends to finding his son and being with his family?" He reached for his blue crab salad sandwich.

Senator Maxine Byte, an inside trader and adulteress said "That's not how the Vice-presidency works. The President has to be incapacitated before you take over."

"He may not know that." Bates said. "And besides, the trauma of recent events may render him incapacitated. It's worth a try."

"Even if you did convince him, the kid will probably show up in a day or two and the bill would still be vetoed." Senator William Bruce said, who had gambling debts. He took a sip of a buttery Willamette Valley Chardonnay.

Representative Vince Rondo, involved in an arms-smuggling deal, said "What if we could find a way to keep the kid from being found?"

The climate of the meeting got a shade darker when Sol said, "the only way we could do that, is to find the kid before the law does and hold him."

"We couldn't hope to compete with everyone who's looking for that kid," Bates said. "What chance would we have?"

"What if we were to use their own information. After all, we have powers that could give us that information," offered Senator Martin as he slid his fork under a slice of smoked portobello mushroom.

"The FBI Director is a friend," Senator Case said, the recipient of oil company bribe money. "If we can get him to hold off finding the kid right away, we might have a chance. Especially if the Director shares what the FBI knows."

"There's a lot of money riding on that bill. I think it's worth a try, "Bates said.

Senator Maxine Byte, her injured arm now in a brace, said, "I'm on the Judiciary Committee and could get access to that information. I also have a friend in the FBI who likes money. He can inform me when they know where young mister Goodwin is. That would give us time to get to him first." She sipped her Hennessy cognac.

"But how would we get him?" Congressman Bireley said, who committed voter fraud.

"I have people for that," Sol said.

That was it. They had a directive. They would find out what the FBI knew, then pass that information on to a small contingent of Middle East operatives holed up in Sol's old hunting lodge. They could do the dirty work. They would immediately start looking for the President's son. If they found him, they could hold him long enough for Vice-president Bates to sign the bills into law or long enough to prevent the President from seeing it. They needed four days. Senate Majority Leader Melvin Case would coordinate. Lunch ended.

Fred Ferguson, still searching for corruption, had followed Senator Jim Tubbs to the Jefferson Hotel to see if he was having a rendezvous with his elusive other wife. Tubbs had eluded to the bigamy, but no one could find either the wife or the marriage certificate. Fred sat in the lobby waiting to see if the Senator would be with a woman. Eventually, Tubbs came through the lobby in the company of a woman, but it was Senator Maxine Byte whom Fred had investigated and found to be Involved with insider trading and a clandestine love affair with the Deputy Director of the FBI. She couldn't be the other wife. Then he saw other congressmen he had investigated. Each of them was found to be corrupt. Fred stayed seated and noted each one who left the hotel. All but one was a subject of his investigations. The odd one, dressed all in black, looked vaguely familiar. Fred didn't know what was going on, but it couldn't be good. He arranged a meeting with Marion West to discuss his new findings.

A few blocks in another direction from Josh, Al and Mark sat together in the President's dining room near the Oval Office, having a late lunch of grilled cheese sandwiches and coffee. Both had been awake most of the night; Al awaiting word about Josh, and Mark driving around town. Al had just hung up the phone with the FBI Director. "Here's the latest," he told Mark. "It looks like Josh's friend Cole is on his way here. The FBI questioned people in Centralia, and it looks like Cole lied about his whereabouts and disappeared. Checking by state, they learned that he received a warning ticket for speeding in Illinois. He also ran a toll gate in Chicago.

He could be here now. The FBI is issuing a description of Cole's car. They could have him any time."

"I don't think he should be stopped until after he picks up Josh."

Al saw the logic in this and got back to the FBI. The director said not to worry. They would follow Cole until he picked up Josh.

"Looks like things might work out okay," Mark said. "I'll check back later. I'm going to see if I can intercept Cole as he comes to town. I know his old beat-up Jetta. My Mustang is out front."

Over at the Capitol, Senate Majority Leader Case received the same information from Senator Byte. She assured him that the FBI would delay picking up Cole long enough for Sol's people to grab him first. Case in turn called Sol, who activated the Middle East operatives.

Three men in a brown van were on the streets looking for Cole before the FBI could go through their purposely delayed formalities of notifying other law enforcement agencies.

The Vice-president walked into the President's dining room just as Mark walked out. He sat down in Mark's chair. Any news about Josh?"

"The FBI thinks they might find him pretty soon."

"I know this is stressful for you and your wife. Why don't you take some time to be with the family until Josh comes home? I can keep an eye on things here until you get back. That's what vice-presidents are for."

"Thanks, Lyle. I'll be in the residence. The Chief of Staff and Amy can keep a handle on_things around here. What I really want to do, is go look for him. Can you imagine me doing that? Back home I would just jump in the truck and go find him. All I can do here is wait."

"You've got the best people looking for him. They should find him in no time."

"I don't trust the best people. The FBI Deputy Director didn't strike me as being very sincere. Maybe he doesn't think Josh is worthy of an all-out search. Al got up and headed for his Chief of Staff's office. Lyle cracked a half grin. He headed for Al's desk.

CHAPTER 28

A blue Volkswagen Jetta turned onto Pennsylvania Avenue. It moved to the outside lane. Josh saw it coming. He jumped to the sidewalk and waved his hand. Cole flashed his headlights in recognition. As soon as he stopped, Josh jumped in. "You got anything to eat in here. I'm starving."

Cole and Josh headed for the beltway. Not far behind followed a brown Chrysler minivan. At the same time, the FBI was purposely delaying their briefing of Cole's anticipated arrival in Washington. Other law enforcement agencies only got the news after Cole arrived in town, leaving enough time for Sol's men to intercept Josh.

With Washington behind them, Cole pulled into a gas station to fill up. Josh stayed out of sight in the car while Cole went inside to pay for the gas and grab a few snacks. As soon as Cole was out of sight, the brown minivan swooped in between the front of the station and Cole's car. Two men jumped out of the passenger side, leaving the sliding door open. One man jerked open the Jetta's passenger door. The other reached in and yanked Josh out of the car. With one continuous pull, Josh landed in the minivan. By the time the minivan was back on the highway, Josh was zip tied and blindfolded.

Cole came out of the gas station with his hands full of snacks and drinks. Unconcerned about the minivan that just sped out of the station, he continued to his car, but Josh wasn't there. He went back into the station to see if he was in the restroom. No Josh. As he hurried out of the station, he saw a Maryland State Police car pull-up behind his car. A policeman looked in the Jetta, then headed straight for Cole.

The cop pointed his thumb over his shoulder and said, "That your car?"

"Yeah."

Cole was asked for his ID. "Do you know Joshua Goodwin?"

"No."

"Where is he?"

Another cop pulled up.

"I don't know any Josh."

"Listen kid, we know that Joshua Goodwin was in your car. Now, where is he?"

"Am I in some kind of trouble?"

"You better believe you are. If you don't start telling the truth, it's going to get a whole lot worse for you."

"I think someone in a brown minivan took him. When I came out from paying for my gas, a brown minivan was pulling out of the station and Josh was gone."

"When did this happen?"

"Three or four minutes ago."

"Which way did the van go?"

Josh pointed in the direction of Washington. The cop yelled the information to another cop, who took off after the minivan. The cop asked questions about Josh, then read him his rights and asked, "do you understand your rights?"

"No. I haven't done anything wrong,"

"One more time. Do you understand your rights?"

"I guess. What did I do wrong?"

"You're implicated in the disappearance of a minor." The cop placed Cole in the back of the patrol car. After half an hour, a black Chevrolet Suburban pulled up. Two men in black suits got out.

More cops thought Cole. But these guys were FBI. They handcuffed Cole and transferred him to the back seat of their Suburban.

Cops kept coming, then news trucks showed up. He looked out of the Suburban at cameras that broadcast his image everywhere. The FBI towed his car away and impounded it for investigation, then took Cole to a building in Washington.

Senator Case picked up his phone. It was Sol Solomon. "We've got the kid. "

President Goodwin's phone rang. It was the Deputy Director of the FBI. "We have Joshua's friend Cole Stendahl, in custody. Unfortunately, Joshua is not with him. It looks like Joshua was picked up by someone in a brown Chrysler minivan. We believe he was kidnapped."

"Kidnapped?" Al's heart pounded. "What do you mean, kidnapped?"

"All we know is that Joshua and his friend Cole stopped for gas. When Cole came back from paying for it, Joshua was gone, and a brown Chrysler minivan was speeding out of the station. This is according to Stendahl. We've got a bulletin out on the minivan. I'm sorry to have to report this to you. We're doing everything we know how to do, Mister President."

"What was he doing in Cole's car? I thought you guys were apprehending him?"

"It happened that mister Stendhal found him first."

"Why do you think anyone would kidnap him?"

"We have no way of knowing that at this time."

"Where's Cole?"

"We're holding him."

"What for?"

"We're considering charges of harboring a runaway, custodial interference, contributing to the delinquency of a minor, and whatever else may materialize."

"Don't you think that's a little stiff, for some kid helping his friend run away from home?"

"Also, by his actions he is involved with the kidnapping of your son. He may even be a participant."

"I want young Mister Stendahl brought to my office."

"We can't just let him go."

"Are you denying my directive?"

"Not exactly. It's just that he hasn't been arraigned yet and isn't eligible for bail."

"I want him in my office now."

Al had the dreaded duty of telling Josh's mother the terrible turn of events.

Just South of Washington, the brown minivan followed a secondary road toward the Potomac River. It turned off onto a muddy driveway with an open iron gate and continued to a large rustic lodge near the water's edge. The van came to a stop next to a blue Ford Escape. The place lay dark, wet, hidden under wide-spreading maples and dogwoods.

It was Sol's lodge. As a real estate broker, he purchased it from an estate left by a World-War-One era Army general whose family kept it mothballed for decades until the last owner died. The ancient building was once a safe alternative to prohibition era speak-easies and a hotspot for Washington insiders.

In the unlikely event that the lodge was raided, it had a hidden tunnel that stretched under the building to a large boathouse and dock where boats waited to whisk away drinkers into the dark of night. The same boats delivered booze from offshore suppliers. It was never used after the twenty-first amendment repealed prohibition in 1933. Sol received the building just as it was left in the mid 1930's. The doors and windows were boarded over. The basement still had a huge pile of coal ready, to fire the furnace that heated the building's hot water radiators. The furniture remained, covered with dirt-laden white sheets. Sol had hired a contractor who patched and scrubbed it back into a semblance of the of the way it once was. This time capsule of a bygone era sat ready for its new purpose.

Josh's three captors led him through the damp air to the side door. Once inside, an older man grabbed him by the arm and propelled him to an overstuffed chair. The old man pulled the blindfold from Josh's eyes, and cut the zip ties off his wrists, then pushed him into the chair. The old man looked to be sixty something; short, stocky, and dark completed with thick white hair. He had a semi-automatic pistol tucked under his belt. He told Josh to pull up his pant leg, then he snapped a GPS tracker around his ankle. "If you try to leave, I'll know it," he said, "there are video cams out there too. There's no neighbors around here either, so you might as well make yourself at home in that chair." The old man walked away.

Josh looked around. He sat in one of a dozen antique, overstuffed green mohair chairs that formed an oval around a large polar bear rug in the center of a long room. The walls were age-darkened knotty pine. At the far end of the room a large stone fireplace rose to a vaulted ceiling, where a set of chandeliers made of elk antlers hung from a peeled log ridge beam. The floor was worn hardwood. A row of hunting trophies lined one long wall beneath the balcony where they gazed forever across the expanse of the Potomac River. A yellow Lab lay next to the fireplace, eying Josh.

At the other end of the room, the old man stood at a carved oak bar. Over it hung a broadly antlered moose head, under which a wooden plaque read, Bull Moose Sportsman's Club.

When Josh was abducted, his cell phone and wallet were immediately taken from him, but they missed his new phone, that was in his pocket behind his wallet. He now slipped it out and shoved it down beside the cushion.

Josh called out to the old man. "I have to go to the bathroom."

The old man pointed to a hallway next to the bar. "At the end of the hall. I'll be right behind you."

There were two stalls, and a long porcelain urinal. The place smelled of age. There were no windows. The floor was tiny black and white tiles with a corroded brass drain cover in the center of the room. A silver painted radiator stood against the outside wall. When Josh came out, the old man escorted him back to his chair.

"Why was I kidnapped?"

"None of your business."

"When can I leave?"

"Don't know yet. Maybe a few days."

"I'm hungry."

"You'll eat when I eat."

"What are you going to do with me?"

"Nothing, unless you try to leave. Then, I'll use you for target practice."

Josh sat imprisoned in his chair with no idea of where he was or what would happen to him. The one thing he did understand was that he was the president's son, and these guys were using him to get at his dad.

Around midnight, Cole and an FBI agent arrived at the White House. The FBI kept all of Cole's belongings. He had only the clothes on his back, and he hadn't bathed since leaving home. Maybe it was unrealistic to expect the FBI to deliver Cole any sooner, but Al didn't like being treated this way by the director of the FBI. Tracy led Cole to Josh's room, where he could shower and find something to wear.

A much fresher Cole walked into the room. "What's going on?"

"We're getting ready to hit the sack," Al said, "Tracy has a bed for you. We'll go look for Josh in the morning."

Al went to the Treaty Room where Mark and Leo were waiting. Al dropped heavily onto the end of a couch. "Mark, they could have delivered Cole on time, with a change of clothes and his toothbrush. Why do you think the FBI is acting this way?"

"My opinion? I think the Director is trying to assert his authority. He doesn't want you telling him what to do. They probably took a while grilling Cole. I'm sure they still intend to charge him."

"Mark, if this is a kidnap for ransom, don't you think we should have heard something from them by now?"

"I think this is a political kidnapping. Anybody could be in on it. Including members of our own government. Why did the secret Service make it public that Josh ran away? That's a security risk they should never have taken. Why didn't the FBI follow Cole?"

Al contemplated the possibility. "Knowing Josh was on his own, anyone could have hunted him down, but only the FBI knew Cole was driving out here from Washington State. The kidnappers had to have gotten their information, in some way, from the FBI. How else would they have known to follow Cole's car? Maybe there's a leak at the FBI and maybe even collusion with the kidnappers. The first question to ask, is who could the FBI have told about Cole arriving in Washington, and the description of his car? I also want to know which agent told the press Josh ran away, and who directed him to do it. I'm going to call those guys in for a meeting first thing in the morning."

"If the FBI can leak information, then it's possible that someone at the FBI may have stalled the search for Josh."

"I don't trust those guys, Mark."

"Which of your activities have changed, since Josh left?"

"Plenty. I can't concentrate on anything. I've spent most of my time here with Tracy and Mom, waiting and worrying. I had to cancel talks with the Mexican President about automobile parts. Why would anyone want to take Josh?"

"What about your appointments and meetings?"

"Amy is rescheduling what she can, and Bates offered to fill in as VP if I can't be available in this crisis. I appreciate his help."

"We have to ask how this could affect what you are doing as president? I think you should be in your office in the morning conducting business as usual. You can't let anyone see you falter. There's nothing you can do, anyway. In addition to that, I think you should do something bold and unexpected. It might be good idea to let that Navy task force stay in place with no further action until Josh is safe.

"I'm seeking international cooperation for the rescue mission. I have to keep everything on hold until other nations get on board. Hopefully Josh will be back by then."

"I know this is hard for you. Let me handle finding Josh. Tracy and your mom will understand."

"You're right, Mark. I'd feel better knowing you were looking."

CHAPTER 29

At eight O'clock the next morning Mark and Leo sat over coffee and pastry at the Capital Grind, discussing what they could do to find Josh. At the same time, Al sat at his desk instructing Amy to arrange meetings with the Directors of the FBI and the Secret Service. She would include the Attorney General, whom Al had appointed from Oregon. They would be sandwiched into his already tight schedule.

Later that morning, Al's phone rang. It was Mark. "Leo and I talked to a private investigator who knows the area and is willing to help us. Leo spotted his office while we were grabbing breakfast. It's right across the street from the Capital Grind. His name is Fred Ferguson. He's an ex-military police investigator who worked the DC area for several years before he retired and became a PI. He said he'd been following the kidnapping in the news. He wants to help find Josh. Is this something you would support?"

"Go for it. You handle it any way you see fit. Consider yourself completely in charge. I'll cover the cost. Thanks, Mark. I gotta run."

Mark hired Fred. Fred wanted to know everything about Josh. He took copious notes as Mark and Leo described as much as they could about the President's son. Fred would start immediately.

"We can't just sit around," Mark said. "We've got to help you in some way."

"The kidnappers surely have him hidden somewhere around here," Fred said. "Until they make a move all we can do is follow the line of evidence that the FBI has been following. I've found from experience, that a different approach to the same investigation can get different answers. I'll start by visiting the gas station where Josh got abducted. Then work back from there, following in the direction of the abductor's vehicle. If you want to help, get me in touch with Cole. You might also do some internet searching. Maybe someone has mentioned something on Facebook or Twitter or whatever."

Mark arranged a meeting with Fred and Cole. It would be at the White House. Fred was issued a White House pass.

Cole was nervous. He was way out of his element. Here he was in the White House with the first family. It wasn't the same as hanging out at the Goodwin's place back home. Not only that, the FBI scared him. They threatened prison and they kept all his stuff. They accused him of things he never did, and asked questions he couldn't answer. On top of that, everyone back home knew he lied about what he was doing. The news even had him implicated in the kidnapping. When he sat down with Fred, he saw him as another threat. Fred sensed this and showed compassion.

"I'm here to help you find Josh," Fred started. He then assured him he had nothing to do with the law or the FBI. They talked for a while about Cole's trip east and then what he remembered about the kidnapping and what questions the FBI asked.

Finally, Fred asked, "how would you like to ride with me while I do some snooping around? I could use your help."

"Yes, I would. I feel like I'm responsible. If I hadn't come to get him none of this would be happening." A measure of fear lifted from Cole as he followed Fred to his car.

At the gas station where Josh was abducted, Fred had Cole walk through everything he did the day before. The young woman at the counter was the same person who waited on Cole during the kidnapping. Fred introduced himself as a private investigator helping in the search for the President's son. "Have you been interviewed by the FBI?"

"Yes."

"Anyone else?"

"I'll say. I was even on TV last night. You should have seen this place. They had police tape strung up everywhere. It caused us to lose our evening business."

"I'm sorry to hear that. As a private investigator, my only interest is helping to locate the missing boy. Can you tell me what you told the FBI?"

"I saw the whole thing. I never would have noticed, but the van came in fast, facing the wrong direction, so I looked. All the action happened between the van and the car at the pumps. I could tell something was going on, but I couldn't see what. Then the van took off."

"What else did you tell them?"

"I got a good look at the driver. He looked like a youngish guy with black hair and a dark completion. That's all I know."

"You got a good look at the van, so describe it as completely as you can."

"That's easy. It's a gold Chrysler minivan just like one my mom used to have. Maybe about ten years old."

"Are you sure? It's being reported as brown."

"It's just dirty. There's mud all over it. If anybody ever washed it, it would be gold just like my mom's. there was so much mud that some of it fell off when they slammed the door."

"Really? Can you show me?"

The attendant led them out to the pumps where she pointed at what remained of a little pile of dirt on the concrete. Fred went back into the store and got a paper cup and a plastic spoon. He scooped up the dirt.

"Did you see the back of the van as it left?" Fred asked.

"Yes. It was just like my mom's, but muddy."

"The license plate in the back, did you see that? I want you to think hard about that. It's important."

The attendant stood pensively for a moment then said, "It was a Virginia plate, but I can't remember the numbers, except I got a real weird feeling. There were two or three sixes in the number. Yeah, three. Doesn't that just give you the creeps?"

"Did you tell anyone the numbers?"

"No, I wasn't sure, and besides I was afraid they'd think I was nuts if I said the number was '666'. You know what I mean?"

"Could I have a look at your security camera videos."

"The FBI guys took them, and the recorder too."

"Thanks anyway. You've been very helpful."

"Oh, and by the way." She addressed Cole. "You left all your snacks here yesterday. Let me get them for you."

Fred and Cole left with all the goodies that were intended to feed a very hungry Josh Goodwin.

On the way back to Washington, Fred called Mark with the information that the van was a ten-year-old gold Chrysler minivan covered with dirt, and the partial Virginia license number. He told Mark that he had a soil sample that needed to be analyzed. "Unfortunately," he said, "the best forensic geologists are known to the FBI. Do you think you guys can find an alternative soil analysis? That mud could tell us where the van has been."

"I'll get right on it," Mark said.

Fred then turned his attention to Cole, "If you were the one trying to find Josh, what would you do?"

"I'd try and locate his cell phone."

"Don't you think the kidnappers would have taken that?"

"Probably, but he has two phones."

"Two?"

"Right. When he ran away, he went to Walmart and bought a second phone. He was afraid to use his regular phone because he thought the Secret Service, or somebody, was tracking it. It's kind of hard to run away when the cops can read your texts and follow your cell tower pings. One more thing. There's an army veteran that Josh hung out with while he waited for me."

"What about him?"

"He was with Josh when I picked him up. He might have seen the van that followed me."

Cole had listened to Josh tell about the veteran. A good enough description that Fred thought he could find him. Especially with his beard and black Labrador dog.

On the way to Pennsylvania Avenue Fred asked about what plans he and Josh had.

"Pretty simple really. All Josh wanted to do, was be with his friends back home. We figured he could hide out at my place until he turned eighteen and then he would be free to do whatever he wanted."

"I understand that. When I was Josh's age, my dad moved us across town to a different school district. I refused to enroll in school. After all, this school was our rival. We didn't like them, and they didn't like us. If I showed up in that school, I'd be dead meat. Instead, I ran away and joined the army. I lied about my age and got away with it. Once I did that, there was no turning back. When I went home on leave a year later, I found that my friends had graduated and moved on. Everything I looked forward to, was gone." Fred chose his next advice, carefully. "Josh's dad moved him across the nation. He's now the President's son and always will be. In a few months, both you and Josh will be out of school and so will all your friends. Then what?"

The events of the last twenty-four hours ruined Cole's plans of returning home with Josh. His car was impounded, and he had none of his things. Even if the FBI gave everything back, all he could do was to drive home alone. But for now, his thoughts were filled with the hope of finding Josh safe, accompanied by the dread that something terrible had happened to him.

"You're right, Mr. Ferguson. Make one mistake and nothing will ever be the same again."

The FBI Director arrived at the White House in the late afternoon. The Attorney General was already there. Both were ushered into the Oval Office.

During introductions, Al's cell phone rang. It was Mark.

"Have you talked to the FBI yet?"

"No."

"When you do, find out if they found any cell phones in Josh's stuff. I just learned he had two phones, but don't share that information."

"Will do. I'll get back to you."

Amy led the FBI Director into the Oval Office. "How's the search for Josh coming along?" Al asked.

"I'm sorry Mister President, we don't have a lot to go on. We took the video from the gas station. It showed the van come into the station, the abduction, and the departure. What we know, is that there were possibly three kidnappers in an older brown Chrysler minivan with a Virginia license plate. Witnesses said they saw the van leave the station eastbound."

"I'd like to see that video?"

"That's not available right now. It's being evaluated."

"I'm the President of the United States, and that's a video of my son. I want the original."

"Yes sir."

"So?"

"We tracked Joshua's activities after he left Nordstrom's. We got as far as a Subway shop where he called a cab. The cab driver said he took Joshua to Walmart. That's where the trail went cold. We have video of Josh buying outdoor equipment. We don't know where he went after that. I have agents on it as well as cooperation from other law enforcement agencies, including the Metropolitan Police Department. We think our break will come when they try to contact someone. Perhaps for ransom."

"Is that all? What about cell phone activity?"

"Cell phone activity ended shortly after Joshua ditched his grandmother. I'm sorry sir, that's it for now."

"How come the kidnappers knew to follow Cole's car when only the FBI knew about Cole coming to Washington?"

"I don't know. We told other agencies about Cole as soon as we learned he was coming here. They could have told someone."

"Your protocol delayed informing local law enforcement until only minutes before Josh was kidnapped.

The leak is in your department. I want you to find out who did it."

"I don't see how that could happen. Only a few of our agents had that information."

"Good. Then that should narrow your search. When you went through Josh's belongings did you find his cell phone?"

"What we have is his backpack with a charger in it but no cell phone."

"When are you releasing Cole's car and belongings?"

"Where is he?"

"He's with my personal assistant who is out getting a change of clothes for him, among other things. Answer my question."

"Everything is being held as evidence."

Al turned to the Attorney General. "What do you think?"

"Cole and Joshua are almost the same age, eighteen and seventeen, and are both high school seniors. All that I see happening, is that Joshua ran away from home and his friend Cole picked him up. This goes on all the time. Just because Joshua is the President's son doesn't make what he did a crime. I don't see that Cole has committed even a misdemeanor."

"He crossed a state line to do it," the Director said.

"Since he didn't commit a crime, then crossing a state line is of no consequence," the AG said. Furthermore, you already let him go and there are no valid charges under which to arrest him."

"We didn't just let him go. He was remanded to the custody of the President."

"Only a judge can remand a prisoner. No court has contacted the President."

Al had it. He got out of his chair and pointed a thick working man's finger at the FBI Director. "That's enough. It's clear to me that Cole broke no laws. Stop worrying about Cole and put your energy into finding my boy! And one more thing. I want Cole's car and every bit of his belongings in my driveway as soon as possible and I don't mean midnight."

"There's an impoundment fee."

Al changed the direction of his finger toward the door. "This meeting is over."

The AG stayed on for the meeting with the Director of the Secret Service. Al called Mark to report that no cell phone was found.

The Secret Service Director arrived.

Al asked, "Why did your agency tell the press my son ran away?"

"That's not exactly what happened. When Vice-president Bates was told, he asked the agent to get the word out so that as many eyes as possible would be looking for Josh. He even suggested that an Amber Alert would be appropriate. When told the President should be consulted, he said you were indisposed, and he would have to make that decision. We then followed his advice."

That was all Al needed to hear. He excused the Director. The AG stayed long enough for Al to tell him the kidnappers drove a gold – not brown – ten-year-old Chrysler minivan with a Virginia plate containing two or three sixes. "Do you think you can find someone to trace that plate?" Al asked.

"Can do."

"One more thing. We have a mud sample coming that needs to be forensically analyzed. Is that something you can get done without the FBI knowing about it?"

"Yes sir. I'll get right on it."

"When you find something out let me know, but don't tell anyone else."

"Don't you think it would be a good idea to let the FBI have that information?"

"No. Under no circumstances are you to share that information. It's important that you expedite this. Let me know the moment you find something, no matter the time."

When the AG left, Al updated Mark, and Mark called Fred. "The FBI found no phones in Josh's backpack or Cole's car. Also, the President met with the FBI Director. It looks like they're not going to charge Cole with anything. He can expect to get his car and the rest of his stuff back tonight. One more thing, can you stop somewhere and get Cole a change of clothes and some toiletries before you bring him back?"

When Cole learned that no cell phone was found, he explained to Fred that both he and Josh had GPS locator apps on their phones. All Josh had to do was turn on one of his phones and Cole would know his exact location. Cole then set an alert tone to the app — a bird call. Fred took note of the sound.

When Fred got Mark's call, he was busy retracing Cole and Josh's path from the gas station where Josh was kidnapped, back to where Josh jumped into Cole's car on Pennsylvania Avenue. He stopped at each business that looked like it could have a camera aimed at the highway. With each inquiry, Fred showed his ID and then said he was looking for a wanted man. If Fred stopped at a motel, then the man was wanted for a violent motel holdup. If it was a convenience store, then the man was wanted for armed robbery of a convenience store, and so on. Most were eager to help. By the time

Fred reached Washington, he had viewed several tapes. Two of them showed Cole's car being followed by a dirty brown minivan. The tapes also showed the minivan heading east as far as I-95 after the kidnapping. No one Fred met had been questioned by the FBI.

When they reached Pennsylvania Avenue, Fred found the veteran Josh had been keeping company with. The vet was surprised to learn that he was hanging out with the President's son. He said Josh acted as if he were afraid of everything. The vet didn't find that unusual amongst street people who often were paranoid. Except, he thought Josh was a runaway. Street people don't wear new clothes. The vet said he remembered Josh dashing to a stopped car. He also thought it odd that a van stopped in another lane, while Josh got in the car. The van then took the lane behind the green Jetta as both vehicles drove away.

"Can you describe the van?"

"Sure. It was a brown minivan with two dark complicated guys in the front seat. The window was rolled down, and another guy was leaning forward from the back seat. They were all looking at the green Jetta that the President's kid got into. There were three of them in the van. It just didn't fit in with the rest of the cars on the street."

"How's that?"

"It had muddy tires."

CHAPTER 30

While Fred was busy searching for Josh, Sol sat in the back seat of his car as it turned on to Rhode Island Avenue heading toward a meeting with Marion West. These days Sol had his own car and chauffeur. The car was the paragon of extravagance; a Mercedes Maybach S600 protected by armored floors, side panels, and bullet proof glass. His driver knew martial arts and carried a nine-millimeter handgun. After what that horrible cockroach of a man, Congressman Roger Carlson, tried to do to him he wasn't taking any chances. The big car rolled to a stop in front of the offices of Leonard Government Relations. The chauffeur hopped out. He looked around carefully, before opening Sol's door. Once Sol entered the building, the car pulled away from the curb.

Across the lobby, behind a counter that separated the waiting room from the inner offices, sat a business-like middle-aged woman. She smiled at Sol as he approached. "How may I help you?" she said.

"Arthur Bishop to see Marion West." He answered in a pleasant voice, pleased at the simple opulence of the waiting room.

"Please be seated. I'll tell her you are here."

Sol picked up a newspaper from a coffee table and sat down. The headline article was about the abduction of the President's son. He scanned through the paragraphs to see what the Article had to say about the kidnapping. He learned the president's office had nothing at all to say, except the President had entrusted the recovery of his son to the best law enforcement agencies on earth. He added that since he couldn't participate in the search, he would devote his time to the duties of his office. He asked for prayers for his son and his family. Further down the column he saw a description of the van the crew used in the kidnapping with a low-grade surveillance camera picture of the brown van. *They gotta get rid of that van*, Sol thought.

"Come with me, Mister Bishop." The receptionist lead Sol a short distance down a hall to a small meeting room. "Ms. West will arrive in a moment." She left Sol alone at a small conference table.

To Marion, Sol was Arthur Bishop, the executive Director of The American Anti-Corruption league. She had the name of another corrupt congressmen for him. It included incriminating photos and written information provided by her investigator. She placed the folder on the table.

"What do you have for me this time?" Sol asked.

"We have one prospect. Senator Douglas Boyd has accepted a large amount of money from a British pharmaceutical company and did so while in the company of a woman other than his wife." Marion handed Sol a manila folder.

"I'm curious." She added. "We have for some time provided you with the names of congressmen we find to be corrupt, but we haven't noticed more than a couple of them being exposed. Why is that?"

"I appreciate your concern. Like you said, a couple of them have been exposed and are no longer in congress, but it takes time to build a case against people. We must be sure of our actions before we expose someone. A lot is at stake when we do this. We must consider not only the congressman, but his family and colleagues as well as his constituents. There is also the need to adhere to the law. We can't run the risk of unanticipated consequences. Some may never be exposed. Finally, we must consider our budget. Sometimes we must sit on a case until we can afford to move forward. Don't worry. We're close to exposing several congressmen."

Sol looked through the new folder thinking about the possibility of another million dollars. "Look at this. The Brits are paying off a congressman. No wonder drugs cost too much."

"Maybe you can do something about it."

After the meeting Sol called his driver who met him at the curb. As Sol's car merged into traffic, his phone rang. It was Speaker Case.

"Lyle told me the President vetoed our caliphate bill. Now we've got to find enough votes to override his veto. It's possible. To make matters worse, he told the Joint Chiefs of Staff to get ready to implement his plans to rescue ethnic groups in the Middle East. He told Lyle that he has been working on this for some time. He said he has the authority to protect American interests in the area, as well as that of our allies. He thinks he can do this without consulting congress. He even believes he has a moral obligation."

"I think we can find ways to stop him."

"He's addressing the nation at six. We can talk after that."

Sol felt the pressure. He had to satisfy Ibrahim Bin Jabar. "Let's meet at the Hay-Adams hotel. We can watch the President's address there. We've got to work out a solution. See how many of our colleagues you can round up. I'll be waiting in the bar." He then called his brokerage and instructed his administrative assistant to reserve a banquet room at the Hay Adams to watch the President's address.

Sol called Jameel, his contact with the crew of the Middle Easterners staying at the lodge, alerting him to this new turn of events.

Since Fred's chance encounter with the dozen corrupt congressmen at the Jefferson, he took every opportunity to check on their whereabouts. His best source of information was Marion West, whose lobbying organization could tell him what some of the congressmen were doing after hours. She just informed him that at least two were going to the Hay-Adams to watch the President's address. Fred got there early.

At four o'clock, Sol sat in the bar at the Hay-Adams having an early dinner and sipping a martini. Later, his congressional faithfuls would arrive to watch the President's speech. As he ate, a man lowered himself into a chair across from him. He rolled a familiar looking gold coin between his fingers. Sol recognized him.

"May I join you?" he said.

"Of course, Mister...?"

"It looks like your plan to have the Vice-president sign our bill has failed."

"The President is addressing the nation at six. I'll be watching it with some of our cooperating congressmen. We'll have a chance to talk about things then. I can let you know more after that. Where can I find you?"

"Just come back to the bar. I'll find you here. As you watch the President's speech remember, we are depending upon you and your congressmen to achieve our goals. So far you have done well, but should you stumble now, there will be consequences."

Sol shifted uneasily in his char.

"I want you to know that we are most able to assist you. We have many more agents in your country than you know of. More can arrive any time through the secret conduit of our fishing charter. Any one of them would give his life for our cause. We expect no less from you."

Sol waited for the man to leave the room, then pushed his dinner aside. a few congressmen came in and took seats at his table. From a smaller table at the far end of the room, Fred surreptitiously took cell phone photos.

Shortly before six, Sol and his congressmen adjourned to a banquet room where they settled in to hear what the President would say.

As soon as a few Pharmaceutical ads ended, the President came on. "I'm sure you all know," the President began. "My son Joshua has been abducted. We have heard nothing from the kidnappers. We have no idea why he was taken or who took him. I have this to say to the kidnappers. If any harm comes to my son you will feel the full force of the American justice system come down on you, no matter who you are or where you are. If you think using my son for personal or political gain is a good idea, then think again. We want our son home safe. Josh, if you can hear me, know that we are doing everything possible to locate you. Be brave.

"There are other families just as worried about their children as my family is about Josh. Throughout the world terrorists are randomly and wickedly extinguishing life to further their cause. As their caliphate grows, entire communities of people who do not share the beliefs of their conquerors are being conscripted, enslaved, and murdered. Thousands have become refugees whose fleeing masses serve as conduits to insert terrorists into any country humane enough to give shelter.

"I am not the only parent worried about one's child. To parents suppressed by the caliphate, I say this: I have ordered the United Sates armed forces into the Mediterranean region on a rescue mission to stop the savage atrocities committed against victims of war. The Secretary of State and I have been gathering our allies to this cause. As part of this effort the USA and our allies will welcome any and all refugees. For too long, innocent lives have been sacrificed while nations discuss protocol, but do little. It's time for action. Goodnight and may God bless us all."

Senate Majority Leader Melvin Case spoke first. "Not only has he vetoed our bill, now he wants to raid the Middle East. We've got to stop him."

"We still have the kid," Sol said.

"So, what's that doing for us?" Senator Case said, "the reason to take him, in the first place, was to let Lyle take over the presidency long enough to sign our bill, while the President dealt with his missing kid. That idea backfired on us. Lyle assured us that President Goodwin was too uneducated and too ignorant to handle the office of the President. Competent or not, he's making international deals and directing the armed forces. We have a great investment in keeping America out of the Middle East. Not just for personal reasons but for the welfare of every American. If we fail at this, there could be grave consequences for each of us. The President is about to ruin it all."

"Nobody could tell the last president anything either, until he was threatened with assassination. After that, he stopped interfering, we have threatened the President's son Conner. I think we need to follow through with that, "Sol said.

The room was filled with criminalized congressmen eager to serve their Middle East benefactors by preventing the President from acting on his intention of rescuing the so-called victims of war. The congressmen were enthusiastic about thwarting terrorism, having convinced themselves that they really were protecting America from terrorist harm. They were allowing themselves to be deceived for the love of money, while simultaneously being blackmailed. There were now thirty-three congressmen in Sol's stable, each a millionaire.

When the last of Sol's guests were gone, he went back to the bar to wait for his contact. He was in the middle of nursing a martini when the man with the coin arrived at his table.

"I watched the speech," the man said. "This is exactly what you are commissioned to prevent. How do you plan to do so?"

"We can use the War Powers Act. It prevents the President from committing to an armed conflict without the permission of congress. Then there's the United Nations Charter that requires the UN Security Council to agree with hostilities. We can also tie up funding. We'll be getting the ball rolling first thing tomorrow. As for our bill, we can't be sure that we can override the veto, but there is a strong possibility. Senator Chase is lining up the votes already."

"Your President needs to be reined in. Maybe he needs a little intimidation."

"We haven't figured out how to do that, but We think it is time to use the threat to his son Connor as an incentive to keep him out of the Middle East. What's more, he employed illegal aliens to manage his farm and has been seen in the company of white supremacists. He's also breaking the law with his so-called rescue mission. Impeachment proceeding are underway based these offenses. Hiring illegals is a felony. While we wait for impeachment proceedings, the immigration people are ready to arrest the Mexican Nationals he hired. We can hold them as witnesses in an impeachment trial. There will be several subpoenas of witnesses who will testify to his felony of hiring of illegals and incompetence in office."

"I am not sure of his incompetence, just make sure he stays out of our business. Remember, each one of your Congressmen was handpicked as a person with their own impeachable background. If they don't perform, we'll see that their nasty little secrets come to light."

"It's time to release the boy. I can see no value in holding him any longer."

"We keep the kid. You may not know how to intimidate the resident, but we do."

The next day, Fred took the time for a lunch meeting with Marion West at a Denny's restaurant. He got to the point. "Something funny is going on. A couple of days ago I followed a congressman to the Jefferson Hotel. The one who we think has a second wife that nobody seems to have seen. I thought I might spot her. While I was waiting in the lobby, I saw him walk out with several other congressmen and the Vice-president. Each of them a congressman that I had identified to you as engaging in corrupt behavior."

Marion, with her mouth around a big bite of French dip sandwich, mumbled, "All of them together?" As she maneuvered to keep au jus from running down her chin.

"Yup. There were fourteen of them. When I checked with the front desk to see who reserved the room, I was told it was Sol Solomon. I photographed him. See for yourself." Fred handed Marion a four-by-six print. "I checked into this guy. He's a real estate broker and fundraiser for the Republican National Committee. I believe he is the man-in-black we've been looking for.

Marion studied the photograph. "I know this guy. He's Arthur Bishop, the executive director of the American Anti-Corruption League."

"No. That's Sol Solomon."

"I said I know that man. He's Arthur Bishop. He's the one who contracts for the information on the corrupt congressmen.

"I'm certain he's Solomon. I did my research."

"How can he be both?"

"It looks like Solomon, posing as Bishop, is collecting corrupt congressmen. No wonder you're not seeing anyone being exposed. But since exposure is not his objective, what is?"

Marion sat stiff with her sandwich in mid-air. She looked dumbfounded. "We were commissioned to investigate suspected wrongdoing and make reports on our findings. It's entirely up to the client to use that information as they see fit."

"They're not being honest with you, Marion."

"We're fulfilling our contract."

"Why would lobbyists take this kind of work in the first place? You're supposed to influence congressmen, not tell on them."

"We are well paid to represent Mister Bishop and his organization. They believe that corruption in government is costing Americans money and lives. One of the great symptoms of this corruption was the ratification of the presidential lottery. If states had any faith in their government that would never have happened. I am happy to contribute to their altruistic ambitions. They also argue that we know people in congress well enough to seek out their misconducts."

"Don't you care that this guy is a phony?"

"It hasn't hurt your pocketbook any."

"Here's something interesting for you to think about. Solomon, your Bishop, was with fourteen of the congressmen I referred to you as corrupt. I have a picture." He showed it to Marion. Several of her referred congressmen, and Solomon walking through a lobby. "If he wants to blow the whistle on these guys why is he going to a lunch meeting with them?

Marion got caught off guard with another bite of sandwich in her mouth. "I see what you mean."

"I think you've been lied to and we have both been participating in that lie. Also, I have fulfilled your request to identify the man-in-black. Now I have another pressing investigation to attend to and have no more time or desire to follow congressman around. I am no longer in your employ. We've been had."

CHAPTER 31

Josh stared-at his ankle bracelet. It looked cheap. Maybe he could get it off. He pulled it down to his heel, but it would go no farther.

"Hey! Leave that alone!" The old man stood on the balcony above the trophy heads watching him. He came down the stairs at the end of the balcony, walked to Josh and slapped him across the head. "Next time you mess with that I'll hurt you."

"Take it easy, will ya? I wasn't doing anything. So, what is this thing?"

"That tells me where you are at all times." He pulled out his cell phone and opened an app. He showed it to Josh. "See. You're right there." His finger pointed at a red dot in the center of the screen. "Anywhere you go, the red dot goes"

Josh saw a map of about one square mile. Not far from his red dot he saw a highway. Almost half the map was blue for the river. No other landmarks were visible. He also noticed that the old man's phone looked like his.

The old man went behind the bar and disappeared into the kitchen. Josh ran his hand down beside the chair cushion, nervously reassuring himself that his phone was still there. But he felt something small, cold and metallic. He pulled it out. Pinched between his fingers he saw a nickel. It had a buffalo on it. He turned it over and saw an American Indian with a couple of feathers in his hair. The number 1927 was under the Indian. It looked new. He wondered what else might be down there. He ran his hand all the way around the cushion. He found an old penny. It, too, had an Indian on it.

The old man came out of the kitchen with a plate of food that he sat on a table. He summoned Josh to eat.

At the end of the room near the bar were six round wooden tables with six matching chairs each. Another large antler chandelier hung above them. The old man sat a plate on the table. It looked like beans, with a fried egg on top and some kind of flatbread. The old man returned to the kitchen. The food smelled strange, but hunger made it taste good.

The dog walked across the room and sat down to watch Josh eat. When he was finished, Josh put the plate on the floor for the dog.

"Don't feed Dog," the old man yelled. "Get in here and wash the dishes."

Other than trips to the bathroom, this would be Josh's first time out of the great room. The kitchen looked like a restaurant kitchen; big and old like the rest of the place, except for the refrigerator and stove. They looked new. The large stainless-steel sink was filled with dirty dishes.

"Use lots of hot water, rinse them good, and put them in the rack to dry."

"I know how to do dishes."

"Shut up!" He slapped Josh across the head again.

Josh filled the drying rack to overflowing. The dog watched the whole time. When the dishes were done, Josh asked if he should return to his chair.

"You're not done yet. Sweep the floor and mop it with hot water and soap. I want it rinsed too."

"What do I do with the dog?"

"Put it outside. Use the kitchen door."

"What's the dog's name?"

"Dog. The dog's name is Dog."

When Josh let Dog out, he heard the old man's cell phone sound an alarm from the motion detectors. The parking lot became illuminated by one large light which switched on when Dog walked into the yard. The light was motion sensitive. It too set off an alert on the old man's phone. The light reached into the thick brush and trees that surrounded the yard. Some of it reflected from the muddy ruts in the driveway. The only open space was toward the river where a boathouse and a long dock stood above the river.

"You don't have to wait for Dog. Get back in here."

After Josh cleaned the kitchen, the old man propelled-him back to the great room and told him to sit down. Josh chose a different chair, one that faced the bar where the old man sat down to a small glass of wine.

Josh slid his hand down beside the cushion of his chair. Toward the rear, he hit something hard. He pulled out a small, metal-handled pocketknife. Embossed in the flat metal handle were street scenes and palm trees. Imprinted on it were the words, Souvenir of Habaña. Josh opened it. There was one shiny, little sharp blade folded into the handle. He looked at the old man to be sure he wasn't being watched, then slipped the knife into his pocket.

"What's your name?" Asked Josh.

"None of your business."

"Can I call you Old Man?"

"Why not."

Josh pushed his hand down between the cracks under the cushion to see what else he could find. This was fun. He moved to the next chair. This time he found a whole handful of old coins. One large dollar coin. The old man didn't seem to care about which chair he sat in, so he moved from chair to chair. He found a few more coins and a tiny paper box with the word Sen-Sen on it.

"Hey Old Man, can I let Dog in?"

"No."

"Hey Old Man, you got anything I can read? I'm bored."

"Shut up." The old man got up to let in the dog. "I can fix your boredom. Come with me."

The old man led him down the hall to a door next to the bathroom. It opened to a set of open wooden stairs that went down to a cellar with a dirt floor. One bare light bulb cast shadows everywhere. On one side of the cellar, stood a rusty monster. A flickering yellow flame could be seen through a tiny window in the heavy cast iron door. Near it, was a huge pile of coal.

"You see that thing over there? That's what heats this place. Your job is to keep the fire going."

"How do I do that?"

"I'll show you."

The old man walked over to the furnace. He grabbed the handle, swung the door open, then shoveled in some coal. "Do this about every two hours and don't burn yourself. At night you bank up the coal inside and close the draft. I'll show you that later."

Hearing the old man say "at night" made Josh wonder how many nights he would be there.

He looked around the shadowy, dark cellar covered with age-old spider webs and dirt. Unidentifiable stuff lay everywhere, like a junk yard. He was glad to climb the stairs out of there.

On their way back, the old man reached under the bar and pulled out a gallon jug of red wine and his glass. Josh went to an overstuffed chair and searched around the cushion. The old man stared into his glass between sips, then filled it again. After a few refills, the old man muttered slow incomprehensible words as he poured more wine. Dog curled up by Josh's feet.

Josh now sat in a chair facing the windows. Lights reflected from the far side of the river as he softly stroked Dog's head. He heard the incoherent words of the old man who rested his head on his arm. He was crying. Josh got up, walked over, and sat on a stool next to him. "Are you okay?"

"I was a kid like you once, but I wasn't as important as you are." It was the alcohol speaking. "We were Palestinians living in a Lebanese refugee camp. My father was killed in 1967 fighting for our liberation, which we never got. My brother died trying to even the score. My mother wanted to go to America to be free from it all. I wanted to go too, but for different reasons. I wanted to be in America to do as much harm as I could. America is the natural enemy of my people. My mom died a couple of years after we got here. My sisters all went their own way. I did what I could to help my people. Now I'm old and alone and have nothing, stuck babysitting some brat in an old drafty lodge."

He continued blabbering his heartaches, his hand clutching an empty glass. "I wish I could be young again like you. Things would be different. I have nobody just my memories. I want to go home." His tears continued to roll down his cheeks as he fell asleep.

Josh wanted to go home too, back to Centralia. *Would I someday be an old man living on memories and regrets?*

While the old man slept, Josh decided to cut the GPS anklet off to see what would happen. He slid the blade of his newly found pocketknife behind the strap and pulled. It cut right through. Nothing happened. He slipped the GPS under the chair. He knew he couldn't run for it because the yard was rigged with motion sensors that turned on yard lights and alerted an app on the old man's phone. Josh clearly remembered what the old man said, "I'll use you for target practice." That scared Josh, but he had to explore the lodge. There may be way out — maybe a telephone.

He went straight to the kitchen. He opened the refrigerator. He saw beer and some strange looking food, and a beef log. He grabbed it. He searched the rest of the kitchen and the bar. Behind the bar he saw the old man's phone charger. He found a small box of Ziplock bags. He put his coins into one of them.

The kitchen opened into a hallway that had several doors. The first one led to a room that held a large table and several chairs. At the end, a new looking TV sat on an old, green metal serving cart. The next door opened to a large closet with house cleaning tools. He went in to see what he could use, but it looked like it would be wasted time. Then he saw a set of shelves that stood at an angle from the wall, he pulled it easily away and found himself looking into a dark hole. Then, a narrow staircase that curved out of sight into the darkness appeared.

An old-fashioned ceramic light switch was mounted just above the metal pipe handrail. Josh turned it. A string of bare bulbs, mostly burned out, lit the way down. The shelved door could be locked shut from the stair side. He stepped onto the stairs, quietly locking the door behind him.

The stairs opened to a large wine cellar and pantry. It had rows of shelves once filled with kitchen supplies and bottles. There were other abandoned things. Piled against one wall were several one-armed bandit slot machines. Odds and ends of household items were everywhere. A stack of empty wooden boxes labeled; "Canadian Club" sat next to an old wood burning kitchen stove. Next to it, he saw a concrete tunnel. It too had a set of shelves for a door that hung open.

He followed the tunnel until it came out in the boathouse, through yet another disguised door. The small windows in boathouse let in just enough light to illuminate a large old rum-running boat that sat on blocks well above the floor. It looked as though it had remained high and dry for decades. A wooden canoe leaned against a wall. Josh saw his chance for escape.

He pulled the old canoe toward the side door. Suddenly he saw headlights coming into the yard up by the lodge. They illuminated the boat house. He dropped everything and ran for the tunnel. He dashed through the pantry, then up the stairs. AS he unlocked the shelf door, he heard car doors slam outside. He made it back to his chair just as the kitchen door opened.

Two men and a woman came in, talking in their strange language. When they saw the old man sleeping, the two men shook him awake and yelled at him. They guided him to one of the many easy chairs that surrounded the polar bear rug. One of the men took the old man's gun and cell phone. The old man looked sheepishly at Josh, then curled up and went back to sleep. Josh shoved the beef log and Ziplock bag full of old coins, down beside the cushion.

The new arrivals hung around the bar eating from a paper tub of fried chicken and drinking beer, with occasional glances at Josh. They were two of the guys who kidnapped him. The older, taller one seemed to be in charge. It was he who had bound and blindfolded Josh during the kidnapping.

The woman said nothing while eating most of the chicken and washing it down with cans of beer. Her greasy-lipped smiles made Josh nervous. When she finished eating, she grabbed her beer and headed toward Josh. Too much beer and high heels kept her off balance. She looked down at Josh's GPS anklet. He held it steady between his ankles, so it wouldn't fall to the floor. Her watery brown eyes looked down at him. Her lips glistened with chicken fat.

CHAPTER 32

Dog arrived to stick his nose in the cushion crack where the beef log lay hidden.

"So, you're the President's kid." She didn't have a foreign accent like the others. She didn't look like them either.

"That's right. My name is Josh. What's your name?"

"Danielle."

"Why are you here?"

"I'm Jameel's girlfriend."

"Which one is Jameel?"

"He's the tall guy."

This chick was a bundle of information. Josh made mental notes. "So, what's the name of that water out there?"

"Why everybody knows that's the Potomac River."

"Really? Which way is Washington?"

Danielle pointed toward the kitchen. Dog pushed his nose deeper into the crack between the cushion and arm of the chair, making Josh very nervous. "I think Dog wants to go out."

Danielle coaxed Dog to the front door, and he left. As he walked across the veranda and down the steps, the motion detector alarm sounded on the old man's cell phone.

"Hey what are you doing?" Jameel yelled.

"The dog wanted out," Danielle said.

"Leave that dog alone and don't talk to the kid."

Josh leaned over and stuffed the GPS into his sock. "I have to go to the bathroom."

Jameel pointed toward the hallway. "You know where it is."

Once inside a stall, Josh cut off a length of shoelace and tied the GPS in place on his ankle. On the way back to his chair, he saw that the closet door was all the way open. The shelf door also hung open, exposing the dimly lighted wine cellar stairs. It was just as he had left it, rushing in from the boathouse. He quickly stepped into the closet, turned off the lights, and carefully pushed the shelf door shut. Then he returned to his chair. Dog ran around outside setting off motion detector alarms. Jameel called it in, then turned his attention to Josh. "Stand up."

Josh stood to be patted down. "When can I go home?"

"You should have thought of that before you ran away."

"So, when?"

"That's not up to me. Maybe never."

"Do I have to stay in this chair?"

"Consider it your home." Jameel took out his pocketknife, grabbed a hank of Josh's hair and cut it off.

"Ouch! That hurt. What are you doing?"

"Shut up."

Josh eventually calmed down and fell asleep listening to the old man snore.

The next morning the old man handed Josh a chicken bucket with the remaining pieces left over from the night before. That would be his breakfast.

Partway through a wing Josh yelled out, "Old man, you got anything to drink?"

"You like coffee?"

"Sure."

"There's a pot in the kitchen. Help yourself."

Josh went to the kitchen with Dog close behind. On return he sat his chicken bucket on the table where the old man. drank coffee. "So how are you this morning, Old Man?"

"What do you care?"

"I like you."

"Don't try getting friendly with me. You mean no more to me than a babysitting job."

"Sorry about that. Where is everybody?"

"None of your business."

"I'm tired of sitting in those chairs and you're tired of babysitting, so why don't we do something? We could take Dog for a walk, or maybe if that's your car out there we could go for a ride."

"I can fix your boredom. This place needs cleaning. There a men's room and a women's room at the end of the hall and four more bathrooms upstairs. You'll find everything you need in the hall closet. You can get started after you clean the kitchen."

Josh tossed a piece of not-so-crispy chicken skin at Dog and left for the kitchen.

At the same time, Jameel pulled up to a post office drop box, and tossed in a letter,

the one that contained Josh's lock of hair. Being careful to leave no fingerprints, he wore surgical gloves. He smiled. The letter would find its way to the White House and affirm that Josh was being held for political reasons.

When Josh finished cleaning the kitchen he went upstairs. He stopped on the balcony where he looked across the river to a housing development, and some larger buildings - maybe a half mile away. The land beyond lay flat and wooded. Because the sun rose in that direction, he knew he was on the west side of the river and south of Washington.

Josh alternated between cleaning and snooping. The upstairs bedrooms were like hotel rooms. The ones that opened onto the balcony were suites, each with its own bathroom, bedroom and sitting room. The ones opening onto the halls were single rooms without bathrooms. Each hall had a large communal bathroom at the end. All the rooms were wallpapered and there were no showers, just free-standing tubs. The floors were hardwood with large carpets. The bathrooms were white tile like the ones downstairs, but these had small windows through which Josh could see a long, muddy driveway winding westward through the trees.

Five of the rooms looked lived in. In one suite, clothes lay on the floor and a shirt draped over the back of an easy chair. Josh recognized it to be Jameel's. Odds and ends of personal things were scattered about on the dresser and other furniture.

Josh put his cleaning tools in the bathroom and snooped around Jameel's room. A notepad on the nightstand caught his eye. He flipped through several pages, stopping at some phone numbers. Suddenly, he heard footsteps on the balcony. He stuck the notepad in his back pocket and made it to the bathroom just as Jameel entered the room.

"Hey, what are doing in here?"

"The old man told me to clean the bathrooms."

"Not my room. You get out of my room." He grabbed Josh by the arm and pushed him onto the balcony while yelling at the old man. "Hadi, did you send this punk to clean my room?"

"No. I would never do that. Just the bathrooms."

Jameel dragged Josh down the stairs and pushed him into an easy chair. "Don't get out of that chair or I'll hurt you." He kicked Josh in the shin for emphasis, knocking his poorly attached ankle bracelet to the floor. Jameel immediately turned his attention to yelling at the old man in the strange language that these people used.

Josh shoved his Ziplock bag of coins down beside the chair cushion along with Jameel's notebook. He re-tied his ankle bracelet. As soon as Jameel finished yelling at the old man, he returned and searched Josh.

The day dragged on. By late afternoon Jameel's dirty van headed back up the driveway, leaving Josh and the old man alone.

"Old man. Can I get some water?"

"Go ahead."

After getting a drink, Josh went to the bar where the old man nursed a freshly poured glass of wine. He sat down next to him, and asked, "Did you ever go back to where you came from?" For once, the old man seemed to soften a bit.

"Once I did. After a few years in your country I got homesick. I wanted to be around people like me and do things I did in the old days, but it wasn't the same. I didn't know anybody. Things looked different, and people were doing different things. My world lived only in my memory."

"I want to go home too. That's why I ran away. I just don't belong in Washington DC. It's not home."

The old man poured another glass of wine.

"Do you think I could have some of that?" Josh asked.

"Get a glass."

Josh got a glass from behind the bar. The old man's cell charger still lay back there. The two sipped wine and talked.

"So how long did you visit home?" Josh asked.

"Just long enough to know that I had no home. Anyway, I had to get back to work."

"What kind of work?"

"I drove a cab in New York. I knew every street in Manhattan. I used that knowledge to help my countrymen do their work."

"What kind of work?"

"That's not important." The old man poured more wine. Now, instead of being caustic, the wine seemed to mellow him out.

"I don't understand you. You have everything you could possibly want, and you want to run off somewhere. Don't you know you have nowhere to run too? You can never return to your old life. It's gone. If it's something you love, then cherish the memory. You need to find new things to do and new places. Don't wind up like me, chasing a cause that I no longer believe in, with nothing to show for it but regret."

"Do you think I could have a little more wine?"

"Sure. If it makes you feel better, have some more wine."

Josh woke up sleeping next to Dog in the middle of the polar bear rug. He could hear the old man busy in the kitchen. After a breakfast of hard-boiled eggs and beans, the beginning of another boring day began. Josh decided to teach Dog some tricks. He worked on high five and sit and stay, all the while thinking about his escape. Every moment of every day, Josh waited for his chance to disappear to the boathouse and freedom. That afternoon, the old man tossed him a couple of National Geographic magazines.

"Thanks, Old Man. Where did these come from?"

"There's all kinds of old crap around here."

"Your name is Hadi. Isn't it?"

"How did you find that out?"

"Jameel called you that."

"So, you know his name too. How many more names do you know?"

"Just Danielle. That's all."

"You keep calling me Old Man and forget those other names. Never mention them again. Do you understand me?"

"Yeah, I got it."

Josh spent the rest of the afternoon reading about life along the Amazon River. It was like a time capsule from the 1930s, inspiring his hope of escape as he saw a man in a dugout canoe paddling across a broad expanse of water.

Josh lifted his gaze to the Potomac River beyond the boathouse. He let his imagination loose as he saw *himself* gliding across that expanse of water, as free as an aboriginal Amazonian.

That afternoon, the old man put a chess board on the table.

"Hey kid, you know how to play chess?"

"No"

"You want to learn?"

"Sure."

Once Josh got the hang of it, they played until dinner. The daily routine included boring days followed by wine and conversation. Three men and the old man lived there, and sometimes Danielle, but only the old man was his steady babysitter. He never went anywhere. One of the others would watch both of them at night.

After a dinner of cold convenience store pizza that Jameel brought, the old man and Josh continued sipping wine and talking.

Josh said, "You know that every law enforcement agency in the county is looking for me. They'll find me and when they do, they'll find you and the rest of these guys. You and your buddies will spend the rest of your life in prison."

"Are you threatening me?"

"I like you. I don't want to see you get in trouble. Why don't you just pack up and leave before it's too late."

"It's not that easy. Besides, where you're going nobody will find you."

CHAPTER 33

Security screeners pulled a business sized envelope out of the White House mail and put it aside. Because it contained a suspicious lump, an X-ray was taken showing a lock of hair. That's when the Secret Service was called in. If cleared, it would be filed away or delivered to the President. If not cleared, the FBI would investigate.

Amy stuck her head in the door. "Mister President, you'll want to see this. It's about Josh."

Al jumped to his feet and met Amy at his office door. The Director of the Office of Presidential Corr-espondence stood at her side. He handed Al an already opened envelope. Al pulled out a lock of hair and a handwritten note that read, "Your son is safe and well. When it is clear the United States will not interfere in the Middle East, your son Joshua will be released unharmed. We are responsible for Connor's incident at school and could harm any one of your friends and family. Leave the caliphate alone."

Al stared at the lock of hair. He knew it was Josh's. "Who all knows about this?"

"It's been thoroughly tested," the director said. "No fingerprints or harmful chemicals were found. It was post marked in Alexandria Virginia The FBI and NSA are on it."

"I can see the postmark. It's three days ago. Why am I the last to know?"

"Sorry sir. Bear in mind, you receive thousands of pieces of mail every day. Sometimes one looks suspicious and will be X-rayed or tested to ensure that no dangerous mail is forwarded to the White House. This is one such letter. The moment it cleared I hand carried it to your office."

"Three days. My son's life is at stake and you spend three days investigating a letter?"

"No sir. The postal service had it for two of those days. We got it for you as soon we were able."

"You get any more mail about my son and I want to know immediately. I don't care how dangerous it looks."

"We will sir. What we know is that the author of this letter is right-handed, and probably a foreigner, because the handwriting is not the way most Americans write. Poor command of the English language could mean that English is not his first language. The FBI thinks it's from someone of Middle Eastern origin. Handwriting, like language, has a kind of accent to it."

"So, this looks like Josh's hair but how can I be sure?"

"FBI is doing a DNA test. My job is to take care of the mail. I really don't know much else."

"Of course, thank you. "

Al called an immediate press briefing. He had Tracy at his side. He delivered a simple message. "Terrorists have Joshua. I have received a lock of his hair with a message that says he will be returned if we turn away from our rescue mission to the Mediterranean. I can't do that. Americans don't make deals with terrorists. You will return our son, and you will return him safely. Several agencies are following leads right now that will find Joshua and find you. We are closer than you might think. When we find you, expect to suffer the consequences of your crimes. Do you feel safe? A SWAT team could come at you, or a swarm of drones could annihilate you anywhere. You must let him go."

Senator Case conference-called Vice-president Bates and Sol. "This kidnapping fiasco has gone far enough," Case said. "It has to stop."

"How? If the kid is released, he'll identify his captors," Bates said.

"Then get the kidnappers out of the country," Case said.

"Do you know where those stupid kidnappers are keeping that kid?" Sol interrupted. "In a place I own on the Potomac River. If the kid goes free, how long do you think it would take to find out who owns that place? The caliphate wants the kid. They think they can use him to intimidate the President. If they want to keep the kid, they have to pull him out of the country."

The three agreed. Joshua would have to leave the United States. Sol notified his contact. Jameel arranged for a charter fishing boat for the next day.

Fred's phone rang. It was Mark. The assistant AG had a soil type analysis ready, on the mud taken from the gas station where Josh was abducted. The kidnappers had picked up the mud somewhere in the rather broad area of the lower Potomac River Valley. This, combined with information from various videos that showed the kidnappers van heading South on I-95 and the letter with the hair sample being mailed in Virginia caused Fred to believe that Josh might be held somewhere near the river south of Washington, on the Virginia side. To develop his hunch, he outlined a grid of secondary roads east of I-95 and south of Washington. He would start with the highway closest to the river. He drove south, stopping at each gas station and convenience store to ask if anyone had seen the dirty brown van. He showed them a surveillance camera picture of the dirty van. He used the same story he told people before; that he was trying to solve a string of convenience story robberies. Everyone was eager to help. After several stops, Fred showed an attendant the photo and got a hit.

"Sure, I've seen that van," the young man at the minimart said.

"Tell me what you know about it."

"I've seen it a couple of times. Easy to remember. The guy who drives it paid cash for gas both times and loaded up with snacks and cheap red wine."

"Can you describe him?"

"Tall, slim and has thick, black hair and a short black beard, and he's rude. Who could forget him?" He went on. "He's maybe thirty-five or so and has a strong foreign accent." He let Fred see a video. There were several frames of the van taken at various times. The kidnappers were regulars at this store. In frames where the van was parked at a pump heading south, the tires showed some mud. In frames where the van was heading north, the tires were thick with mud. The kidnappers had to be somewhere nearby and south of the store.

Fred drove south searching the side of the road for any sign of a dirt road or muddy driveway. Less than a mile from the store he saw it. An old iron gate hung open between two stone pillars. Between them a muddy drive with fresh, deep ruts ran toward the river. Muddy tire tracks headed north onto the pavement. Other than the ruts the property looked abandoned. Because it was late in the day, Fred could see bits of light through the trees and some dark chimney smoke a hundred yards from the road. He stopped just past the driveway. There was enough daylight light left to photograph the muddy tire prints. He moved his car a few hundred feet down the road to a pullout next to some mailboxes where he could watch the driveway without being seen. While he waited, he called Mark. "I think I found where the kidnappers are staying," he explained. He then texted the photos of the tire tracks and a photo of the mailboxes with addresses showing.

Mark and Al decided to give Fred's information to the FBI. The FBI agent was skeptical of information provided by some private detective. He wanted to check out Fred's background. They couldn't just barge onto private property on someone's hunch. While Fred sat in his car watching what he found, his phone rang. It was the FBI. He explained how he found the property, and all that had led him to the muddy driveway.

"We have to talk," the agent said, "stop your surveillance now."

Fred was given an address for the meeting. He pulled onto the highway and headed back to Washington.

An hour after Fred left for Washington a brown van turned into the muddy drive to the lodge. It was the fifth night of Josh's captivity. Jameel walked into the lodge with Danielle and the two other kidnappers. He handed Josh a shopping bag. "Go to the bathroom and change clothes. While you're in there, clean up. Tomorrow morning you're going on a fishing trip."

Josh stayed awake into the night. By midnight, only Jameel remained in the room, slumped over the bar and sound asleep. Josh got up and walked toward the door. The dog followed. He let it out. Just as before, the motion detector sounded on the old man's cell phone lying on the bar. Jameel raised his head and looked at Josh. "What are you doing?"

"Dog wanted out."

"Don't do that again."

Josh stood at the window watching the dog walk around the yard. It set off another motion alarm and the yard light came on – enough light to illuminate the end of the canoe where it stuck out of the side door of the boathouse door.

"Can I let Dog in?" Josh asked.

"I'll do it. You stay away from the windows."

Josh knew he had to make a run for it. He didn't want to find out what kind of fishing trip he would be going on. As soon as his captor returned to sleep, Josh sneaked over and opened the door. He threw a piece of the beef log through the opening and went back to his chair. The dog took off after it, followed by a motion detector alarm. Jameel jumped out of his chair. "What's going on? I told you not to let the dog out?"

The dog came running back in. Dog stood looking at Josh.

"The woman did it before she went upstairs," Josh said.

Jameel walked over and slammed the door. "Are you sure?"

"Yeah. She woke me up. She wanted to talk. Can't you keep her away from me?"

Jameel headed for the rooms upstairs. Josh took off his ankle monitor and tied it to Dog's collar. As soon as Jameel was out of sight, Josh grabbed his cellphone and crammed the Ziplock bag and notebook into his pocket. He ran. He grabbed the old man's charger from under the bar as he headed through the kitchen. He opened the door and threw the beef log as far as he could across the yard and into the woods. Dog shot out the door after it. Alarms went off. Josh ran for the tunnel. He locked the shelf door behind him and ran down the tunnel to the boat house. He grabbed the canoe and dragged it into the water. He looked back at the lodge as he cast off.

Lights were coming on and Josh heard someone crashing through the brush. With one push of an oar he moved out of sight of the lodge into the protection of the trees that hung over the river. He could hear his captors shouting and searching the brush as he drifted quietly with the current. A low fog hung over the river dimming the lights from the far shore. The cold air chilled him. Josh slipped his oar in the water, guiding the canoe as close to the shore as he dared. He paddled with the current, moving steadily away from the lodge. But the crashing in the brush grew closer. Then a splash in the water and the sound of someone swimming toward him. Josh dug his ore deeper into the water.

Suddenly, through the moonlit water, his pursuer could be seen. It was Dog. Josh helped Dog into the canoe. He pulled the GPS from its collar and threw it in the river. The shore was silent as he paddled downriver hugging the bank for cover. In his snooping around the lodge, Josh saw no other boat except the big one in the boathouse. He felt safe that his kidnappers couldn't chase him on the water. He paddled steadily down-stream, his feet were wet from launching the canoe, but they seemed to be getting wetter. The old canoe was leaking. Down river, a row of docks protruded out over the water. As he approached, Josh saw a row of houses from which they jutted. Only a few lights were on, giving evidence of a community asleep. Josh had to get across the river, but not in a leaky canoe. He paddled close to the docks, looking for any kind of boat to cross the Potomac. Suddenly headlights appeared, as a car headed down a driveway. Over this shoulder, Josh saw the brown minivan. They weren't coming for him by water, they were coming by land.

Other docks appeared ahead of him, as he paddled past the first one. The water in the canoe now reached his ankles. Each dock had at least one boat tied up. The car stopped near the water. Two men jumped out. A flashlight beam swept across lawns and docks toward Josh.

Josh ducked down and guided his canoe under a dock. He ditched the canoe and climbed onto the dock where three fishing boats were moored. Jameel was a couple of hundred feet away and closing fast. Josh pulled Dog along as he ducked under the edge of a boat cover. He found himself in the pitch dark of an aluminum fishing boat. He groped his way quickly to the driver's seat. He took out his knife and slashed open the cover above the windshield. It gave enough light to see the dashboard, and an ignition key slot.

Josh felt wires under the dash. This thing could be hot-wired. He moved quietly to the port side of the boat and loosened the lines to let it drift in the river current. As he did, he looked out to see two men with a flashlight getting closer. He returned to the dashboard, took a large silver coin from his pocket and placed it underneath, across the contacts of the ignition. He had learned about things like this, working around his dad's shop. The dash lights came on. He pushed the starter button. The outboard motor cranked and roared to life as Jameel jumped onto the front deck of the boat. He had a flashlight in one hand and a gun in the other. Josh pulled the throttle back hard. Jameel fell back grasping for the dock, where he hit his head and splashed into the river. Once clear of the dock, Josh sped toward the center of the river.

Shots popped behind him. Two bullets pierced the plastic windshield. Josh looked back. Lights were coming on in the houses. He saw Jameel climbing a ladder out of the water, as his buddy stood on the dock squeezing off one last round in Josh's direction. It pierced the transom and continued into the gas can. Josh kept one hand on the wheel and one hand under the dash, pressing his old coin against the ignition terminals. He could smell the leaking fuel. How long would it be until all the gas leaked out, or caught on fire?

On the far side of the river he slowed down and followed the shore looking for a good place to hide the boat. After a few minutes, he saw an inlet where large trees overhung the river. He nosed the boat under the branches and beached it in the mud.

Police arrived at the riverfront home where shots were reported. Homeowners said they saw two men running across lawns to a brown minivan. They were last seen backing up a driveway. Several neighbors came out to see what had happened. Most of them called the cops. One homeowner ran yelling to the police that his fishing boat was stolen. The owner said he could hear the boat cross the river toward the Maryland side, where it disappeared into the fog.

At the stolen fishing boat's empty moorage, the deputies found wet footprints and drops of blood. Nine-millimeter shell casings lay on the deck. More cops showed up. A police boat arrived to search the river for a possible shooting victim and the stolen boat. Soon a helicopter joined the search. Crime scene investigators showed up to collect evidence. A news helicopter circled above the river, but the boat was hidden under the overhanging trees and the early morning fog. The FBI was not notified.

CHAPTER 34

Josh and Dog slogged through the mud to dry ground, where they entered a quiet street in a nice housing development. They walked through the neighborhood together, avoiding any cars that passed. Dog trailed along on a leash fashioned from a rope from the boat cover. Soon, the glow of morning affirmed that they were headed east.

As the sky lightened, traffic increased. Eventually, they approached a shopping mall that had a Safeway. He tied Dog to a pillar in front and entered, sure he could find a plug-in for the phone charger. It would be safe, as no one knew of his new phone except Cole. And there it was; next to the pharmacy and a blood pressure cuff. It worked!

Cole's phone chirped. He whipped it out and stared at the display. "It's Josh!" he shouted to the President's family at the breakfast table. "His phone is active!"

"Call Fred right now." Al ordered.

Cole did so immediately. "Fred, I know where Josh is. His phone went active just a minute ago."

"Don't say anything more. Your phone may be monitored. Where's Mark?"

"Right here, having breakfast with the Goodwin's."

"Give Mark your phone."

Mark's Mustang was parked near the North Portico. He and Cole ran to it, with Al right behind. A secret service agent caught up. "What's going on?"

"Tell you later," Al said.

Mark's Mustang pealed out of the White House driveway. Nothing more would be said until the two were with Fred. An anxious President Goodwin stood at the White House door.

Mark screeched to a stop across the street from the Capital Grind. Fred jumped in. The car left a trail of black rubber, as they hastened to find Josh. Cole gave Fred the coordinates of Josh's phone; located East of the Potomac river and south of Washington. Mark keyed this into his GPS, and the threesome headed for Pennsylvania Avenue and the east side of the river.

While a police boat searched for the stolen fishing boat, Sol's phone rang. It was Jameel. "Bad news Sol. The kid got away."

"What do you mean, got away?"

"The kid tricked us. He snuck down river in an old canoe. We caught up with him while he was stealing a fishing boat. We shot at him, but we had to get away fast. Lights were coming on in a row of houses. I didn't know if we hit him or not. He headed across the river. We just now arrived on the Maryland side of the Potomac. We're looking for him. I think the kid ditched the boat and took off on foot on the Maryland side. We think he has a yellow Labrador retriever with him."

"You listen to me, Jameel, and you listen good. Your boss expects that boy to be on the Midnight Express. Some dumb kid with a yellow dog shouldn't be all that hard to find. The cops probably don't yet know who they're looking for. A stolen boat and some shots fired aren't that unusual. You have a head start on catching that kid. He can't be allowed to talk. When you find him, finish him off. And get rid of that van like I told you to, then get out of the country. No one must know that you had that kid in my lodge. Do you understand?"

When the President walked into the West Wing, Amy was waiting. "You need to watch the news," she said, "an early morning shooting on the Potomac River involved a minivan and two men that match the description of those involved in the kidnapping of Josh. It all happened less than a mile from where Fred found that property yesterday." Amy played a recording for Al. "It had to be Josh who stole the boat."

"Amy, call the sheriff's office and see what you can find out. Get the FBI too. They had better be on top of this."

Being visible in a Safeway store made Josh nervous. He wanted to get going. A partial phone charge was good enough. He unplugged his phone and headed for the front door. As it opened a dirty, brown Minivan came into view in the parking lot. Josh looked for a place to hide.

"Hey look. Doesn't that look like Hadi's dog?" Jameel pointed to the front of the Safeway store where Dog stood tied to a pillar. The van skidded to a stop in front of the store. Jameel and his companion jumped out of the van and ran into the store. They split up. Jameel would search the front, his cohort, the rear.

Josh hunkered down under an organic fruit display in the produce section at the front of the store and pulled out his phone.

Cole's phone rang. It was Josh. "I'm in a Safeway store hiding from the kidnappers. They're here in the store looking for me. I don't know where the store is."

"We've got your location and we're almost there. Stay hidden."

Josh heard footsteps nearby. He silenced his phone. When the sounds faded, he peeked out and saw no one. He could, however, see out the front door, where the van sat near to where Dog was tied. The engine was running, and the driver's door hung open. Josh saw his chance.

He bolted from his hiding place, grabbed Dog and jumped into the van, cramming it into reverse. Jameel reached the van in time to grab the passenger door and pull it open. Josh slammed on the brakes and shifted into drive. Jameel hung onto the door handle, trying to point his gun at Josh, but he lost his balance and fell free of the van. Josh sped onto the highway in the direction of Washington. Jameel and his companion ran after him and kept running until they were out of the mall.

Out of breath, the two kidnappers ducked by a dumpster behind a church. Jameel called another operative who was nearby searching for Josh, driving the blue Ford Escape. Soon all three of the kidnappers were together in the Escape heading after Josh.

The commotion of the two men running through the store toward their disappearing van, guns in hand, caused the store manager to dial 911, as did a couple of concerned customers.

Mark pulled into the Safeway parking lot. A sheriff's cruiser idled at the curb in front of the store. "What now?" Cole asked.

Mark got out of the car. "I have to see what's going on. I'll be right back." He walked nonchalantly into the store and rushed out a moment later. "Grocery checker said some kid ran out of the store and jumped into a brown minivan. He drove onto the highway going north, with two men chasing him on foot. Looks like Josh stole the kidnapper's van."

"Alright!" Yelled Cole as he bounced up and down in the confined back seat of the Mustang.

"We can't do anything here," Fred said. "Let's go after Josh."

Mark called Al. "Josh has escaped in his his captors van. He's heading north on the Indian Head highway. So are we."

The deputies, responding to the call at Safeway, linked it with the boat theft and shooting, and notified the FBI. The FBI connected it with the kidnapping.

Josh reasoned that Jameel wouldn't report his van stolen, so he felt safe to drive on toward Washington. He didn't know that one of Jameel's men had picked him up in the blue Ford Escape and were only a couple of miles behind.

As Josh drove, he remembered what the old man told him about returning home where he found everything had changed. Josh knew that life would be different for him too. People wanted to harm him. There would be no going back. It wasn't even safe to be in public. He just wanted to be with his family, and the security of their new home. He was tired, cold, hungry, and thirsty. He bounced in his seat to stay awake. He rolled down the window. Cold air buffeted his face, barely keeping him awake. He took an off-ramp into a large parking lot and stopped at a Burger King, which occupied its most visible corner.

Jameel was a slob. The inside of the van looked like the bottom of a dumpster. Josh dug through it and put on a dirty sweatshirt. In the armrest he found a handful of coins and garbage. Enough money to drive through Burger King. He ordered two breakfast burritos and a large water. He and Dog wolfed them down and then he called Cole.

"Where are you?" Cole answered.

"I don't know. I'm in the parking lot of a Burger King. According to the road signs I'm almost in Washington on highway 210."

Mark grabbed the phone. "Don't go anywhere. We're almost there."

Josh backed the van into a corner of the parking lot where he could watch the entrance. He waited.

Fred, Mark and Cole were still a few miles away, when Josh saw a blue Ford Escape enter the parking lot. He recognized it as the one parked by the lodge. It had muddy tires just like the van. He recognized the driver as one of the kidnappers. *How many more people are looking for me*, Josh wondered. The Ford Escape drove to the far end of the lot. As soon as the Escape disappeared behind a building, Josh pulled onto the highway in the direction of Washington. He took the first exit he saw, into an industrial park. He ditched the van at the end of a row of trucks, threw the keys in the bushes and took off on foot between warehouses until he saw a well-manicured office building. Before entering it, Josh called Cole and told him what was happening.

Inside the building, a stylish young woman at a spotless desk asked what he wanted. Josh said he was expecting to meet someone, and could he wait for them here, "for just a few minutes." The young lady sized him up. A skinny, unkempt kid in a dirty navy-blue sweat-shirt, one size too large. He held a rope tied around the neck of a damp, smelly dog. She sensed trouble. "Who are you waiting for?" asked the young lady.

"A ride home. They should be here soon." He spotted a small table with coffee and doughnuts. "May I?" He asked.

She hesitated, afraid to say no. "Sure. You look familiar. Have you been here before?" From his appearance, she knew otherwise. *Perhaps he's a street person. Maybe he's running from the law.* She placed her cell phone on her lap and dialed 911.

"No. I'm not from around here." He handed Dog a doughnut. He ate it in one gulp.

"I know I've seen you somewhere. Do you work around here someplace?"

"No."

"Where do you live?"

"Washington -- both of them."

"Both? What do you mean?"

"I have a home in Washington State, and I live in Washington DC."

A Forest green Mustang Bullitt pulled up in front. "That's my ride. I have to go."

"Isn't the President from Washington State? Hey, I know who you are."

Josh and Dog dashed out the door. "Thanks for the doughnuts," Josh called back. They squeezed into the small backseat next to Cole. Fred scooted his seat forward to make room. Mark stepped on it, pipes roaring as the Mustang shot out of the industrial park and onto the highway. The young lady in the office reported to 911 that the President's son had just left her office.

Beyond the parking lot, Jameel's Ford Escape came in sight. they had seen Josh and Dog squeeze into the Mustang and speed off. The Explorer gave chase. Tires screaming, it fishtailed onto the highway directly behind Mark. A passenger in the Escape rolled down his window and leaned out, pistol in hand. Every time Mark found an opening in the heavy morning traffic, so did Jameel. Just as Mark gunned it through a red light, Jameel's passenger started shooting. but his bullets went wide. While Mark dodged around several cars, weaving away from his pursuers, Fred held his phone to his ear and talked to police. The Mustang pressed on, driven by a man with the skills of a race car driver.

When sirens could be heard in the distance. Jameel lost hope. He pulled into a parking lot and hid while the cops, with lights flashing and siren wailing, cleared a path toward the Mustang. As soon as they passed, Jameel headed toward I-95 and the Salt Breeze Charter in Florida.

Police cars surrounded Mark's car. As they traveled toward the White House, more law enforcement vehicles joined in, forming a motorcade. Mark presented his pass at the White House gate. Surprised by what he saw, the agent at the checkpoint smiled at Josh. He waved them through with a "Welcome home."

Josh, Cole, Mark and Fred unpacked from Mark's Mustang, all smelling like wet dog. They were met by FBI agents, secret service agents and the President. Al grabbed Josh in his arms. Josh was glad to be back, but not enough to be hugged. He wiggled free. There was no time for sentiments or conversation. Everyone went to the Green Room, where more agents waited. The interrogation began immediately. As tired as he was, Josh had to endure a debriefing of his ordeal. He told them everything. Each of the others were also questioned. Soon, The FBI had names and descriptions including Jameel's notebook with all of its phone numbers, including Sol's and Ibrahim Bin Jabar's. The questioning went on into the afternoon. Eventually, Josh was handed over to his mom who took him upstairs. During the whole ordeal, Josh refused to let go of Dog.

The FBI took Fred to his office where he gave them the names of all thirty-three congressmen and the Vice-president. His report included the evidence given to Marion West, who in turn gave detailed personal information to Sol Solomon. Sol used that information to blackmail congressmen into supporting a caliphate. Fred's office computers and files were confiscated. He thought he would be arrested, but he was left standing alone in his ransacked office.

Ironically, he had accomplished what the fraudulent American Anti-Corruption League said they would do. Through his activities, he caused at least thirty-three corrupted congressmen to be exposed.

Fred called Marion. "I suppose you know by now that the President's son is home safe."

"How could I not? There's nothing else on the news."

"Because of my involvement in the rescue, I had to answer a lot of questions. The FBI took all my files, both from my office and from home. I already destroyed any evidence of witnessing the Carlson assassination. You should destroy all the information you have about these investigations. If you don't, the FBI with grab it. They already know who the corrupt congressmen are, including the man-in-black who is in fact Sol Solomon —your Arthur Bishop — just like I told you. You should expect a visit from the FBI real soon. Be ready to own up to our investigation."

"Own up to what? We had a legitimate contract to provide information. How was I to know we were employed by phonies. You're the one who figured that out. All I wanted were names. I'll deny any wrongdoing."

"Tell the truth, Marion. The worst that can happen would be charges of illegal surveillance of members of congress. After they find out what these congressmen did, they'll probably forget all about you. Play this up as a service to your country."

"I didn't tell you to do any illegal surveillance. That was your doing."

Fred hung up.

The next morning found a congress in chaos. Overriding the caliphate bill veto became impossible and opposition to Al's rescue mission evaporated. Congress was too busy cleaning house to worry about the President. Thirty-three corrupt congressman had to be dealt with. The impeachment trial went on hold — maybe permanently.

Senator Morris Weinberg and Secretary of Defense Tory Thorson discussed recent events over tea and Fig Newtons in Weinberg's office.

"From the looks of things, we should have gotten congress elected by lottery, instead of the President."

"You might be right," Weinberg said, "When our constitution was drafted, John Adams wrote that the legislature should be a 'portrait, in miniature, of the people at large.' We don't fit that picture. We are mostly white, protestant and male. Most of us are lawyers and millionaires. Some of us are criminals. We spend huge sums of money on endless campaigning, resulting in new congresses indistinguishable from the old."

"Would we be better off picking people at random for congress?"

"Why not? We select juries from lists of registered voters. That works. Jurors get their jobs done without being professional jurors. I bet Congress could do the same."

"If congress were as interested in the American people as they are in themselves, we wouldn't be having this conversation."

Ann Mercer heard enough. Instead of pouring more tea, she cleared the cookies and cups from the coffee table. "Don't you boys have something better to do?"

It was Al's turn to ask questions. Josh had a lot to tell him about his abduction and the abductors. When he paused, Al asked. "Do you want to go back to Centralia with Cole? You can if you want."

Josh was dumbfounded. *I don't need to run away anymore. I can go with Cole.* He hesitated a long time before he spoke. "Things are different. I don't think there's much left to go home to. I'd rather stay here."

That afternoon, the FBI released Cole's belongs. Al went through his car, servicing it in the driveway in front of the White House, getting it ready for Cole's trip home. The press finally had what they hoped for; pictures of the President, all greasy, bent over the engine of an old beat-up car.

It was late. Al and Tracy could finally relax. Their boy was safe at home, and threats to the family were at an end. Al grabbed the remote. A few clicks, and the Night Show with Archie MacArthur came on. Archie's giant screen showed the guilty faces of congress — the ones so far identified. Archie danced his way on stage while the band played a rendition of Jail House Rock. Archie wore a black and white striped prison uniform.

"I'm wearing the new fashion trend of congress. In Washington yesterday, the President's son broke loose from his captors. In the process, crimes of treason and a catalogue of other offenses, were uncovered in congress. Take a good look at those pictured behind me and ask yourself, how do these people get in congress?"

The pictures were photoshopped with black and white striped uniforms like Archie's. The band switched to playing, You're in the Jailhouse Now.

"Check out the photo top center. You should recognize Vice-president Lyle Bates, or should I say former vice-president. He hasn't been seen since yesterday morning. This afternoon the President Announced that his personal advisor, Mark Pierce — another mechanic, would become vice-president. Pretty soon you'll be able to take the White House tour while getting your oil changed." The screen switched to a picture of Al and Mark with their heads under the hood of Cole's beat up old Volkswagen Jetta.

Chapter 35

With a fresh warrant in hand, several FBI agents converged on the hunting lodge. Vehicles filled the yard, including an armored SWAT personnel carrier. Snipers trained their sights on the doors, and windows, grenade launchers were armed with tear gas, an agent with a bullhorn addressed the building. "You, inside! We have you surrounded. Come out with your hands above your head. You must come out now!"

Since they found no cars on the property, the agents weren't even sure anyone was in the lodge. One agent stealthy climbed through a coal shoot door and up into the lodge. An upstairs window swung open, revealing a waving hand. "Don't shoot. Don't shoot. Please, please." It was Danielle.

"Put both your hands out where I can see them, and don't move," the bullhorn continued.

She showed her hands, afraid to do anything else.

"Who all is in there with you?" The bullhorn said.

"I don't know," Danielle replied. "I just woke up. What are you doing?"

"Never mind. Do exactly as I say. Come out of the house with your hands above your head."

"I have to get dressed first"

"Right now."

Danielle was scared. She quickly pulled on her jeans and blouse. Suddenly her door opened. A man in black uniform rushed her, frisked her and handcuffed her. It was the agent who had crawled through the coal shoot.

With her hands cuffed and her feet bare, she was escorted through the kitchen door and removed to the far side of the SWAT vehicle, where she stood with cold mud squeezing between her toes. The SWAT team entered the building. More FBI agents arrived to process the lodge as a crime scene.

As soon as Hadi heard the SWAT team arrive, he grabbed the wine jug from under the counter and ran into the tunnel beneath the lodge and the hidden wine cellar. He locked the door behind him and crept down the dark stairs. There, he slid an empty wooden box next to a wall and waited, afraid to even breathe – but the secret tunnel did just as it was designed to do. Even the FBI couldn't find it.

Once in custody, Danielle couldn't stop talking. She gave the names of the kidnappers, what kind of cars they drove, and that the President's son had been a captive in the lodge. She couldn't remember Hadi's name. She referred to him as some old guy. She didn't know where he went. She didn't know where anybody went. Most importantly for Hadi, she didn't know about the secret speakeasy era wine cellar. She didn't know much of anything; just a naive girlfriend, arrested as an accomplice.

After two days of quietly staying hidden, Hadi realized that the investigating agents were gone. Having only a half-gallon of red wine to sustain him he was cold, dehydrated, and hungry. He opened the secret door that led into the house, where he drank water and found food. Then he sneaked up to the second floor where he found furniture tipped over and items scattered. A thorough search was obvious. Gathering warm clothes, he prepared himself to be outside for a long time.

Still on edge, he made his way back through the secret tunnel to the boathouse where he emerged into the moonlight. Careful not to go near any motion detectors, he snuck through the dark woods. At daybreak, he entered the road well away from the lodge and walked until he reached public transportation. He kept going until he disappeared into New York City.

While the lodge was being raided, Sol was hurrying to leave the country. At his condo, he gathered his most important documents into his briefcase and stuck his fake ID into his wallet. Sol was now Arthur Bishop. He drove to his bank where he closed his account and took as much cash as the bank would allow and stuffed it into his coat pocket. The rest of his money he transferred to his Cayman Islands account. Next, he went to a shipping agent where he crated his possessions along with his briefcase and all the ID that showed him to be Sol Solomon. The crates were addressed to Arthur Bishop in the Cayman Islands. With that done, he called his housekeeper, Marla, to say he would soon be on the island, then he smashed his phone and dropped it in a trash receptacle. Finally, he had an Uber drive him out to Dulles airport where he had booked a flight to the Cayman Islands.

Sol flew South, knowing the FBI would quickly make the connection between him and the kidnapping. It was all Jameel's fault for taking the President's kid to his lodge. But it was too late to do anything about that. He made Sol Solomon disappear and was now Arthur Bishop, the alternate identity provided by Ibrahim.

Sol looked below as his plane passed over the last bit of the United States and then the Gulf of Mexico. He left behind a lifestyle and way of living that he loved. Now he must embrace a new lifestyle, one of wealth and Leisure. He looked forward to his small waterfront house in West Bay on Grand Cayman Island, and the marina where his cabin cruiser waited. Arthur Bishop was ready for some serious deep-sea fishing and island living.

Marla met him at the airport and drove him to his house at the marina. On the island he was known only as Arthur Bishop except at his bank and he was about to take care of that. At his house he changed into shorts, Hawaiian shirt, and sandals. Thus, began the first day of his new island life. He opened his garage door and jumped into his roadster. While the FBI searched for Sol Solomon, Art drove to his Cayman Island bank to transfer his money into a new account under his new name. But when he presented his credentials, the teller said, "that's a closed account."

"Closed! What do mean closed. That's my account."

"Yes sir, it is yours, but it was closed by the co-owner of the account."

Sol didn't know he had a co-owner, but he knew that Ibrahim made the deposits. As he let this sink in, the teller apologized. "I 'm sorry, Mister Solomon. There is nothing else I can tell you. You will have to contact your co-owner."

"But...but... is there money in the account?"

"No sir, all the money has been withdrawn and the account is closed."

Sol's usefulness to Ibrahim was over. He felt betrayed.

All he had left was his stash of valuables in his home safe at the marina, but it was enough to live well for a long time. Sol tried to relax, with no clue that this was only the beginning of troubles.

Marla had a late lunch ready for him, but he just couldn't eat. Millions of his dollars had disappeared,

Even though he had a stash worth a few million dollars, Life would not be as lavish as he had dreamed, but he was glad to have escaped prosecution for his crimes.

While his housekeeper was in the kitchen cleaning up, Sol called out, "Marla, we need to talk."

"Sure." she said

, placing his martini on the coffee table.

"I have decided to live here full-time. I'll still need someone to keep an eye on the place, but I can take care of my own cooking. I want you to continue with the maintenance of the house and boat as before. Does that sound alright?"

"Sure. Any way you want it is fine with me." Marla sensed that Sol was in trouble.

"I'm glad to hear that. You're still welcome to use the boat.

"Thank you, Mister Bishop. That's more than generous."

"I have a favor to ask. I have to pick up my stuff at the airport tomorrow. Could you drive me in your husband's truck? My car's too small."

Next morning, Marla parked in front of the airfreight office and Sol went in to clear his shipment with customs. Sol signed the necessary paperwork, while a man loaded the crates into Marla's truck. Sol felt a tap on his shoulder. He turned to see three men. One held out a gold coin. Surprised, Sol Said, "What are you doing here?"

"We have been waiting for you. Mister Jabar wants to see you."

"I don't understand. What does he want?"

"I do not have details. He will explain when he sees you. Just come with us. He is waiting for you."

"Where?"

"We have a car waiting."

The two men with the coin bearer moved to flank Sol and steered him toward the door.

Marla watched from her parking spot. Sol had a man gripping each arm. They muscled him toward a waiting car. She didn't know what was happening. Sol wasn't expecting anyone. When the car left, she followed it at a distance, straight to the waterfront where a fishing boat waited. She could only watch, as the men shoved Sol onto the boat and pushed him into a small cabin. A narrow door slammed shut and locked.

When the boat was out to sea, Marla called her husband. "Manuel you won't believe what just happened." Her voice shook as she explained what she had just witnessed.

"Shouldn't we report this to somebody?"

"No. I don't think so. Meet me at his house."

When she got to Sol's house, she and her husband discussed the events and decided Sol might not be coming back.

Manuel unloaded Sol's crates from his pickup, then said, "Why don't we open this stuff. Maybe there's something in there that would help us find out what happened to him."

They pried open the smallest crate first. It contained books, pictures, some odds and ends of personal stuff, and a briefcase. Marla opened it.

On top of some file folders were a Social Security card, credit cards and various other ID. All of it identified Sol Solomon including a drivers license with what looked to Marla like Arthur Bishop's picture. Marla went online and Googled Sol Solomon then turned to Manuel. "Bishop is a phony. His real name is Sol Solomon and he's wanted in the US for helping kidnap President Goodwin's son. I'm sure we'll never see Mister Bishop again."

"So what should we do with his stuff?"

"Take what we want and donate the rest. What you don't know, is Sol keeps a safe in the living room wall behind the picture of his boat. I saw him open it. It's full of money, lots of money, gold and diamonds too."

"Are you sure?"

"Yes. I know what I saw. Since Bishop isn't coming back, why don't we just take it?"

"I don't know," Manuel said.

"We're doing it and that's final."

The two of them spent the night breaking into the safe, counting money, and estimating the value of the gold and diamonds. The whole thing was worth a few million. By sunrise, the two of them were standing at the barbecue grill burning everything with Sol's name on it.

Since there was no real Arthur Bishop and Sol Solomon was gone, Marla decided she would take everything the non-existent man owned, the boat, the car, and the house. She forged the name of Arthur Bishop on sales contracts giving her and Manuel ownership of Sol's property. Since Marla and her husband had been seen around Sol's place for the past two years, no one thought it odd when the two of them moved in. They would enjoy everything Sol had ever wanted but would never get.

Sol endured a long boat ride in the sweltering heat to the Grand Bahama Island and Ibrahim's secret runway to await a flight to Dubai. Ibrahim's private jet touched down on a moonless night at the Dubai

International Airport. On a remote, dark corner, Sol was escorted off the plane. Ibrahim and two Syrian policemen stood waiting on the tarmac.

Ibrahim extended his hand in greeting. "I am sorry to have to bring you here, but you are a wanted man. We cannot take the chance that you would be apprehended. We need to be sure you do not disclose what you know about us and how we operate. These two officers are here to take you into custody. You will be held using your alternate ID. Americans aren't looking for Arthur Bishop, and Sol Solomon has disappeared."

Sol was in shock. How could this be happening? "Mister Jabar, I would never divulge anything. You are safe with me. I don't need to be held for security reasons. Please. I've done well for you."

"Yes, you have been faithful to our cause, but you also ruined our influence in the United States Congress."

"It wasn't me who screwed up the kidnapping. it was Jameel."

"I must apologize for this needed action, but our security is paramount. You may not remember, but the last time you were here, it would appear you left the country with documents stolen from the Syrian Embassy. These officers are here to arrest you on charges of espionage. You will be taken to Syria."

Sol was searched. Ibrahim must be sure that Sol had no ID other than that of Arthur Bishop. He also took Sol's cash and put it into his own pocket.

"That's not possible. I wasn't anywhere near any embassy," Sol pleaded.

"I have photographs." He showed Sol one taken during their meeting in the Skyview Bar three years earlier. It showed Sol sitting behind a stack of gold coins with the skyline of Dubai in the distance. There were several official looking documents sticking out from Ibrahim's folder. Enough of them were showing to identify them as missing from the Syrian embassy.

"But you were at that table too. That was *your* folder!"

"Yes, but I am not in the photo." Ibrahim nodded to the two officers.